MARK OF THE FALLEN--A DEVILISH FATED MATES PARANORMAL ROMANCE

Dark Fallen Angels #1

EVE ARCHER

Broadmoor Books

For Janet, who brings so much joy to everyone she knows (and who loves a steamy romance)!

1

Ella

"I can't believe it."

I stumbled from the restaurant, grateful to be away from the loud buzz of conversation and the hearty congratulations floating above the din.

My heels rapped on the marble floor as I walked away from the hotel restaurant and toward the doors leading outside. Fresh air. That's what I needed.

"Yeah, right," I muttered to myself, scraping my hand through my long hair and not caring that I was ruining my carefully styled curls. No amount of fresh air would fix this disaster of a trip and neither would my perfectly demure hair.

This was supposed to be *the* trip. I'd been busting my ass for the Clifton Hotel Group for years, and a guy fresh out of business school who I'd barely finished training gets the promotion over me? "What the actual fuck?"

I managed to make it down the polished stairs without falling and ducked under the enormous arched ironwork doors, sucking in a lungful of the night air. Even though the hotel was a stone's throw away from Istanbul's Spice Bazaar, it startled me that the rich cacophony of scents hung in the air. Then again, the entire ancient city seemed to carry exotic scents and sounds that were foreign to me.

I stepped off the red carpet leading into the hotel and leaned against the wall underneath a massive brass sconce, wishing I was anywhere but halfway around the world on a business trip that had gone from bad to worse. How could I have been so wrong—about everything?

A dark-haired valet glanced at me, but quickly looked away as a shiny black sedan swept up to the hotel entrance and he rushed forward to open the door.

A hand closed over my shoulder. "There you are."

I didn't need to look up to know it was my boyfriend of three years giving me a look of curious amusement.

"I needed to get some air," I said, trying to ignore how composed he looked with his sandy-blond hair swept back in a perfect wave from his forehead.

He nodded, while lifting one eyebrow. "You mean you came out here to pout?"

Fresh anger rose in my chest. "Pout? How can you say that? You know how hard I've worked for that promotion, and then..." My words trailed off as emotion caused my throat to tighten.

"Come on, babe. It's not the end of the world."

"For you, maybe." My cheeks still burned from the humiliation of keeping a gracious smile plastered to my face while my boss gave my promotion to someone else. "I'm the one who trained him, and now he's getting promoted *over* me?"

Christopher gave me a look that told me he was humoring me—one I'd seen far too many times to count. "These things happen. You'll get it next time."

I shot him a look. Next time? Was he serious? This was supposed to be *the* time. I'd convinced myself that this big, company trip to Istanbul would be it—the trip where I got the promotion and bump in pay I so desperately needed, and that it would be the magical weekend where my longtime boyfriend finally proposed to me.

I stifled a laugh as I thought how wrong I'd been about that. When I'd invited Christopher to join me for my first international work trip, I'd thought that the romantic setting of Istanbul, coupled with the fact that it was falling the week before my thirtieth birthday would have made it the ideal time for him to pop the question. But as the days of the trip had passed, it had become clear that proposing was not on my boyfriend's mind.

He'd been happier to hang out with my male colleagues at the pool bar and talk sports than spend time with me. I swallowed hard as I allowed a traitorous thought to creep into my mind. Maybe marriage had never been on his mind. Maybe the proposal, like the promotion, was only my pipe dream, and had no connection with the reality I was living.

I tipped my head up to stare at the deep-blue evening sky as clouds shifted across it and the moon glowed down. "This was not how it was supposed to happen."

He let out a breath and shifted from one foot to the next, clearly tiring of my emotional scene. He tucked his blue, button-down shirt more snugly into his pants. "I don't know what to say, Ella. Maybe Clark has more of what the company needs in terms of leadership."

I snapped my head to him. "Clark?" Before he'd come on this trip, he hadn't even known the guy's name, even though I'd complained for months about having to train the recent hire. "Since when has Clark shown leadership?"

Christopher shrugged. "He's a decent guy, and he seems to get along with your boss really well."

I pressed my lips together. Clark and my boss had gone to the same business school, which seemed to bond them together in a way I could never match. Frustration made me fist my hands. "But he barely knows how to do *his* job. How is he going to handle being a regional director?"

Christopher barely concealed a roll of his eyes. "It's not like you lost your job, Ella. You just didn't get this one promotion. Don't make such a big deal out of it, babe."

But it was a big deal. I was drowning in debt, and the pay raise that came with the promotion would have made a huge difference. Tears stung the backs of my eyes. Not that my boyfriend would understand about money problems. Both of his parents were still alive and eager to give him financial "loans" whenever he overdrew his accounts. Mine had died when I was a freshman in college, and I'd assumed all my college expenses, along with their outstanding debts. Even though I'd been chipping away at it for years, it felt like I'd never be out from under the smothering heap.

"Look at it this way," my boyfriend said. "At least you got this baller trip out of it."

He was trying to be positive, but even that pissed me off. Yeah, I'd gotten a great trip to check out the newest property in the company's international expansion, but I'd barely seen anything of the stunning city. I'd spent most of the time in meetings in the hotel, or making calls for my boss. Christopher, on the other hand, had been free to hang out with all the men from my company—including Clark—who apparently hadn't been burdened with the same tasks. I wasn't one to play the feminist card often, but you couldn't tell me that my male boss hadn't treated me like his personal secretary because I was a woman, especially when no one else on the trip—including guys below me in position and seniority—had been given menial tasks all week.

I twisted around so I could see the tops of the Blue Mosque minarets extending into the sky like grey, pointy hats. The most famous building in the city was within walking distance, and I was leaving tomorrow without having even set foot inside it. Sara would kill me.

Sara. My stomach lurched. I'd promised to call my best friend as soon as Christopher proposed, or I got the promotion. She'd be waiting back in New York and wondering why I'd gone radio silent on her.

I steadied my breath and looked at Christopher, reminding myself that he was only trying to help. I should try to salvage the trip, so I didn't have such a pathetic story to tell my best friend. "You're right. What's done is done. We should make the most of our last night in Istanbul." I held out my hand. "Any interest in a moonlight stroll around Sultanahmet?"

He made a face and cringed. "Sorry, babe. I wish you'd said something sooner. I already promised your colleagues I'd join them for celebratory drinks on the roof."

"Celebrator—?" The word died on my lips as I snatched my hand away from him. "You mean you're celebrating Clark getting the promotion over your own girlfriend?"

He put a hand on my arm as the valets glanced over. "Ella, you're being dramatic again."

As I peered into his blue eyes, a calm settled over me. "You're right. What was I thinking?" I wrenched my arm away from him. "Enjoy your evening, *babe*."

His tortured sigh reached me as I strode away, my heels tapping rapidly on the pavement. I didn't know where I was going, but at least I was walking away from him. Part of me hoped he'd run after me, but another part knew he wouldn't. I'd been with Christopher long enough to know that he wasn't the type to pursue me and apologize. Or even just catch up to me and convince me to come back to the hotel.

I barreled forward, ignoring the valets calling after me asking if I wanted a cab. I should get a cab, but I had no idea where I was going. For the moment, I was walking. Away from my snake of a boyfriend and away from my louse of a boss. Pausing at the corner, I wished that I wasn't wearing my highest heels. Then again, I knew these heels made my legs look great, so at least I'd looked good as I'd stormed off.

Using the spires of the famous mosque as a guide, I kept walking as I took my phone from the small, black purse I wore across my body. I might be in ridiculous heels and my only black cocktail dress, but at least I knew enough to wear my purse crossbody when walking in a city. I hadn't lost all my New York common sense.

"Ella?" My best friend's voice cut through the hum of the city around me as she answered my call, making fresh tears spring to my eyes. "Finally, girl. I was starting to worry."

"I'm fine," I said, stopping on the corner and glancing at a Turkish restaurant with a brown awning and pictures of food hanging in the window. The scent of braised meat and fresh bread wafting from the open glass door made my stomach growl and made me wish I'd eaten more at dinner.

"No, you're not. I can hear it in your voice. What's wrong?"

Of course, my best friend would know I wasn't okay from thousands of miles away, when my boyfriend didn't seem to clue in when he was standing right next to me. I drew in a shaky breath. "I'm not engaged, and I didn't get the promotion."

"Shit." Sara let out her own long breath. "Ella, I'm so sorry."

I put a hand over my mouth to keep the stifled sob from escaping my lips. I did not want to start crying on a street corner in the middle of Istanbul.

Her usually forceful voice softened. "What happened?"

I squared my shoulders. "I was an idiot, that's what happened. Clark got the promotion, and Christopher never had any intention of proposing." I peered up at the dome of the Blue Mosque, illuminated pale blue against the midnight blue of the night sky. "Not because we're in a romantic city or because it's almost my birthday."

"Clark? The putz you trained?"

I laughed, despite the tears pricking my eyes. "Now, that's the response I wanted. Christopher told me that Clark's a decent guy, and I should get over it."

"Of course, he did," Sara muttered. "And before you say that I'm saying this because I think your boyfriend is a colossal asshat, you're one hundred percent right. I do think he's a total douchebag, and he should have had your back."

Sara had never made it much of a secret that she didn't like my boyfriend, but she managed to be polite to him the rare times they were together. It wasn't that I didn't totally disagree with her. Christopher could be a jerk, but we'd been together for so long that it felt inevitable that we'd stay together and end up getting married. At least, that's what I'd always thought. Now, I was starting to doubt he had the same ideas.

Even so, I'd been so busy with my work that the thought of breaking up and finding someone new (and a new place to live in New York City) had seemed like more trouble than it was worth, considering he was only occasionally an ass. At least, I only noticed it every so often. According to Sara, he was full douche all the time, and I was too distracted to notice.

"You're right." I stepped back so a family pushing a stroller could walk by, their smiles and laughter highlighting my loneliness even more. "This trip has been a disaster."

"But you're coming home tomorrow, right? And at least you've been to Istanbul. Not everyone can say that." She let out a wistful sigh. "Is it as breathtaking as it looks in photos?'

I crossed the street and walked closer to the enormous mosque, letting the stacked domes and surrounding spires draw me toward it like a moth to an incandescent blue flame. "It's beautiful. Not that I've seen much of it."

"I thought you were staying in the heart of the historic district. How could you not see much of it?"

"Meetings." I frowned as I thought back over all the tasks I'd taken on for my boss, trying to impress him with my work ethic as my male colleagues had made no attempt to deprive themselves. "My last-ditch effort to secure the promotion."

"Screw them," Sara said, her voice back to its usual decibel level and sharpness. "If they can't see how great you are, then they can all go fuck themselves."

I grinned, while pressing my phone close to my ear so passersby wouldn't hear the curse words that fell so easily from my best friend's lips. "Except I still have to work with them all and live with Christopher."

"Not tonight you don't. Did you at least get to go to the rooftop bar at the Four Seasons? Please tell me you didn't miss that. You've been talking about that forever."

Having a drink at the luxurious Four Seasons hotel rooftop bar that overlooked the Blue Mosque had been on my bucket list, and of course, it had gotten pushed aside. I'd imagined sharing a cocktail in the romantic setting with my boyfriend, but Sara was right. No way was I going to miss a once-in-a-lifetime experience because he was being a jerk.

"I'm on my way there right now," I told her, angling my path toward where I knew the famous hotel was located on the other side of the mosque. Even though my heart tripped nervously at the thought of sitting alone in a bar in a foreign country, my pulse quickened with excitement. Who knew what could happen on a perfect night in a magical city? Maybe my trip wasn't a total loss after all.

2

Dominick

I sat on the open-air terrace with my arms stretched along the back of a low, armless divan. Tall lamps glowed behind me, while I looked out at the illuminated Blue Mosque beyond the balcony's stone railing. The sight was enough to take anyone's breath away, but it was one I'd seen many times over many millennia. The final call to prayer had already sounded across the city, the undulating Arabic words bathing the ancient stones and reminding me of times before crackling loudspeakers. When long-dead languages had been spoken across the arid lands and before stone mosques had flanked the shores of the Bosphorus. Before the Bosphorus had been called the Bosphorus.

I inhaled the scent of charred meat, a savory tang that did not change over time, and a familiarity washed over me. I'd been here countless times over countless years, yet the city of Istanbul that I would always think of as Constantinople was still not home.

There was no home for those of us who'd been exiled. Not on the mortal plane, at least.

Twisting my head, I took in the crowd gathered on the hotel's rooftop bar, the A'ya lounge, eating from trays of sizzling *mezze* and sipping cocktails. These were not the observant, who prayed on their knees and abstained from drink. These were people who indulged themselves in all pleasures of the flesh and enjoyed the finest things mortal life could offer.

"Just like me," I whispered, the deep purr of my voice melting away beneath the buzz of eager conversation swirling into the air like fragrant smoke. These were my people. Well-heeled and well-dressed, their dark secrets swathed under a cloak of respectability, they were exactly who I'd expect to find at one of my properties.

Of course, barely anyone knew that this hotel was one of my properties since my collection of luxury hotels, exclusive resorts, and hedonistic nightclubs were held in shell companies. It made most people uncomfortable to knowingly patronize a property owned by one of the most notorious members of the criminal underworld. Like typical humans, they were happier not knowing.

It didn't bother me. I preferred my businesses to have an air of respectability about them, and I didn't mind if my name wasn't listed on the deeds. The people who needed to know that Dominick Vicario controlled some of the most luxurious properties in the world knew.

But if only they *really* knew.

I thought of some of my more secret clubs. No one would ever connect this luxury brand with them, and I doubted many of the clientele dining and drinking on this terrace would crave such abandon. My gaze slid to a young couple in the corner nuzzling close, his hand wandering up her bare thigh. I gave a throaty sigh that only I heard. Some clearly relished my own thrill at the forbidden. I smiled to myself, wondering if the couple might be open to a little more adventure with me later. My fingers tingled as I imagined running my own hand up the woman's long leg.

My sigh became a low chuckle as I contemplated the encounter. While my pulse thrummed at the thought, a cocktail waitress delivered my single-malt whiskey, placing the rocks glass on the low, polishedwood table in front of me. Candlelight refracted off the etches in the glass and sent slivers of colored light cavorting across the table, pulling my gaze away from the couple. The waitress gave me a lingering look from beneath long lashes, her fingers reluctant to release the glass, so I bestowed a smile on her as she backed away, her cheeks betraying a flush even in the fading evening light. Or maybe I would charm *her* into coming to my suite, and relish in peeling off the conservative black pencil skirt and top that was the hotel uniform.

I shifted as my cock swelled with desire, reminding me of my very human needs. Perhaps I was no longer a holy watcher, but human women never failed to draw my attention. They were as lovely today as they were when their beauty had beguiled me and tempted me to fall from grace. I seared a hot look at the retreating waitress, enjoying how her step faltered and her lips parted for me. It had never been difficult to persuade females to savor the forbidden. Or the fallen.

"Dominick." My top advisor, Rami, gave me a small nod that could be mistaken for a bow as he took the canvas director's chair next to the divan. "Enjoying the view again?"

I inclined my head at the dark-haired man who moved, unquestioned as a native through any land stretching from the Iberian Peninsula to the Middle East. Like me, his skin was bronzed, and his jaw square and rough with stubble. Although I was his leader, we could have passed for brothers, and I had always considered him so.

“It is difficult to beat,” I said, acknowledging his double meaning with an arch of my brow, as I tore my gaze away from the willing female.

He scanned the crowd, his gaze pausing on a group of women sitting on the divan behind me who were laughing a bit too loudly then returning to me. “At least, in Istanbul.”

I uncrossed my legs and leaned forward, resting my elbows on my knees. Even though the hum of conversation would mask my voice, I did not want to risk being overheard. “Any more news?”

Rami dragged a hand through the thick hair he wore spiky and angled his body toward me. “About the increased demon activity?”

I growled low in answer then took a languid sip of my whiskey, the liquid easing down my throat like nectar and firing my core. As fallen angels, Rami and I were partly responsible for the demonic spirits that roamed Earth. They were remnants of our unions with human women at the dawn of humanity, and part of our torment as outcast immortals was to keep them in check. The demons were ruled by their own prince, another former angel called Mastema, but he was less interested in controlling them than in using them to build his own demonic empire. It didn’t help that the corrupted demon spirits despised us for their fate and were constantly battling to keep us from any sort of redemption.

Not that I cared about redeeming myself. I’d given up that possibility long ago. Now I embraced the darkness of humanity and all its delicious pleasures, including punishing humans who aligned themselves with demons. Let the archangels have their perfect divinity. I would take the carnal pleasures of humanity any day.

“Not just demons, Dom.” My friend’s handsome face twisted. “You were right about the Solano family. They are being advised by Jaya.”

"Advised?" I flinched at the name of the succubus who'd been plaguing me for longer than I cared to recall, clenching my hand around the hard rocks glass as the thought stoked fury within me. Once, we'd been lovers—the succubi were hard to resist, even for an immortal like me—but now she was determined to torment me. "Are you sure?"

He cocked an eyebrow, and I sank back on the cushions, releasing both a breath and the burgeoning rage. I knew better than to question Rami. He'd been loyal to me since we'd forged our pact to defy the divine commandment not to mingle with humans, never once betraying me, or going back on our ancient promise of solidarity. Not even when it meant we were cast from heaven and cursed to wander the darkness of Earth.

"Do they move against our business positions?" I asked. It would take more than one seedy mob family to pose a threat to the secret empire I'd spent over a hundred years building, but I'd learned long ago that any threats should be dealt with before they became a real problem. Especially when demons were involved.

Rami gave a curt shake of his head. "Even with the shrewd counsel of Jaya, the Solano family is still operating on the fringe. Small nightclubs, lowlife drug runners. But rumors have reached me that they might be dipping their toes in human trafficking."

I sucked in a breath, the air cool between my teeth. As much as I savored the sins of the flesh, I did not allow anything that happened in my properties to be against anyone's will. There was no pleasure to be taken in the pain of the innocent, although I knew the demons might disagree with me. I forbade any of my fellow fallen to involve themselves in those who did not willingly embrace the hedonism off which my business thrived, and the penalty for disobedience—like all my penalties—was severe.

"Arturo Solano is mistaken, if he thought this would not reach my ears." The old mob boss had never been more than a bit player in the Italian underworld, and he'd never been a threat to my empire. Mostly because he didn't have the advantages of immortality and invincibility to aid in his rise to power like I had. Still, I'd been content to let him run his operation without interference, even if I found him to be unsophisticated and crude.

Rami's upper clip curled. "It is not the Don."

"His son, then."

"You know he has two."

I'd forgotten that Don Solano had two sons because only one was a constant irritant to me. The youngest son didn't even live in Venice anymore, but the eldest was being groomed to step into his father's shoes.

"Mateo," I said, my jaw tight.

It was no secret that Mateo Solano thirsted for more power and control, although he struck me as a boy playing dress-up in his father's slick suits. His undisciplined mind would be the perfect playground for a seasoned demon like Jaya, who feasted on the easily manipulated.

Rami angled his head at me. "He aspires to be like you, Dom."

I huffed out a breath then waved my hand at the uplit mosque and then at the opulent terrace setting where cocktail waitresses moved easily between long, low tables, and the scent of jasmine drifted on the breeze. "It took us thousands of years to build all this." I closed my hand into a tight fist. "I will not let Jaya and her boy toy ruin it."

Rami grinned at my description of Mateo. "So far, their dealings have not come close to ours."

"Not yet." Dread pooled in my stomach. I knew Jaya and her lust for revenge. She would keep coming after me until she'd exacted the pound of flesh she believed she deserved. Even if she was destined to fail, she wished to pull me down with her into the ashes.

Rami met my gaze, his expression knowing. A battle was brewing, one we'd been hoping to avoid.

"I need a drink before you send me out on one of your impossible missions," he said, lifting a hand and summoning a waitress.

"Nothing has ever been impossible for you, especially not when it comes to finding humans who deserve to be punished. Or demons."

He shrugged at the flattery then turned his attention to the cocktail waitress. The pretty woman with dark hair pulled back in a chignon reacted to Rami just as the other female waitress had reacted to me, her pupils dilating and her breath hitching in her throat. It was a reaction we'd become accustomed to in human women. It was as if they sensed our deeply hidden divinity and our sinful fall from it, their bodies reacting viscerally to us. It was not something we took for granted, although we certainly took what we wanted when it came to women. And we did not shy away from using our former divinity as the aphrodisiac it was.

"Your best *raki*." He touched a hand lightly to the woman's arm as he ordered the anise-flavored Turkish drink he favored.

I shook my head at him as she walked away dazed, and he gave me a look of mock innocence.

"Do not tell me you've stopped indulging," he said, successfully changing the subject to something we never tired of discussing.

I sighed, surveying the rooftop again now that almost all the seating was taken. "And rob myself of the true pleasures of humanity? No, but I admit to growing bored of it all sometimes."

"Bored of sex?" He frowned. "I hope that's a curse that never befalls me. Not when there are so many intriguing creatures, with so many appealing talents."

I shook my head at my friend, who knew me better than anyone but still did not understand. It was true that I partook freely of carnal pleasures, taking women to my bed nearly every night, but none of them could ever make up for what had been ripped away from me. No matter how many females submitted to my dark desires, they could never change who I was—an unredeemable outcast.

The waitress returned with the *raki* along with glasses of water and ice, arranging it all in front of Rami with more care than was needed, her gaze locking on his as she straightened. Her arousal was almost palpable, as was the way my friend's sensual gaze raked up and down her body. She didn't know why her inhibitions fell away under his hot gaze, but it was obvious she didn't care.

I cleared my throat, drawing Rami's attention back to me. He mixed the clear raki with small amounts of water and ice, his eyes on the retreating waitress and not the drink that became cloudy-white as the liquids swirled together.

"Have you had her?" he asked.

I cut my eyes to the pretty woman, quickly searching my memory. "I don't believe so." I inclined my head slightly. "Please, be my guest."

He took a sip of his drink and shifted to the edge of the chair. "I believe I will."

"But wait until she's done with work," I continued. "I doubt you wish to make your encounter quick, and the terrace appears to be at capacity."

Rami seemed to become aware of his surroundings again, sweeping his eyes across the bustling crowd. "Of course. We can't have one of our properties getting a bad review."

"Not because you were fucking the waitress in a corner."

He pretended to look scandalized. "A corner? You wound me, Dom. Why would I use a corner when I have a perfectly suitable suite in the hotel?"

I laughed, swallowing more of my eighteen-year-old whiskey and letting the heat roll down my throat. After placing the rocks glass back on the table, my gaze caught on something by the entrance. Not the eager waitress that Ram would no doubt fuck later, but another woman in black.

This woman had loose, auburn curls spilling over her shoulders and an expression that was the perfect blend of trepidation and defiance as she took in the crowded rooftop. My mouth went dry as I watched her approach the hostess, an arrow of desire—and strangely, recognition—shooting through me. I'd seen her before—that I was sure of—but I wasn't sure where.

She was beautiful, but unconsciously so, and it was clear that she rarely wore a dress like the black one that now hugged her curves. But there was something beyond her physical appearance that made it impossible for me to look away. Before I could determine why, I was lifting my hand and beckoning the hostess to seat the woman in the empty spot next to me—one of the only available seats left on the popular terrace. The hostess hesitated—when I was a guest at A'ya, no one was ever seated beside me—but I nodded firmly.

Rami craned his neck to watch as the woman walked hesitantly behind the hostess, her gaze darting to seemingly anything but me as she approached.

When she reached the table, I stood, as did Rami.

"Please." I beckoned for her to take the spot on the divan next to mine. "A visitor to Istanbul should not miss this view."

She glanced over her shoulder at the incandescent mosque looming behind us then back at me. "No, I suppose she shouldn't. You're sure you don't mind, Mr...?"

I extended my hand. "Dominick Vicario."

A blush suffused her cheeks as she took my hand in her own. "Ella Hart."

The warmth that sizzled across my skin almost made me gasp, and I felt Rami's questioning gaze on me. "A pleasure to meet you, Ella."

I waited until she'd sat down to lower myself back to the cushioned divan, my eyes never leaving the woman beside me. Now I knew I'd seen her before, and I remembered where—at my nightclub in New York City over a year ago. At the time, she'd worn significantly more makeup and dramatically less clothing, but it was her.

I gaped at the woman without bothering to mask my shock. She'd run off before I could get her name over a year ago, and I'd had no luck in finding her afterward, although I'd tried. And now she'd walked onto the rooftop terrace of my hotel half a world away.

The promise of destiny sent tingles through my entire body. It had been a long time since I'd felt a jolt like the one Ella had just given me, but you never forget the euphoric burn of an angelic touch.

3

Ella

The view from the rooftop of the Four Seasons hotel was even more impressive than I'd imagined. I smoothed my hands down the front of my dress, shifting it down about an inch on my legs. I was painfully aware of how close I was to the man next to me, our knees so close they were almost touching, and of how fast my heart was beating.

"It's even more beautiful in person," I said, my voice cracking as I looked away from the illuminated domes and spires. When I swiveled my head to him, I noticed that his friend had disappeared.

"Isn't it?" His voice was a deep rumble that seemed to caress my skin and slide down my spine, the hint of an exotic accent making his words like hypnotic music.

I had the distinct sensation that I'd seen this man before, but where would I meet someone as stunning as him? And wealthy, I thought, taking in his expensive clothes and the Cartier watch glittering on his wrist. I didn't exactly travel is circles with men like this.

The last time I'd seen a man I'd been drawn to so instantly had been a year ago in New York, but I'd had way too many drinks that night to determine if this could possibly be him, although both men gave me a fluttery sensation in my stomach. Any memories of the man in the New York nightclub were blurry and marred by an all-too-clear recollection of throwing up the many cocktails I'd downed. Besides, what was the chance I'd encounter the same man half a world away?

I managed to clear my throat and glance at the empty chair. "What happened to your friend?"

"Rami had to leave." He summoned a waitress over to us with a single, effortless flick of his hand and offered no further explanation for his friend vanishing. "What would you like to drink, Ella?"

My mind went blank. I had a usual drink. What was it? I tried to swallow, but my throat was thick. There was no doubt that I needed a drink—and fast.

After a beat, the man who'd introduced himself as Dominick smiled at me, his sinfully dark eyes flashing, and then at the waitress. "Bring her a Romance."

Before I could ask what that was, he dazzled me with another smile. "It's one of the hotel's signature drinks—rose water, pomegranate, vodka. I think you'll enjoy it."

I rubbed my hands down my dress again, this time because my palms were clammy. "Sounds delicious."

What is wrong with you? Get your shit together, Ella. I took a long, steadying breath. *You're just sitting next to a man and having a drink in a public place.*

But he wasn't just any man. He was one of the most stunning men I'd ever laid eyes on and one hundred percent my type.

I cut my eyes to him again and almost sighed out loud. When he'd stood, it had been easy to see that Dominick Vicario was tall, with broad shoulders, but even when he was sitting, the man was imposing, with hard muscles that were defined through his form-fitting, black, button-down shirt. He didn't look much older than me, but he radiated power and control like no thirty-year-old man I'd ever met. His dark hair was cut short, with a couple of thick waves curling down his forehead, and dark stubble shadowed his cheeks.

I dropped my eyes from his face, but not before noticing that his eyes were the same rich, amber hue as the liquid he swirled hypnotically in his glass. When he lifted the glass to his full lips, my gaze was drawn to the wings tattooed across the back of one hand, and I watched him take a slow drink. When he met my eyes over the rim of his glass, I jerked my head away and forced myself to stare at the Blue Mosque.

You came here for the view, Ella, I reminded myself. *Not for some random guy.*

I almost laughed at my own characterization. Dominick was certainly not a random guy. I didn't know who he was, but he was someone.

The waitress reappeared with a tray of drinks including a hand-blown, glass bubble filled with a ruby-hued liquid that I assumed was the drink Dominick had ordered for me. She arranged everything on the low table, including a fresh rocks glass that held two fingers of whatever Dominick was drinking, and then left with her eyes lowered.

Before I could reach for it, Dominick lifted the bubble-shaped glass in his palm and presented it to me. "I hope you enjoy this Romance."

My breath caught in my throat before I remembered that was the name of the drink. "Right. Thanks." My words sounded rushed and much too casual for the setting—and the man. "I mean, thank you."

One side of his mouth quirked up as I took the glass from him, my pinky finger brushing against his and sending fresh tingles across my bare arm. His eyes narrowed at me briefly, the black pupils flaring and turning his amber eyes into pools of darkness.

I pulled away and lifted the thick, glass straw to my lips, grateful to drink the sweet cocktail. He was right, I thought as I swallowed. It was delicious, although I'd never tasted anything that made me think of drinking rose petals. The tang of the pomegranate tempered the flowery flavor, but I didn't detect a hint of the vodka—the sign of a good cocktail. And a dangerous one.

"Tell me about yourself," Dominick said, stretching one long arm across the back of the divan.

"Me?" I almost choked as I sipped down another gulp. "There's not much to tell."

He pinned me with his gaze and made a *tsk*-ing noise. "I doubt that very much, Ella."

Shit. Why did I feel like I was being simultaneously interrogated and seduced? I sucked up more of the cocktail, grateful for the warm buzz that was filling my chest and making my toes tingle. "Okay." I attempted to modulate my voice to his. "I live in New York, and work for a hospitality company. I'm in Istanbul for a work trip. Our company's management team came here to see our newest acquisition." I gave a halfhearted shrug as I thought back to the final dinner and the announcement of promotions. "It was also a reward for a pretty stellar year for the company and the people who made it happen."

One of his dark eyebrows lifted slightly. "You are one of the people who made it happen?"

My outrage from earlier in the evening flared for a moment, but the vodka seemed to mute it. "I'm one of the unappreciated ones who made it happen."

Dominick frowned. "I have a hard time believing you are not appreciated."

I snorted out a laugh then slapped a hand over my mouth, embarrassed that I was coming off so unworldly in front of the most sophisticated man I'd ever met. I dropped my hand and attempted to match his steady voice. "Well, believe it. Both my boss and my boyfriend like Clark more than they like me. He got the promotion I'd been working for, and my boyfriend is out celebrating with *him* right now. Plus, I've barely seen anything of Istanbul, and the trip is almost over."

"Boyfriend?"

I met his eyes, draining the last of my drink and putting the empty bubble on the table. Part of me regretted mentioning a boyfriend, but being dishonest wasn't my style. Even if I really wanted this guy to make me forget everything and everyone. "Yep, we've been together for three years, but I honestly don't know where it's going. I mean, I thought he might propose on this trip since it's such a romantic setting and my birthday is next week, but I'm pretty sure the thought never crossed his mind."

Dominick's gaze never left my eyes. "He doesn't sound like he's worthy of you."

I laughed again, this time without snorting. "You sound like my best friend, Sara. She can't stand him."

Dominick waved the waitress over, nodding at my empty glass, which was whisked away. "I think I agree with your friend Sara."

"I got comfortable, you know. It seemed easier to stay with him than to find someone else. Besides, he looks good on paper. Decent looking guy with a decent job, and an even better apartment in the city. I've been so focused on working and trying to get out of debt that a mediocre boyfriend who isn't even that good in bed seemed like the least of my problems." As soon as I said this, I glanced up at him. "Oh, wow. I don't know why I just told you that. I'm sorry. That was a serious overshare."

"Not at all." His voice was velvety as his gaze finally moved from my eyes down my body. "A woman as beautiful as you should be with someone who does everything he can to please you in bed."

My cheeks burned. How had he made that sound so smooth and off-the-cuff?

"Tell me about your parents," he asked, changing the subject without preamble. Not that I minded. I needed to stop rambling about my boyfriend.

Another drink appeared on the table, and I gratefully picked it up. "My parents?" My gut tightened, so I sucked down more of the sweet cocktail. "They were great. I was an only child, and they gave me everything. Until they were killed in a car crash, and I discovered that all the things they'd given me had put them into major debt. Between their debt and my student loans, I'll be lucky to finish paying it all off before I die."

"I'm sorry."

For some reason, hearing him say those two simple words made tears burn the backs of my eyelids. "Thanks. It's been a while, but sometimes thinking about them still hurts, which is another reason I try to focus on work. It keeps me from having a pity party all the time."

Dominick swirled the contents of his drink as neither of us spoke, and I tried to figure out why I'd just spilled my life secrets to a total stranger.

"What is the name of the company you work for?" He finally asked.

"The Clifton Hotel Group. They're based in New York."

He nodded, tossing back the last of his drink. "I know them."

"You do?" That was odd. Not many people knew the name of the parent company that owned some almost-luxury hotels.

Dominick leaned forward, and his arm brushed my shoulder. "I do. And like I said before, you're too good for them."

Warmth had suffused my entire body, and his arm cocooned my back and sent heat coiling in my belly even as a whisper of trepidation slid shivers down my spine. "Maybe."

"There is no doubt that you deserve better than that company or your boyfriend can give you," he said, his mouth buzzing my ear as he leaned into me. "Don't you want more?"

I did want more, and at that moment the more I wanted was *him*. I tried to answer but it came out as a whimper.

"What if I told you that I could give you more?" His silky whisper sent heat pulsing between my legs.

I'd never had a one-night stand, but it was getting harder and harder to argue against it. The cleverly concealed vodka probably wasn't helping, but it was more than that. I could be stone-cold sober and still want nothing more than to take whatever Dominick was offering.

I'd never reacted to a man like I reacted to him. I'd never experienced such a physical jolt, or the overwhelming sense that meeting him had been fate—not that I believed in that kind of crap.

"What do you mean?" I asked, bracing one hand against his chest as his body touched mine.

"I think you know exactly what I mean, Ella."

I swallowed hard. I should have been thinking about Christopher and the years we'd spent together and the fact that we shared an apartment and would be boarding a plane together the next day, but now I couldn't have cared less. He'd ditched me, after all. But I also wasn't a cheater.

"I have a boyfriend," I said.

"Do you?" Dominick deftly reached into my purse and pulled out my phone.

I stared down at it, excitement and fear filling me. "You want me to..."

"*I* don't want you to," he said. "You want to. You've wanted to for a long time."

He was right. I'd known in my gut what I should do for months, maybe longer. I breathed in deeply and opened my messages. A text breakup wasn't my first choice, but I also didn't think Christopher deserved much better. "He'd definitely break up with *me* by text."

I tapped out a short message, making sure I didn't sound like I'd been sucking down cocktails, and pressed send before I could have second thoughts.

"And your boss?" Dominick prodded.

"He's never going to promote me, is he?" I asked, knowing the answer before I even asked the question. "He's using me because I'm willing to take his shit, but he's always going to give the promotions and the raises to one of the guys who drinks and golfs with him."

I didn't even glance up at Dominick for confirmation, tapping out another short text message to my boss thanking him for the opportunity but giving him my notice. "Effective immediately," I said as I typed out the last words and hit send.

I dropped my phone back in my bag and then slumped back against the cushions and Dominick's arm. "I just broke up with my boyfriend and quit my job."

"How do you feel?" Dominick's gaze was intense as he stared down at me.

"Like I just took a huge plunge off a cliff." I didn't know if the hammering of my heart was because I'd just blown up my life or because of the way he was staring at me.

Dominick curled his arm around my shoulders, his fingers skimming the bare flesh of my arm. "Sometimes a fall can be just what you need."

4

Dominick

I snaked an arm around her waist as we stepped into the hotel's elevator, the soft, instrumental music a stark contrast to the din of the rooftop terrace. I rested a possessive hand on her hip, holding her to me even though she'd made no attempt to flee.

She wouldn't run. I wouldn't let her. Not until I figured why the woman with the angelic trace who'd managed to slip away from me a year earlier had appeared at the very place I was drinking on the very night Rami brought me news of increased demon activity.

Glancing down at the auburn hair falling around her shoulders, I couldn't help lowering my head and inhaling. Even the scent of her was intoxicating. Then again, there was nothing more tempting for me than a human who'd been somehow touched by angelic forces. I clenched my teeth together. Which was exactly why I couldn't trust her.

The muted ding announced that the elevator had reached my floor. Ella hesitated when the doors swished open, but I propelled her forward, flicking my platinum key card at the door panel and pushing the door open before she could think to protest.

She wouldn't protest, I reminded myself. Not after she'd quit her job and dumped her boyfriend after only a well-timed suggestion. The human wanted to do something forbidden. And that something was me.

"This is your room?" she asked, after I'd led her from the suite's foyer into a large room with a loft leading to a second level.

"It's my permanent residence when I'm in town." I scanned the familiar furnishings that were so unlike the rest of the hotel. Although I'd retained the wrought iron details of the room, the rest of the design was more modern than Ottoman, and embraced the dark and not the light, with gunmetal-grey upholstered chairs and tufted sofas. A chandelier dominated the center of the high-ceilinged room featuring a cascade of crystal-winged creatures spilling down from an illuminated orb.

Her eyes were wide as she spotted the massive four poster bed on the loft level, the finials on each of the posts topped with a glittering crystal. A black duvet with white piping covered the bed and was topped with a collection of monogrammed pillows.

"You live in a hotel?"

"Only when I'm in Istanbul." I led her to one of the tufted couches. "I have several homes throughout the world."

She perched on the edge of the couch and tilted her head up at me. "Who are you?"

"A businessman."

"That's vague." Hesitation had crept into her voice.

I crossed to the bar cart by the French doors and doled out a few hand-cut ice cubes from the silver ice bucket into a pair of highball glasses. I poured water into both glasses and walked back to her, holding out one.

She waved me off. "I don't think I should drink any more."

"It's water." I pushed the glass into her hand. "I have no intention of getting you drunk. Or, at least, any drunker than you already are."

She gave me a petulant frown that reminded me that she was a child compared to my thousands of years. "I'm not drunk."

I sat next to her and my knee touched hers, the contact both exhilarating and bothersome. "How long did you work for The Clifton Group?"

She took a tiny sip of the water, as if she wasn't completely convinced I wasn't trying to slip her some gin. "Almost five years."

Five years. The beat of a butterfly's wings for an angel, but a long time for a human who was only... "And how old are you turning next week?"

"Thirty." She grimaced, as if thirty were a scandalous number.

"Trust me. You're younger than you think." I took a gulp of water, allowing the crisp coolness to keep my whirl of thoughts in check.

How had a human with traces of an angelic touch on her end up here? First, she'd appeared at my club in New York and then vanished. Now she popped up in Istanbul. What kind of long game were the demons playing, and what were they hoping to accomplish by putting her in my path? It was a trick I wouldn't put past the demon prince Mastema. He would know Ella would be too alluring for me to resist. More importantly, the leader of the demons knew that claiming a human who'd been marked by an angel would be yet another strike against me to the archangels. Or perhaps the archangels were behind it all.

I frowned at this thought. "How did you end up on my rooftop bar?"

Ella sipped her water as her wide, blue eyes darted around the room, then landed on me. "Your rooftop bar? You own this hotel?"

I saw the glass slip from her hand, and I caught it in my free one. "It's one of my company's holdings, yes."

She shook her head, but her teeth worked her bottom lip as she no doubt thought back to the staff demurring to me on the rooftop as we'd left, each of them addressing me by name. "That's impossible."

I placed both glasses on the table and reclined on the sofa. "Nothing is impossible, Ella. Now, tell me why you were at my bar tonight."

"I told you. I was upset at my boyfriend and my boss. The hotel where I'm staying is just on the other side of the mosque, and I'd heard about how incredible the terrace was at the Four Seasons. I decided to treat myself on the last night of my trip." Her own words seemed to snap her from her daze. "That's right. I'm leaving tomorrow."

So, it was chance that put her in my path? I knew enough about fate and destiny to know that very little happened by accident, especially not with a deity who predetermined so much. "You'd heard about the rooftop?"

Ella nodded and wiped the palms of her hand on her dress again. "Sara sent me a few online articles about it once the company decided to take the staff to Istanbul. She said it was a bucket-list experience."

"Sara?"

Her brow furrowed briefly, then she let out a nervous laugh. "My best friend back in New York. We've known each other since freshman year in college."

"And?" I asked, coiling an arm across the back of the sofa's back. "Was it?"

Her cheeks flushed an even deeper shade of pink. "Was it what?"

"A once-in-a-lifetime experience?"

Ella nodded, her gaze darting past me to the door. She was no practiced seductress, unless she was the best actress I'd ever seen. But she *was* getting more jittery by the minute as the effects of the potent cocktail wore off. No doubt she was questioning her impulsive text messages as well as her decision to come back to my suite with me.

I trailed a finger down the side of her arm. "You can relax. I don't intend to force myself on you."

That was true, but I also couldn't allow her to leave. Not before I knew how she'd come by the angelic trace that almost radiated off her body and what part this beautiful human was playing in the eternal battle between the fallen and the cursed and the anointed. She might be a plant by the archangels or the demons—or she could be something even more significant. Something they hadn't planned and would kill to keep from happening.

She let out a noticeable breath. "I didn't think you were going to force yourself on me. It's just..."

"You're regretting doing what you should have done long ago?"

She blinked rapidly; her eyes bright with impending tears. "I know I should have kicked Christopher to the curb a while ago, and probably found another job, as well, but tomorrow I'm going back to a life with no place to live and no job."

"Not necessarily."

"What do you mean?" She tugged her bottom lip up between her teeth. "Do you know of someone hiring in New York?"

My eyes drifted from her sensual lips to her long neck, and the pulse that fluttered along the side of her throat. "I meant that you shouldn't leave. Not tomorrow."

She laughed. "I have to leave."

I gave in to the urge, running one finger down the side of her neck to the hollow of her throat. "Why? We just met."

She sucked in a quick breath but didn't pull away from me. "Well, for one, I'll need to look for a job. My loans aren't going to pay off themselves."

Her skin was so soft I almost moaned out loud, the desire to skim my lips over it making my cock strain against my pants. "It seems a shame for you to run off so soon when I hardly know you. I would very much like to get to know you better, Ella. Why don't we make a deal?"

"A deal?"

I nodded, my eyes on the pulse that tripped beneath her alabaster skin. "I'm a businessman. I make deals. I'll make a deal with you." I moved my hand around the back of her head and tangled my fingers in her hair. "You stay here in Istanbul with me for a little while longer, and I'll pay off your debts."

Her lips parted as she gaped at me. "My debts? All of them?" She gave her head a small shake. "You don't know what you're promising. I owe a lot of money."

I leaned into her, feathering my lips to her earlobe. "Money is not a problem, and I promise you my bank account won't even flinch. You stay with me a little longer so we can get to know each other better, and I'll pay off everything you owe."

She held her breath for a beat. "Stay with you? Here? For how long?"

I didn't know how long it would take to unravel her origins and what it might mean for me or her. "You already wish to leave?"

"No, but I can't just leave everything forever. I do have a life in New York."

"Do you?" I asked, then felt her stiffen, and I pulled back and locked eyes with her. "You're right. We can't make a deal without parameters." I slid my hand from her hair to cup her chin in my palm. "I will pay all your debts if you stay with me until the end of the summer."

She did a quick mental calculation. "That's almost two months."

"You would rather spend the rest of your life paying off your debt?"

She blinked up at me. "This is crazy. You can't be serious."

I dragged my thumb across her lower lip. "I promise you I am serious, and I have been called a lot of things, but rarely crazy."

"You're willing to pay all that just for..."

The time to unravel the truth of her, I thought. But I couldn't say that. "The pleasure of your company, Ella." I feathered my lips across hers. "I take nothing that is not mine to take."

"But if you pay off all my debts, won't that mean you've bought me? Won't that make me yours?"

A growl rumbled up from deep in my throat, the thought of making the woman mine sending a possessive thrill through me. "If you become mine, it will not be because I paid off your debt. It will be because you want to be mine. It will be because you cannot resist falling from grace with me." I lowered my mouth so that it was a whisper away from hers. "I give you my word I will never force you. I assure you I will not need to do so."

Her breath mingled with mine as she moved her head up and down almost imperceptibly. "I'm in."

"You agree to my deal?" A sinful heat flared in my core as I moved my arm around her, pressing my palm to the small of her back and arching her body so it was flush against mine.

"I agree," she whispered, her words like marks burned in stone that could never be erased. "Do you want me to sign something?"

"Your promise is enough, but you should understand that I will hold you to it. I am what you might call old fashioned. Your word is all I need."

With a dominant sound, I crushed my lips to hers, finally tasting the celestial sweetness of the human. Her intoxicating softness made my heart thunder, and my muscles go taut, lust tearing through me like an inferno.

I felt my resolve slipping even as I fought to maintain control, but there was nowhere for a fallen angel to go but down.

5

Ella

The intensity of his kiss forced me back onto the couch as tremors of desire and fear entwined themselves around my spine. What had I done? What was I doing?

Even as his lips moved hungrily against mine, alarm bells were going off in the back of my head. Alarm bells I ignored, as I pressed my hands against the hard planes of his chest muscles and moaned into his mouth. God, he felt so good. And he tasted like whiskey—expensive whiskey with a slow burn that made me want more of him.

His tongue parted my lips with a hard sweep, taking control of my mouth. His caressing strokes became dominant as his tongue moved deftly against mine. He groaned, and the sound seeped into me and sent heat rushing south.

As his hard body pressed into mine, I realized just how much bigger and stronger Dominick was than me. If he wanted to shove my dress up and take me right there on the couch, there would have been almost nothing I could do to stop him. But did I want to stop him? I should, but I couldn't seem to build up the self-control to push him away. Not when he tasted like sin, yet his touch felt like decadent sanctuary. I moved one hand from his chest to his face, my fingers scraping across his stubble and pulling me from the daze of his touch.

This was *so* not me. I did not hook up with strangers, even if they did look like Dominick Vicario, and even if he did just offer to fix my entire life. Before I could tell him I'd made a horrible mistake, he tore his lips from mine and sat back, panting. His eyes glinted like a barely controlled predator.

Even though the man scared me, he'd also awakened something I'd never felt before. I both desired his touch and feared that I might be consumed by him. This man was way out of my league in every way, and from the moment I'd laid eyes on him I'd known that he was both powerful and dangerous in a manner I'd never encountered before—and honestly didn't know how to handle. I put my fingers to my lips, already missing the feel of him on me even though I knew I shouldn't. "Is something wrong?"

"I told you I will not take anything you don't wish to give me." He drew in a shuddering breath as he stood. "Or anything you're not in the right state to offer."

It took me a moment to decipher his meaning. "You think I'm too impaired to know what I'm doing?" Anger spiked through me, and I glared at him. He was younger than any boss I'd ever had, yet he radiated self-assurance and control like no one I'd ever met. It was annoying as hell. "Don't treat me like I'm a child."

He laughed darkly. "I know very well you aren't a child, Ella."

Even the way he said my name sent an unwanted shiver of pleasure through me, his accent making even my simple name sound exotic.

He dragged a hand through his thick hair, the curls springing back and falling over his forehead again. "I don't want you to do anything you'll regret."

I felt like saying it was way too late for that since I'd already promised to spend two months with the man, and I'd just met him. Dominick's gaze held mine for a moment as if he was reading my thoughts, then he turned and walked toward the bar cart by the windows. He dropped two ice cubes into a glass then poured something amber over them from one of the crystal decanters. Clearly, water wasn't cutting it.

I picked up my water and drank the rest of it, partly to cool off and partly to keep myself from snapping at him. The ice cubes clinked as I set the empty glass back down. "I don't get it," I said once I was sure I could keep my voice calm. "I thought you wanted this. I thought you brought me to your room..."

I didn't say that I'd thought I was about to do something really daring for once and have my first one-night stand, but that wouldn't make me sound very sophisticated.

Even from across the room, his dark eyes blazed hot into my soul. "You have no idea how much I want this." He closed his eyes and braced his hands on the sides of the cart as if steeling himself. Then he opened his eyes, rolled his shoulders back and smiled at me, the fire gone from his eyes. "There's no need to rush anything. You've had an eventful day."

That was an understatement. I'd lost a promotion, quit my job, dumped my boyfriend over text, and agreed to stay with a virtual stranger who both terrified and aroused me for the rest of the summer. My day hadn't been eventful, it had been catastrophic.

Cold chills made my bare arms prickle, and I crossed them. Maybe he was right. The shock of what I'd done was starting to hit me, and the sharp tang of bile rose in the back of my throat.

I closed my eyes and inhaled slowly as I leaned forward, hearing the splash of liquid and feeling cool glass being pressed into my hand.

When I opened my eyes, he was standing over me, holding a full glass of water. "Drink this."

I obeyed him if only so I wouldn't puke all over his expensive-looking shoes, taking the glass in my trembling hand and downing the water.

"This is crazy," I mumbled to myself. "This isn't real. Things like this don't happen. Not to me, at least."

"I assure you; I am very real." The deep timbre of his voice seemed to fill every corner of the suite and every part of my body.

The cold water cleared more of the haze of desire from my brain and reality clenched my gut like a vise. I tipped my head back to look at him looming over me. "How do I know this is real? How do I know that our deal...?" I didn't finish my spoken thoughts but understanding darkened his face almost instantly.

"Trust me." Dominick's voice hummed with suppressed fury. "Your debts will be taken care of by morning. I did not lie to you." He bent down so that his mouth brushed the shell of my ear. "I did not have to. You want to be here as much as I want you to be."

I flinched at the truth of his words, pulling back from him. "I don't know why. This isn't like me at all."

"You really don't know," he whispered after a heavy silence. "Fascinating."

"Know what?"

He shook his head then brushed a strand of hair off my shoulder. "You probably have no idea how alluring you are, either."

I shot him a look. "You don't need to pour on the flattery. I already agreed to your deal." An agreement I was seriously starting to regret.

He lifted my chin with one finger. "It isn't flattery. I have a feeling you aren't flattered very easily."

I twitched one shoulder. "No one's ever pulled a muscle trying before."

A smile teased the corner of his mouth. "Beautiful and amusing. This Christopher was a fool to lose you."

The mention of my boyfriend—correction, ex-boyfriend—made me straighten quickly. He was probably still out partying with the guys from my work—correction, former work—but at some point, he'd go back to our hotel room. "All my things are still at the other hotel, including my passport."

He dropped my chin and absently traced his finger down my arm. "You don't need to worry about any of that. I'll have my people gather your things and bring them here."

"You have people?" I got the idea he was a big deal, but I wasn't sure I understood just how big of a deal he might be.

"I have people," he said smoothly, as he turned and walked toward the door. "People I now need to speak with."

I swallowed hard, glancing around the luxurious room. "You're leaving?"

Dominick turned to face me, giving me a full view of just how magnificent he was in his perfectly tailored black clothes that somehow made him look both menacing and seductive. He was like sex on a stick and anyone's worst nightmare all wrapped up in one tall, dark, deadly package.

"You should get some rest, Ella, but don't worry. You'll be safe. There's always a guard posted near my suite."

A guard? That was far from reassuring. It sounded like I was a captive. Then again, I *had* just bartered away two months of my life.

"I'm not staying in this suite for the entire time, am I?" It struck me that I should have gotten a few more details before I'd verbally agreed to Dominick's deal.

His mouth quirked into a half smile. "Hardly. Tomorrow we're going into the city. You did say you haven't seen much yet, correct?"

"That's right." I tilted my head at him. "You're taking me sightseeing?"

His smile widened slightly. "I am taking you to my favorite place in Istanbul. Someplace dark and secretive." He let out a low laugh at my expression. "It's a tourist attraction, and I promise you will enjoy it."

"Wait," I called out as he turned to go speak with his people. "Am I now one of your people?"

He furrowed his brow. "No, Ella. You are nothing like those who work with me and for me." He closed the distance between us in a few long strides, his gaze scorching me as he leaned down and brushed his lips over mine. "You are something entirely different."

6

Dominick

I tapped a message into my phone as I left my suite and strode down the hall. After so many hundreds of years in the mortal realm, I could no longer communicate with my fellow fallen without the aid of modern technology. Not efficiently, at least.

Stepping into the hotel elevator, I drew in a long breath as the doors closed silently and the car swiftly dropped. I was grateful that it was so late at night and no other guests got on with me. It gave me a few moments of solitude to center myself before I spoke to my top deputy.

Although I trusted Rami with my life, it was an easy statement to make as we were both immortal. Perhaps it would have been more accurate to say that I trusted him with my empire. That was something that could be taken away from me, and it was something we'd both worked hard to build.

Immortality on Earth was much easier to withstand if you had wealth and power and purpose, not to mention the talent to seduce any woman you desired. And as Dominick Vicario, head of an underworld empire, I had all those things. So did the fallen angels who served by my side. I would not let the demons—or even the archangels—destroy what we'd built from the smoldering ashes of our banishment.

Putting aside the prophecy that I didn't even know was real, or if I believed, the chances of Ella stumbling into my sphere twice seemed highly coincidental. And one thing I'd learned over millennia was that things were rarely a coincidence. No, Ella was here for a reason. One she was unaware of, that I was certain. Who had conspired for her to encounter me, if anyone? Of that, I was less sure.

Anger simmered inside me, but it wasn't only anger at whomever was plotting against me. I was angry with myself. I twisted my neck to one side as I suppressed a roar of frustration. I never should have kissed her. Not when I knew what she was and how hard it would be to control my desire for her. It had been more than an indulgence. It had been a lapse of weakness, and weakness was something the head of an underworld organization could not afford. Nor could the leader of the Fallen.

The elevator doors glided open with a single chime, and I stepped out onto the lobby level. Beige marble was edged in a border of pewter, and sconces on the walls alternated with chandeliers to give the corridor a warm glow. I walked briskly to one of the doors that led outside, pushing through double doors and jogging down the short flight of stone steps to reach the hotel's enclosed courtyard.

The mustard-yellow walls of the hotel surrounded the garden and glass-walled octagonal structure tucked to one side, peaked turrets in the corners reminding me that the hotel had once been a jail. I followed the stone path around beds of colorful flowers, breathing in their faint perfume, until I found a wrought iron table flanked by two chairs.

I hadn't been sitting for more than a minute before Rami joined me, flopping down in the other chair and scraping a hand through his hair. His shirt was only partially buttoned, and his face was flushed.

"I've interrupted you," I said, more a statement than an apology. "The waitress?"

He smiled in acknowledgment of my guess. "She probably needed a break anyway. I do hate when they start calling out for a deity."

"But never for angels."

Rami lifted an eyebrow. "Only because they don't know what we truly look like."

I inclined my head at the truth of his statement. When we'd revealed our forms to human women when we'd been Watchers of humanity, they'd been virtually powerless to resist us. There was something intoxicating about divinity in a mortal form. Just ask anyone who'd laid eyes on Lucifer. Now I knew that temptation all too well, myself.

"Is this about the woman you invited to sit with us?" Rami asked, no doubt eager to return to his woman, despite her habit of calling out for a deity we no longer served.

I nodded. "You left quickly, I noticed."

"I've never seen you so captivated. In that case, and that case only, three felt like a crowd."

Like all Fallen, Rami's intuition was supernatural, as was his skill at reading human emotions. "Did you notice anything special about her?"

He leaned back in his chair. "She was more alluring than most humans, but I don't know why I think that. She is certainly beautiful, but many women are just as lovely. But there was something—"

"Yes." I nodded at him. "And that something is an angelic mark."

Rami stared at me for a moment. "You are serious?"

"The moment I touched her, I felt it. It's unmistakable, and it explains why I was drawn to her so powerfully. Just like I was in New York."

Rami narrowed his eyes. "She's the woman you lost over a year ago? The one you had us all searching for?"

I gave him a brief nod. "She didn't look quite the same tonight as she did at *Epicurus New York*, but it's her."

"What are the chances?" he murmured.

"Precisely."

"You are sure it's angelic?" Rami after a short pause, leaning forward in his seat. "You know what this would mean."

I let a rumble escape my throat. "That the archangels are interfering in the mortal realm again. Our realm."

"They are still tasked with monitoring Earth, although it is rare for them to get involved with human dealings."

"They are more concerned that the Fallen never regain status than they are in the activities of humans," I growled. "They leave us to keep demons at bay and gorge ourselves on mortal sins so we can never be redeemed."

Rami eyed me. "I can barely remember a time when you cared about chasing redemption."

"Because it is impossible. We were cast out of heaven for eternity." Anger bubbled inside me at the memory of being cast out from the celestial world forever.

"Unless we guide humanity away from sin," my friend reminded me.

I choked out a bitter laugh. "An impossible task. Humans are weak and especially with demons roaming the Earth and pushing them toward greater evil."

"Which we usually prevent," Rami also reminded me.

"Usually," I said under my breath, thinking back to some of our greatest failures—times when we'd almost lost our ongoing war with the demons, and when humans had embraced hate so fully that we'd barely triumphed.

It was after one of those dark and pivotal moments in history that I'd wholeheartedly embraced hedonism. If I couldn't stop hate, I could at least distract it with unbridled lust. It was hard to commit genocide when you were occupied by the best blowjobs known to man.

"It's been a century since we've encountered a human who's carried an angelic trace," Rami said. "Why would we run into one now?"

"That is exactly what I need to know. Is this part of some large plan by the archangels? Was she sent to me on purpose?"

"For what purpose?"

I slammed my hand on the table and it rattled. "That is what I need to know. You cannot tell me that it's a coincidence that at the same time demon activity is one the rise and a rival family is being led by my greatest enemy, a human female with an angelic mark appears in one of my properties when I am in residence.

Especially after I encountered her at one of our clubs a year ago. I do not believe in this much serendipity."

"You think she is connected to the demons?" Rami's brow creased. "As much as the archangels despise us, they would never work with demons."

I rubbed a hand across my forehead, huffing out a breath. "Maybe you're right. Maybe I'm crazy to imagine a plot, but what are the chances that *she* would waltz into my life for no greater purpose?"

"If she is like others who have carried an angelic mark, she probably doesn't know this about herself."

I nodded reluctantly. "She is either fully unaware, or is an actress skilled beyond anything I've ever seen."

Rami drummed his fingers on the table. "Either she was saved from death by an angel, or her conception was an angelic intervention. If her birth was divinely influenced, she would have no clue. Even those who are saved from death rarely believe—or they become zealots."

"She is no zealot," I said, thinking of how eagerly her body had responded to mine. If she felt any guilt about wanting me, it had nothing to do with religious zeal. "But if she was created by divine force..."

"Then you need to know why."

I curled my hand into a fist on the cold iron tabletop. "I despise being manipulated by the Seven."

"As do we all," Rami said, with a faint shrug. "But it has been a long time since we've seen any evidence of them here."

"Until now."

He pressed his lips together. "Unless they didn't plan for you to meet her. Unless the last thing they would ever want is for one of the Fallen to meet her."

I held his serious gaze. "The prophecy?"

He shrugged one shoulder. "I have never been one to hold it in much regard, but if it is true..."

"If the union between an angelically-marked human and a Fallen could spark the restoration of all the Fallen to angelic status?" I whispered, as if saying the words softly would protect them.

"That would change everything."

I shook my head roughly. "If that was true, then the archangels and demons would do anything to prevent it."

"Which means she would be in danger if it was discovered." Rami frowned. "Which makes it more difficult to determine if she has any connection to our enemies without tipping them off. What do you wish me to do, Dom?"

"Make inquiries. Find out everything you can about her." I pulled a card from my pocket and handed it to him. "Discreetly. Make sure anyone who asks knows she's only my latest sexual conquest."

His eyebrows popped up. "Her driver's license?"

"She will not need it for now."

"Why not?"

"She has agreed to spend the rest of the summer with me."

If it was possible for his eyebrows to go even higher, they did. "She has agreed, or you have—?"

"I have not kidnapped her, if that is what you're implying," I snapped at him before he could finish his question.

Rami held up both hands, palms out. "I am only suggesting that it isn't a small thing for a woman to drop her life for a man. Even for a powerful man such as yourself."

"I might have given her an incentive," I said. "But I need to keep her close to me until I can figure out what role she plays in all of this. Or if she is at risk."

Rami cocked his head at me. "An incentive?"

I blew out an impatient breath, knowing how my deal would sound to him. To anyone. But I didn't care. I needed her close. Not only until I determined what was going on, but because I hadn't felt such a connection in longer than I could remember—possibly ever. Touching her made powerful desires storm through me, and the possibility of feeling more with her was too tempting to give up.

"I have agreed to pay off her debts in exchange for her company until the end of the summer."

Rami only sighed and flipped Ella's license into his pants pocket. "I hope you know what you're doing, Dominick."

I thought about what I hadn't told him. About how I'd almost lost control when I'd kissed her. How I'd barely been able to keep myself from claiming her as mine in a frenzied passion. How I'd felt my last tenuous grasp on my divinity slipping as the dormant wrath deep in my soul had been awakened.

I hoped so, too.

7

Ella

"You were serious?" I rubbed my eyes as I sat up in bed and watched Dominick walking up the stairs to the loft bedroom. If it was possible, he looked even more handsome than he had the night before, and he wore a perfectly tailored, dark suit that didn't boast a single wrinkle. I, on the other hand, felt like a rumpled mess and had a raging headache.

"About showing you the dark underground of Istanbul?" He sat on the foot of the bed and smiled at me. "Of course, I was serious."

The daylight streaming through the windows did nothing to make him look less dangerous, his amber eyes still unnerving me with their intensity as his gaze raked over me without apology.

I glanced down and realized I was only wearing my black bra and panties. The cocktail dress I'd worn the night before nowhere in sight. I tugged the ivory sheet closer to my neck. "I can't exactly go out in this."

"Pity," he purred, his gaze drifting down to the exposed skin of my throat and the sheet that covered the rest of me. "Your other clothes are hanging in the closet. I suggest you wear shoes suitable for walking on uneven stones."

"The underworld isn't paved?"

"Underground," he corrected with a slight smile, as he stood. "And no, it isn't."

My gaze went to the closet doors. "You really got all my stuff from the other hotel?"

"I didn't, but my people did. And before you ask, I hung everything up while you slept. No one else has been in here."

"Thanks." I touched a hand to my temples, wondering for a moment if Christopher had even noticed that my stuff was gone —or cared. If he'd replied to my text, I hadn't gotten it. Come to think of it, where were my purse and phone?

"Coffee and fresh *simit* are on the table." Dominick waved at the living room below as he descended the stairs. "I'll leave you to dress."

Before I could unleash a torrent of questions for him, he'd slipped from the suite and left me alone again. The room was quiet, and the energy that seemed to crackle off the man had vanished with him.

I let out a soft sigh as I kicked off the duvet and swung my legs over the side of the bed. Dominick clearly hadn't slept beside me last night, but he also didn't look like he'd pulled an all-nighter. Was there an extra bedroom I hadn't seen, or had he bunked with that guy who'd been talking with him before I joined them on the terrace?

I shook my head as plucked the plush bathrobe from where it was draped across the end of the bed, then I padded barefoot down the stairs, the rich scent of the coffee and the yeasty aroma of the bread beckoning me. No, powerful men like Dominick Vicario didn't bunk with their male friends. Where he'd gone last night was another one of the mysteries about the man I'd have to add to the growing list.

Sinking onto the dark tufted sofa, I flashed back to the night before and how he'd pressed me into the back of it with the single best kiss I'd ever had in my entire life. I shook that memory from my mind and reached for the cylindrical coffee pot that was silver on the bottom and glass on the top. The cup matched the design with an ornate, silver base and a white, ceramic cup nestled inside.

I filled my cup and added two sugar cubes before taking a sip. It was strong, Turkish coffee, a brew that made American coffee seem like water in comparison, but I liked the flavor and the added kick. I picked up one of the circles of bread—*simit*—that reminded me of bagels, but skinnier and covered with sesame seeds. I took a bite along with another sip of coffee, the ache in my head already fading. I wasn't usually a big fan of breakfast—a blueberry muffin on the way to work was an occasional indulgence—but the combination of the rich coffee and the warm bread was both filling and comforting.

I scanned the room as I chewed. I'd had my black, crossbody purse on me the night before, but it had apparently vanished, along with my cocktail dress. If I hadn't been staying at a well-known hotel in the middle of a busy city, I might have been worried. As it was, I doubted Dominick could drag me from the Four Seasons and away from Istanbul without a lot of people noticing. Even if he did own the hotel. Not that I was so sure I believed that part of his story.

I believed that he was wealthy and powerful. That had been obvious the night before. But just how powerful was he? Powerful enough to own a Four Seasons hotel? Did that mean he was a secret owner of the entire brand? The thought sent a shiver through me.

I gulped down more coffee as I thought about what I'd agreed to last night. Had he seriously promised to pay off my debts—all of them? It would be easy enough to check, if only I had my phone or access to the Web. If the banks were even open on the east coast of the US, which I doubted they were, since it was still morning in Turkey.

"Patience," I whispered to myself. As insane as it was, the prospect of getting over a hundred thousand dollars of debt paid off instantly was too good to screw up, even if I did have to spend a couple of months with a terrifyingly gorgeous businessman.

Sara might tell me I was crazy, but only until she saw Dominick. Yeah, I doubted I'd get much of a pity party about the arrangement after that. Especially if I added the part about staying in a baller suite at the Four Seasons.

I took a final swig of Turkish coffee and stood, hurrying up the stairs and to the closet. Dominick had promised to show me Istanbul, and I was dying to see it. Even if this deal was too good to be true, at least I owed it to myself to take advantage of his tour guide services. Besides, I was curious about this underground Istanbul he'd teased.

I opened the doors and pawed through the clothes on the wooden hangers. As promised, all the clothes I'd already packed up for my flight had been hung, and they even looked like they'd been pressed. Damn, his people were good.

Remembering what he'd said about walking, I picked out a celadon-green, sleeveless sundress and flat sandals, draping the dress across the foot of the bed. But first things, first. I needed a hot shower.

Stepping into the bathroom, I let out a breath as I took in the deep soaking tub underneath an arched window on one side, and a standing, glassed-in shower on the other. A red-and-blue-patterned Turkish rug lay on top of the tile floor, and luxurious bottles of toiletries were lined up on a marble counter than stretched underneath a gilded mirror. Even though Dominick wasn't there, the dark spicy scent of his cologne lingered in the air, making my pulse flutter as I imagined him in the spacious, glass shower.

I groaned as I tried to banish the image from my mind. "Ella, you are so screwed."

"You weren't kidding about the underground." I eyed the darkened stone steps and rested my hand on the crossbody purse Dominick had returned to me. Even though he'd insisted I wouldn't need money or even ID today, I felt a sense of security having it draped over one shoulder.

Dominick rested a hand loosely on the small of my back as we walked down the dimly lit stairs leading underground and into the Basilica Cistern. "I wasn't. It is called Yearbatan Sarayi."

I repeated his words, but they didn't sound nearly as melodic when I said them.

"It means sunken place, and it's one of the most magical sites in the entire city." His hand moved to my hip as the stairs twisted, and we descended further underground. Even though we'd only started down the wide staircase, the distinctive scent of moisture wafted up from below. "If you've seen nothing of Istanbul, this is where to start."

The short walk from the hotel to the basilica in the Sultanahmet district had taken us past the Blue Mosque, which had towered above us in all its white marbled splendor, the bright, midday sunlight making it almost as impressive as it had been in the moonlight. Vendors with street carts had hawked skewers of meat, and tour guides had vied for our attention, waving tourist maps, but then moving away quickly when Dominick waved them off. Electric trams rattled by on rails, and shiny tour buses lined the curbs. I was glad for my flat sandals, even though the walk wasn't long, and I was even grateful for Dominick's hand on my arm when we crossed the street, and now as we were led deeper underground.

Despite my low-key trepidation about the deal I'd made with him, I was enjoying spending time with the man. He might give off a seriously dangerous vibe, but so far, he'd been nothing but a gentleman, waiting patiently for me to get ready for our outing without barging in or telling me to hurry up, something Christopher did constantly. Aside from the one scorching kiss he'd given me the night before, Dominick hadn't tried anything, although I wasn't sure if I was happy about that or disappointed. Even remembering it now made my heart beat faster.

Regardless, Dominick Vicario had been more considerate of me in less than twenty-four hours than Christopher had in three years. He'd held open doors for me, walked on the traffic side of the sidewalk, and listened when I talked. Not to mention the fact that he was the best looking man I'd ever seen in person and drew open-mouthed stares wherever we went. But not once had he seemed to notice the looks he got or let his attention be drawn away from me. Not like my ex, who'd had a seriously roving eye.

Dominick, on the other hand, made me feel like I was the most intriguing woman on the planet. I could get used to it, which was a good thing, considering.

“It’s so quiet,” I whispered, as if my words might break the magical spell that seemed to hang in the air as our footsteps echoed on the stone.

“It isn’t usually this quiet,” he said, his voice also hushed. “I bought out the morning’s tickets.”

My foot faltered on a step as I snapped my head to him. “You did what?”

He caught me before I slipped, his grip around my waist tight as I righted myself with the wooden railing. “I wished you to see it as I used to, before it was crowded with tour groups.”

I was speechless as we continued down the stairs, gold light beginning to seep up from below, as well as the sound of lapping water. How rich did you have to be to buy out all the tours—and how powerful? I doubted just anyone could call up and rent out a major tourist attraction in the heart of Istanbul in June.

At the bottom of the stairs, we stepped down onto a paved path that then opened to a massive space. As my eyes adjusted to the subterranean dimness, I could see that hundreds of massive, marble columns rose into the air, each one uplit with amber light. The light bounced off the water that they sat in, making the entire enormous underground room glow.

“Holy crap,” I said, then slapped a hand over my mouth as my words echoed in the quiet.

Dominick’s throaty laughed also reverberated off the marble. “There are over three hundred columns.”

I peered down the rows that seemed to stretch endlessly. "All of this is under the city?" It was hard to think that we'd just been walking on top of all this. "It looks like a cathedral."

Dominick made a low noise. "Perhaps, but this was built to the glory of water, not God."

Peering into the water below, I spotted fish darting beneath the surface. The water was not deep, but I suspected it was cold.

He took my hand and led me farther down to the columns, pointing to a carved face at the base of one—a face that was upside down. "Medusa."

I peered up at his face, which was cast in shadows. "As in the woman with snakes for hair?"

He nodded. "There are many theories for why the heads are here." He pulled me farther down the wooden walkway. "They're all wrong."

Our shoes tapped on the walkway as we walked among the columns, the cool air making goose bumps prickle my bare arms. Finally, I stopped him.

"This is amazing, but I don't understand how you managed to kick out every single tourist and book it for our private use." I pulled my hand from his and crossed my arms over my chest. "Who are you?"

"I've already told you my name. I did not lie to you."

"Dominick Vicario," I said. "But who are you really? I know you're a businessman, and you claim to own the Four Seasons, but I don't know any businessman who could pull off a trick like this with only a few hours' notice. We did just meet last night." I sucked in air. "Unless you were stalking me and had this planned all along."

He angled his head at me. "You appeared on my hotel's rooftop. How is that *me* stalking *you*?"

"Right." I gave my head a small shake. "Still, who are you to manage something like this?"

He exhaled. "You really wish to know?"

"If I'm going to be spending the next couple of months with you, I think I deserve to know."

He closed the scant distance between us, the heat from his body pulsing into me. "I will tell you only if you promise me that you will not go back on our deal."

I shrugged aside any hesitation. I'd already gone this far, and I had very little to lose that I hadn't already tossed aside. "If you can prove to me that you've truly paid off my debts, I'm in."

He brushed a loose strand of hair off my face and then traced a finger down my cheek. "I am a businessman, like I told you, but I am also the head of the Vicario organization."

My stomach fluttered. "What's that?"

"We used to organize business endeavors that were outside of what was strictly legal, but now most of our holdings are legitimate."

It took me a few beats to process his meaning. "Organized crime? Are you telling me you're the head of an organized crime family?"

He slid his hand from my cheek to my hair, running his fingers through it and cupping my head in his palm. "We're less a family and more like a collection of outcast sons."

My mind whirred with this information. No wonder he could pay off a hundred grand in debts so easily and clear out an entire tourist attraction. It also explained why people in the hotel melted into the shadows when he passed. He was a fucking mob boss. Before I could respond, his grip on me tightened.

"We have to go."

"I don't think so," I said, trying to pull away from him. "You need to—"

He jerked my body flush with his, and the velvet of his voice had a sharp edge. "I do not have time to argue with you, Ella. Not now."

As he tugged me forcefully back toward the entrance, I caught sight of a figure standing at the far end of the walkway. Even though the woman was silhouetted in the light, and I couldn't make out her features, I could feel her gaze searing into me—and I could have sworn her eyes were flaming red.

8

Dominick

I tipped her head up, the desire to kiss her again almost bringing me to my knees. Her angelic connection, whatever it was, made it almost impossible for me to resist her. She'd even managed to get the truth about my business from me, even though now she looked up at me with a mix of shock and horror.

As need stormed through me, the feel of her lithe body rendered my breath ragged and my restraint in tatters. Just a small taste, I thought, as my gaze lingered on the curve of her lips. The subtle tinge of her divinity skimmed over me, unfurling dark desire from my soul that rose like smoke.

Then, my peripheral vision caught a flutter of movement so swift and silent that mortal eyes would have missed it. My spine stiffened at the familiar hiss that indicated the demon's displeasure. I would know that sound anywhere, and across endless millennia. Jaya.

I tightened my grip on the human in my arms, as rage slid scorching tendrils across my skin. How dare Jaya approach me uninvited, especially since I'd banished her from my sight long ago. But my anger was doused by the ice of fear that she was not here for me. At least, not anymore.

I shifted my gaze down the cavernous glowing space to where the succubus stood in her alluring female form, her long, black hair trailing down her back and her eyes flashing through the shadows. It only took a moment to confirm my fears. If she'd come for me, I was no longer her focus. Her gaze was fixed on Ella, her demonic senses alerted to the human's angelic mark even more instantly than mine had been.

I lowered my voice to little more than a whisper of a breath. "We have to go."

"I don't think so," Ella attempted to pull herself from my grip, panic sharpening her words. "You need to—"

I did not have time to explain things to Ella, nor did I think she would believe me. But I did need to get her away from Jaya, especially if the demon was not alone. As powerful as I was as the leader of the Fallen, I did not want to fight off a swarm of demons. Not and attempt to keep Ella safe at the same time.

I jerked her so that her body was flat against mine, silencing her complaints. "I do not have time to argue with you, Ella. Not now."

I didn't wait for her to speak again, practically carrying her toward the stairs leading from the underground cistern. The normally placid water surrounding the pillars churned and bubbled behind us, sending spray into the air. I flicked my wrist and sent the water shooting backward so that it spiraled around Jaya. It took all my control not to unfurl my wings and fly us out, but that would require much more explaining than I was ready for—or that I suspected Ella could handle. Still, her feet barely brushed the floor as I rushed us up, my gaze catching one final glimpse of Jaya's molten glare through the swirling wall of water before she vanished behind a marble column.

When we reached the top and were standing outside the entrance—trams clacking by and tourists chattering loudly as they peered up at the Blue Mosque—I slammed the glass doors behind us, pulled my phone from my pocket, and speed-dialed Rami.

"What the hell was that about?" Ella's face was flushed as she finally wiggled from my grasp and stumbled back.

I ignored her question and the furtive stares from a passing couple, instead giving quick orders to Rami when he answered on the second ring. "Prepare the jet. We're leaving early." I took Ella's arm and pulled her to me, moving us both swiftly away from the basilica entrance while she swatted at me.

"Dom?" Rami's single word response held a torrent of questions.

"Jaya."

That was all the explanation he needed, a thick silence falling over the line. Then he growled low. "And the woman? Did Jaya see her?"

Ella still attempted to free herself from my embrace, but she was no match for my strength—or my will. I squeezed my eyes shut for a beat before biting out the answer. "Yes. And she knows what she is."

"Where are you?" In the background, Rami gave succinct orders to our brethren amid a flurry of snapped fingers and dark murmurs.

"We just left the Yearbatan Sarayi." I scanned the bustling street. "I see no evidence of others."

"Jaya always preferred to work alone," Rami said, then hesitated. "What about the woman, Dom?"

Ella was cursing as I held her, but I didn't loosen the arm pinning her to me. "She's coming with us. Pack her things for the plane."

"Understood." If he disagreed with my actions, his tone didn't reveal it. "The car should be to you in a few seconds."

I disconnected and slid the phone back into my pants, turning my attention back to Ella, whose cheeks were mottled pink as she looked up at me.

"I hope you weren't talking about me," she said, as I allowed her to take a small step away. "I'm not going with you anywhere."

I sighed, casting a quick glance behind us to the basilica cistern entrance. My distractions would not hold off the demon for long, although I knew Jaya well enough to know she would not wish a battle in the middle of the day in front of humans.

"Of course, you are." I closed the distance between us again and looped an arm around her waist. "Or have you forgotten our deal already?"

Even though her body trembled, she did her best to give me a ferocious glare. "That was before I knew..."

A sleek, black limousine glided up to the curb. I didn't wait for the driver to jump out and open the door, pulling it open myself as I cut my eyes behind me. "Like I said, now isn't the time or the place to discuss this."

I scooped her up, bent over, and tossed her inside the vehicle. Luckily, only a few passersby gawked as Elle screamed from inside the limo, but I ducked in after her and quickly slammed the door.

Ella scrambled to sit up and tug down the skirt of her dress as we pulled away and began weaving through Istanbul.

"What the fuck was that?" Her blue eyes were wild, as she smoothed her tousled hair.

I leaned back against the buttery, black leather, my pulse already calming in the cool air of the luxury car. "It was important we get away from the basilica."

She studied me for a second. "Because of the woman standing at the end of the walkway?"

My heart missed a beat. "You saw her?"

Ella nodded. "No one else was supposed to be down there since you bought out the entire place, so it seemed weird. And she didn't look...normal."

"Well put," I said, thinking that was the understatement of the century.

"Okay." Ella rearranged herself on the banquette that curved around the length of the limo, taking in the polished wood, the inset bar stocked with crystal decanters, and the privacy screen between us and the driver. "That still doesn't explain why you told someone on the phone that I was going with you on a plane."

"We're leaving Istanbul."

She stared at me as if waiting for more. "And going where? I never agreed to leave the city with you."

"You didn't agree not to. Our deal specified that you would spend the summer with me." I leaned forward and my knees brushed hers. "That means you go where I go."

"And where are we going?"

"For now, we're going to Venice." I thought of the Fallen who would be there, and my shoulders uncoiled. "We have a palazzo that is well-guarded."

"Guarded?" She opened her mouth and then closed it again. "Am I to be your prisoner?"

"You are my guest," I said, choosing my words carefully and trying not to let my gaze be drawn to her seductively soft lips. "But in my business, I need to be careful. That means protecting you as well."

"You weren't guarded here in Istanbul. Unless your bodyguards were really stealthy."

"My guards are skilled at being inconspicuous, but you're right. I did not bring many guards with me to Istanbul." I thought about the increased demon activity and scowled. "I did not think they would be necessary."

She sank back into the seat, her gaze going everywhere but to me. Finally, she locked eyes with mine. "You also didn't tell me everything about yourself before we made our deal."

It was difficult to be so close to her and not touch her. My skin longed to feel the electric hum of her flesh. Instead, I reached for one of the decanters and poured a glass of whiskey then offered it to her. "You didn't ask."

Ella waved away the glass. "It never occurred to me that you could be a..." She darted her gaze at the divider between us and the driver. "A mob boss."

I huffed out a laugh and took a sip of the single malt that I favored. "I would hardly call us a mob. And I told you that I've moved our business into legitimate enterprises."

Her scowl softened. "So, you aren't a crime boss?"

"Crime?" I shook my head and took a significant gulp, letting the heat of the whiskey roll around my tongue and then sear its way down my throat. "I do not deny that our holdings focus primarily on luxury and pleasure, but hedonism and indulgence are hardly crimes."

The pink returned to her cheeks. "I don't even know what that means."

My pulse quickened as I saw her pupils flare and the skin on her chest flush. "You will soon."

Ella shifted on her seat, glancing out the tinted windows as we made our way farther from the center of the city. "You don't break kneecaps and have people murdered?"

The whiskey burned in my stomach as I thought about the demons and humans I'd punished. "Breaking kneecaps isn't my style. I have never inflicted pain on anyone who didn't richly deserve it. Those who are truly wicked and corrupted by evil need to be corrected."

"You're kidding, right?" Her voice trembled.

"I would never joke about something as serious as evil." I drained my glass and tucked it back into the holder, then slid over to sit next to her. "But you don't need to worry about any of that. You are far from corrupt."

"What if I've decided not to go through with our deal? What if I want out?"

If Ella had said no before she'd been spotted by Jaya, I might have considered letting her go. At least, that's what I told myself. But now that a demon like Jaya knew about the angelically-marked human, I had no choice. The only way to keep her out of demon hands was to hold her tightly in mine.

I rested a hand on her leg, my thumb lazily caressing the bare skin of her lower thigh. "I'm afraid it's too late for that, *amor*. I've already paid your debts." I inched the fabric of her dress up a fraction. "Now it's time to pay yours."

9

Ella

The private jet sat on the tarmac as the sun sank low in the sky behind it, the horizon suffused with gold. Outside the limousine, Dominick and the friend who'd been with him the night before—Rami, I think he'd called him—stood close together, talking.

I glanced down at my phone, trying to comprehend what I'd just learned. Unless Dominick Vicario had the influence to alter credit card and bank websites, he'd done what he'd promised he'd do. He'd eliminated all my debt.

My breath was shallow as the reality sank in. According to my financial records, I now had zero student-loan debt and all the balances on my credit cards had been wiped out. I still didn't know how he'd managed to do it so quickly, but the proof was undeniable. I'd refreshed each page several times.

"Fuck," I whispered. As thrilled as I was to lose my choking debt, now there was no going back.

I peered out the tinted windows at the tall, broad-shouldered figure of Dominick Vicario. That is, if I even wanted to. There was no denying that the man was used to getting his way, and that obviously included with women, but I also couldn't deny that his dominant gaze made my heart race and heat throb between my legs.

I was a successful professional who'd been supporting myself since I was eighteen years old. No way should I be drawn to a mob boss who'd paid off my debts so he could keep me. I would have rolled my eyes if I'd heard about a woman falling for something like this, thinking she was an idiot not to run as fast and as far as she could. But there was something about the way Dominick looked at me and the way he touched me that was both familiar and made me crave more. And it had been a long time since I'd allowed myself anything that I truly craved.

I gave my head a hard shake. "This can't be real."

Things like this didn't happen to regular women like me. It wasn't like I was some supermodel, or blonde bombshell with fake boobs and a spray-on tan. I was a sort of redhead with a decent rack and skin that required SPF 100, at least according to my best friend.

Sara!

She would be expecting me back home soon or at least to report on what happened on my solo night out in Istanbul. I scrolled my recent calls and hovered my finger over her name. How was I going to explain this to her? My boss and boyfriend might not expect to see me again, but my best friend would send out a search party if I disappeared without a word.

I glanced at Dominick again, taking a shuddering breath as he twisted his head around as if sensing that I was staring at him. Even though he couldn't see through the dark windows, his hot gaze felt like it was boring into me.

I pressed Sara's number, the blood rushing in my ear as I waited for her to pick up.

"Ella! I was dying to hear from you." Her voice was muffled, and I assumed she was still at work. "Are you calling me from your layover?"

"Not exactly," I said. "I'm still in Istanbul."

"Really? Did your flight get delayed?"

"Nope, but I didn't get on it." I took a deep breath. "A lot has happened since I talked to you. I quit my job and broke up with Christopher."

She was silent for a beat before letting out a quiet whoop. "It's about fucking time, girl. What finally convinced you?"

"You remember how I was heading to the rooftop terrace at the Four Seasons? Well, I met someone there."

"As in a guy? Oh my God, this is so romantic. I can't believe you met someone in Istanbul."

"I broke up with Christopher before anything happened with Dominick," I added quickly.

"As if I care about that. Your ex was a tool and did not deserve your loyalty. Now tell me more about this Dominick. Damn, that's a sexy name."

"He's pretty incredible." I peeked at him again, my stomach somersaulting. He was by far the most gorgeous man I'd ever dated. My mouth went dry. Was I dating him? Would you call our arrangement dating?

"And?" Sara prodded. "He's why you're staying in Istanbul?"

"Yeah. I mean, I don't have a job or a boyfriend to go home to, so I figured I might as well hang out here and get to know him."

"Okay." Hesitation had crept into her voice. "So, what's his deal? What do you know about him?"

I smiled. Sara was always the protector. I could almost envision her sitting at her desk, with her stick-straight, black hair in a messy bun and her almond eyes narrowed in concentration. "He's a hotelier, a successful one."

"Successful is good. I'm assuming he's not a punk-ass boy like your ex?"

I laughed. Sara did not mince words. "He's definitely not a boy."

"An older man?" Sara made a humming sound. "I like it. You need someone more mature and experienced."

Dominick didn't look much older than me, but he exuded power and control that no thirty something did. "He's definitely experienced."

"Ella! Did you already—?"

"No, no," I cut her off before she could finish. "I didn't sleep with him. Not yet. Give me some credit."

She let out a disappointed huff. "I always said you needed a really wild one-night stand."

"Well, this is going to be more than one night. Dominick has invited me to stay for the summer."

The line went silent.

"Sara?"

"You're spending the rest of the summer with a man you just met? That doesn't sound like you at all, Ella."

"I know, it's crazy," I said, the words spilling from me in a nervous rush. "But maybe it's exactly what I need. Aren't you always telling me that I need to break out of my rut? Well, I'm breaking out."

"I meant you should try a different flavor of ice cream or change up your hair. Not run off with a perfect stranger." Her tone shifted. "Ella, what do you really know about this guy?"

Way too much, I thought. No way was I telling my best friend that Dominick was the head of a former crime family and that he'd paid off all my debts in exchange for me staying with him. Not only would she freak out, but she'd also probably hop on a plane to come rescue me.

"You worry too much," I told her. "I'm perfectly fine, and Dominick hasn't even tried anything." That was mostly true. "Besides, he's the first guy in a long time who's made me feel special. After Christopher, I really need this."

Sara released a reluctant sigh. "I get that, but does it have to be for two months?"

"You know I haven't had much of a chance to travel. This is my chance to have a real adventure and see a part of the world I may never get to again."

"You're really good at presenting logical arguments, you know that?"

I laughed quietly. "I am, I know."

"Fine. But do you promise me that this guy deserves you? Your judgment hasn't always been stellar where men are concerned."

My good judgment—whatever was left of it—was sending up serious alarm bells when it came to Dominick, but it didn't do any good to tell Sara that. "I promise. And I'll call you again in a few days, okay?"

"I would say don't do anything I wouldn't do, but that leaves you with just about everything." Her voice cracked. "Just come home safe."

I told her I would, my own throat constricting as I said goodbye and disconnected. When I'd blinked away the tears that stung the back of my eyelids, I opened the limousine door.

Dominick turned, his gaze tracking me as I walked over to the stairs extending from the plane. His friend nodded at me in acknowledgement as Dominick rested a hand possessively on my hip.

"Did you confirm everything?"

I lifted a hand to shield my eyes as I looked up at him. "You were telling the truth."

"I told you that I wouldn't lie to you, Ella."

His gaze was slow and scorching as it moved over my face, lingering on my lips. Dominick Vicario did not look like a man who could be trusted. He looked like a man who should be feared and avoided, but I couldn't seem to stop myself from being pulled into his orbit. For some strange reason, it felt like I was destined to be wrapped up with this deadly man who was so different from everything I'd ever known. Nothing about being with him made sense, but I couldn't resist the inevitable fall.

The warm air around us shifted suddenly, a hot breeze sending my hair flying into my face. I closed my eyes as bits of grit stung my bare skin, and I wondered if Istanbul got sandstorms.

"We need to go." Dominick's voice was a bellow over the roar c the plane engine, and his hand closed hard around mine as he pulled me up the stairs of the plane.

I stole a glance behind me before we ducked inside. The black-suited men who'd been on the tarmac with Dominick seemed to almost fly across the pavement toward us, as a dark cloud billowed in the distance and barreled across the sky, obscuring the glow of the setting sun. And were those winged silhouettes emerging from the dark swirling mass?

Impossible, I thought as I was jerked into the plane, and the stairs were pulled up as the jet lurched forward. I barely had a moment to take in the luxurious, plush interior, before Dominick was strapping me into a cream-colored seat. Dominick's men stood in the aisle and peered out the small windows, their bodies tense with anticipation as we rocketed down the runway, outrunning the storm.

"Things might get a little bumpy," Dominick said, as he took the seat next to me, then pulled my lips to his in a hard, claiming kiss as we lifted off the ground.

10

Dominick

The plane trembled as it rumbled down the runway, dark clouds swirling outside the windows. My fellow Fallen had rushed inside right behind us and now watched with trepidation as the demon storm raced across the sky.

Ella's expression was a mixture of shock and confusion while I hurriedly strapped her into one of the seats. If the demon winds overtook us, it would be a bumpy ride. If we survived.

"It's *her*," one of my guards muttered darkly, his palms splayed on either side of an oval window.

I ignored this, although I knew precisely who he meant. Instead, I took the seat next to Ella and buckled in. My stomach churned at the thought that she was now in danger because of me. "This might get a little bumpy."

She managed a weak smile, her hands gripping the armrests tightly as the plane shuddered and the interior dimmed as the sky outside became black. The demon storm had reached us.

Driven by a pang of regret, I crushed my mouth to hers as the plane lifted off the ground, wobbling in the air and pitching forward roughly. But I didn't notice the rest of the jerky takeoff. Instead, I lost myself in the softness of her lips as they yielded to mine and the sweetness of her mouth as she opened to me.

Yearning morphed to desire as I scraped a hand into her hair and held her to me, my mouth moving more urgently. The roar of the plane and the rage of the storm were mercifully drowned out by the thundering of blood in my ears as my tongue tangled with hers. Like before, her touch rendered me senseless like nothing ever had, and I desired nothing but to lose myself in her. When she fisted a hand around my collar and moaned, I was pulled back to reality and the plane—which was still flying.

Tearing my mouth from hers, I glanced around as if coming out of a trance. Turgid clouds no longer swirled outside the windows, and my fellow Fallen weren't poised for battle in the aisle. They sat in seats with belts fastened across their waists as the plane cruised through white clouds.

I glanced down at Ella, her lips puffy and her expression dazed. We'd kissed long enough for both of us to miss most of the dramatic takeoff, which had been one of the reasons I'd distracted her with a kiss. Not that I'd intended to be so distracted myself that I'd lost all track of time or place.

I smoothed her tousled hair and brushed a gentle kiss over her forehead. "You're all right?"

She nodded, sweeping her gaze around the cabin. "Did we outrun the storm?"

"It appears so." I let out a relieved breath that she hadn't noticed anything odd about the storm. Not that a human would know the difference between a regular storm and one that was demonically created. But I did.

I unhooked myself from the seat and stood. "I'll get us some Champagne."

I cut a meaningful look at Rami as I passed him, motioning with my head for him to follow me to the back of the plane. When we reached the back, the flight attendant, a curvy blonde who was pouring Champagne into glass flutes, glanced up.

"Mr. Vicario," she said, clearly surprised to see me out of my seat. Her cheeks reddened when she slid her gaze to Rami, and I remembered one particularly long flight when he'd sampled much more than the bubbly.

I took one of the glasses without a word and slammed it back in a single gulp, the bubbles tickling my throat as they went down. The attendant silently refilled my glass and then handed one to Rami.

"Would you mind taking a glass to my guest?" I asked her, shifting my gaze to Ella.

"Of course. Right away." She hurried down the aisle with the bottle of Champagne and an empty flute, her ass swishing for Rami's benefit, no doubt.

"Was that what I think it was?" I asked my second-in-command, taking a more measured sip.

"Unless Istanbul's weather is becoming more unpredictable."

"I'm assuming there were no storms called for today?" I asked, glancing at Ella again, who was chatting with the flight attendant.

Rami frowned. "None. The storm came out of nowhere."

I let out a low rumble. "I wish that were true."

Rami scraped a hand across his stubbly cheeks. "You truly believe Jaya would do this?"

"She's been after me for over a year, Ram. Maybe she's getting desperate."

"It's one thing to appear at your clubs and try to lure you back into her clutches. It's another to send a demon storm after you."

"You have another explanation?" I asked. "She was in the Basilica."

My friend leaned against the back of the plane. "But she's a succubus, a pleasure demon. Since when are her kind so vindictive?"

"They feast on sex and desire. I rejected her and deprived her of that. She's clearly out to punish me."

Rami folded his arms over his chest and gave me a wry smile. "I don't mean to disparage your immense charms, Dom, but she's a skilled succubus. She can seduce anyone she wants. Why obsess over you?"

Regret pooled in my gut like bile as I remembered nights spent with the she-demon. "Because our union was demented and cursed. What could be more twisted than the mating of an angel and a demon?"

Rami didn't answer. He didn't need to. We both knew I was right.

Redemption had been so far from our minds for so long that there were few carnal sins we hadn't indulged in, although I didn't know of many other fallen angels who'd been lured in by one of the pleasure demons. I'd been weak and eager to quicken my rush to damnation. Apparently, I'd been successful, since the succubus was now summoning her demonic powers against me.

"You said she saw you at the Basilica Cistern," Rami asked. "How could she have known you'd be there?"

I drained the last drops of Champagne, setting the glass down on the half-full tray the flight attendant had abandoned. Even though the plane was now flying smoothly, the tray rattled gently from the same vibrations I felt in my feet. "No idea, but Jaya is resourceful. Obviously, she knows all our properties, and we allow pleasure demons to hunt in our clubs. One of her fellow succubi could have tipped her off that I was in Istanbul. After that, it would only take a few well-placed bribes to discover I'd rented out the Basilica."

"I don't remember seeing any she-demons on the rooftop last night."

I thought back to the crowd lounging on the banquettes the night before. Giggling tourists and amorous couples. "Neither do I."

Rami waved a hand. "It doesn't matter how she found you. She did, and now she knows about the female."

"She doesn't *know* about her," I clarified. "She saw her from a distance."

Rami's expression told me he'd didn't buy it. "If we can sense Ella's angelic trace, she might be able to as well. Even from far away. Regardless, she saw you with Ella and that made her angry enough to try to stop you from leaving."

"Jaya wasn't trying to stop me from leaving Istanbul." I glanced at Ella again, the bile rising in my throat. "I think she was trying to kill us."

❧ 11 ❧

Dominick

The glossy, wooden boat powered through the canals, sending water churning behind in its wake. I stood at the front of the boat, looking over the glass shield that buffered little of the cool breeze, and kept one arm wrapped snugly around Ella.

Night had fallen over Venice, and the dark water glimmered from the light spilling from stone palazzos and brick homes that rose on both sides. Gondolas glided slowly along as love songs drifted through the air, laughter spilling from waterfront restaurants and fading as we sped past.

I inhaled the salty air, glad to be back in the old city which always felt like it had been created for angels. We passed underneath the Bridge of Sighs, the ornate scrollwork of the covered stone bridge seeming to glow from the lights shining on it from below, and I thought of Casanova's fate. We took a series of turns and skirted under another bridge, this one with a twisted gargoyle looking down. Or maybe Venice had been created for the Fallen after all.

My kind had always been more comfortable in the ancient cities. The new world, for all its shiny cities and unchecked greed, did not remind us of centuries past like the ruins of Constantinople, or the crumbling stone of Venice, or the desert cities of Jordan. We had witnessed civilizations—and cities—rise and fall, yet we remained. It was nice to return to an old city that also remained.

The boat took a series of deft turns, and I glanced at Rami on my other side as he steered. I had no doubt he could navigate the canals to our palazzo blindfolded, although in the dark was nearly the same. When he slowed the boat around the inside of the wooden post and brought it to a stop at the dock, I leapt out, lifting Ella effortlessly with me, and hurrying through the massive arched entrance and up wide, marble stairs.

"This is yours?" She asked, tipping her head back to look at the ceiling that soared above us, painted with a scene of winged warriors cavorting among the clouds.

"Not only mine," I said, not bothering to glance at the mural overhead. My gaze was drawn to the two men who stood at the top of the stairs, their stances wide and their expressions ominous. Despite their obvious anxiety at the news Rami had imparted to them from the plane, I was glad to see them.

I released Ella once I reached them, pulling each into a one-armed hug. "Dan, Gad. It is good to see you."

They thumped me hard on the back as we embraced, then their eyes flitted to the woman next to me. I had no doubt that Rami had already informed the rest of the Fallen, but I also suspected they were picking up on her angelic trace.

"This is Ella," I said, curling an arm around her back as both Daniel and Gadriel eyed her with fascination.

"It's nice to meet you." She extended her hand, which both took in their own briefly, their pupils flaring for an instant at the contact.

I cleared my throat, and they snapped their gaze back to me. Rami had come up behind us, after securing the boat to the dock, and he nodded to the two men standing guard. None of them would speak in front of the human, but the air hummed with tension.

I turned to Ella, sweeping a hand over her hair, which had been blown asunder on the boat ride. "Rami will show you to our room. I'll join you later."

"Okay." Her tone was questioning, but I suspected she was too self-conscious around the others to voice a challenge to sharing a room with me.

I almost laughed at her obvious nerves, leaning close to her ear and whispering, "Don't worry. I have no plans to maul you while you sleep." I ran one hand down the length of her arm. "You have nothing to fear from me, Ella."

She flinched but nodded, falling into step behind Rami once I released her. I let my gaze follow her as she walked up the staircase that swept around one side of the foyer, her own head moving to take in the collection of gilded paintings that covered the walls. Even against the overly embellished backdrop of the celestially inspired art, she struck me as the most beautiful thing in the room. Watching her move, her hips swaying slightly and her delicate hand trailing along the marble banister, made my breath falter and my cock swell.

I tore my eyes away and cursed my weakness. I would not be able to resist her for long, no matter how much I wished to—or needed to. When she and Rami had vanished down a corridor, I turned to Daniel and Gadriel.

"Tell me what you know."

Gadriel arched an eyebrow slowly, his trademark wicked grin splitting his ebony face and white teeth flashing. He ran a hand over his close-cropped, black hair. "Shouldn't we be asking that of you, Dominick?"

I growled at him, my top lip curling. "She is none of your concern, Gad."

Of the Fallen, Gadriel had been one of the most eager to embrace the sins of the flesh, and especially when it came to women. It had taken very little prodding to convince him to taste the forbidden pleasures of humans so many millennia ago, and even now, his hunger for them had been barely slaked.

"I do not desire your human in that way," he said, glancing at the stairs she'd just ascended. "Although I will concede that she's beautiful, and her relative innocence is appealing, but you know what I mean."

Daniel elbowed him. "Don't provoke him, Gad. He isn't in the mood, and I'm not in the mood for a fight."

Always the peacemaker. I inclined my head at Dan, who stood almost as tall as Gadriel, but who wore his dark hair pulled back in a low ponytail at the nape of his neck. "I don't know much yet. Only that she carries the angelic mark, and she appeared in my hotel last night."

"And Jaya saw her today?" Gad asked, his mischievous smile gone.

I nodded as we walked three astride toward the back of the palazzo, turning until we reached the entrance to our gathering room. Two towering arches greeted us, carved, stone angels entwined over the top, wings unfurled as they appeared to plummet. I pushed through one of the heavy wooden doors into the long room that stretched the length of the building and served as the Fallen headquarters in Venice. Books lined the far wall, with mahogany tables covering Persian carpets, and a fireplace crackling at one end. Even though it was summer, the old stone palazzo was difficult to heat, which meant we kept a fire burning most of the year.

I walked the hearth, eager to warm my fingers after the boat ride in the cool, night air. I braced my arms on the thick marble mantle and stared into the flames. "I cannot imagine that the human's appearance and Jaya's reappearance are wholly unconnected."

"You cannot think the human is involved with the demons," Gad said with a dismissive laugh.

"No." I didn't think that Ella was aware of demons at all, or of fallen angels, or of her own angelic connection. Not anymore. "But a human with an angelic mark appears just as demon activity is increasing?"

"You think the demons are using her as a distraction?" Dan asked.

If they were, it was working. I'd rarely felt as unmoored and out of control as I did when I was around Ella.

"It is not the demons who most worry me," I said, twisting my head to look at him.

"Then who—?" Daniel began, then shook his head. "The archangels? But why?"

I pivoted fully and spread my arms wide. "Why do they do anything? To ensure we remain fallen? To prolong our torture? To maintain the conflict between the Fallen and our demon offspring?"

Gad made a low, rumbling noise in his throat. He felt as we all did, that there was scant connection left between the half-angel, half-human children of the Fallen, and the corrupted and twisted demons they'd become.

"There may be no correlation," Rami said, joining us in the room and taking one of the leather wingback chairs angled in front of the fire. "There are coincidences in this mortal world."

It had been no coincidence that Ella had walked onto that terrace last night. Even though I no longer thought she was involved in a plot against me, I believed that she was meant to enter my life. I also believed without a shadow of a doubt that she was meant to be mine.

"There is also one more explanation," Rami added, his voice barely rising above the snapping and hissing of the burning wood.

Dan and Gad glanced at him, then at me.

Dan furrowed his brow. "You don't truly think...?"

"That prophecy has never been verified. You can't count on—" Gad began.

"I am not counting on the prophecy," I said, cutting off both their protests. "Bur Rami is right. I cannot discount it. If there is even a chance it holds truth..."

"Then this human could be the key to the Fallen being restored," Dan said, his gaze locked on me.

I scraped a hand through my hair and swiveled back to the fire, letting the flames warm my skin. "Regardless of why she came to me, or what she could mean to us, she is now in danger because of it."

"Humans with the angelic trace on them do not fare well when hunted by demons," Gadriel said.

Rami grunted. "We might have gotten a glimpse of that as we were leaving Istanbul."

Both Gad and Dan swung their gaze from him to me. "What happened?"

I didn't want to admit how the sight of the storm had rattled me, but there was no use hiding my fear from my fellow Fallen. "Dark winds appeared as we were boarding the plane. The pilot barely outflew them."

"A demon storm?" Dan shook his head. "That would take more than a single demon."

Rami crossed one leg at the knee. "Even more than one as powerful as Jaya."

"Then they were tracking you," Dan said.

"Or her, now that they are aware of her existence. And her connection to us." Rami pinned his gaze on me. "To you."

A rumble of frustration simmered in my gut. In my foolish attempt to protect her, I'd put her in graver danger.

"There is little doubt Jaya will be hunting both of you," Gadriel added. "Especially if she saw the way you look at her, Dom."

I clenched my fingers tight around the carved mantle, the sharp curves of the design biting into my flesh. "Then it is up to me to keep her hidden."

"You know you have the blades of the Fallen," Daniel said.

"We will protect her as one of our own, Dom. You know that without asking," Rami added. "But I'm not sure how long you can keep her tucked away here without her wanting to leave."

Gadriel let out a throaty laugh. "I doubt Dominick will have any problem keeping her distracted in his bedroom. He is a Fallen, after all. What do we do best, if not charm others to savor the forbidden with us?"

12

Ella

I stood in the room trying not to let my jaw hit the floor. "This is my bedroom?"

"Not only yours," Rami had said quietly, before closing the door and leaving me alone.

I gulped, remembering that Dominick had said he'd be joining me. Okay, I guessed the sleeping-separately portion of the deal was over. Not that we'd be crowded in this bedroom. Although, calling the space a bedroom was a bit of an understatement.

Like the rest of the palazzo, the ceiling soared above me and was embellished with a vividly colored fresco of celestial beings with outstretched wings and bare chests. Tall windows interrupted the ornately patterned ivory wallpaper down one long wall, and heavy, midnight blue drapes adorned with gold tassels covered the glass. Gilded chandeliers hung from the ceiling, the light from the electric candles glowing. The floors were hardwood and covered with woven carpets, while gilded chairs and settees were arranged in a sitting area in front of the king-sized bed that boasted a glittering, gold headboard carved with swirls and florets. A fireplace on the far wall was topped with a marble mantelpiece, and a mirror that extended to the ceiling.

I crossed to the crackling fire and held my hands to the warmth. The palazzo was impressive, but the heating system—if it had one—was not, and I was grateful for the burning logs heating the room. The mansion's decor was exactly what I would have expected from such an old building in a historic city, but it didn't strike me as very much like Dominick. The suite in Istanbul had been more his style—sleek and bold and dark. This room felt like it had seen history unfold, and held dark secrets jealously within its walls.

"And it's bigger than my apartment," I whispered to myself as I walked across the floor, the tapping of my sandals the only sound, save the crackling of the burning fire.

Thinking of my apartment in New York made me think of Christopher, which made my blood boil. When I'd checked my phone, the only response I'd gotten from my breakup text was one word—*Whatever*.

That just about summed up him and our relationship. It really had been *whatever,* and I could barely fault him for wording it so perfectly. Still, after three years, the typically immature reply stung.

Three years. I shook my head. What had I been thinking?

Even though I'd only broken up with him yesterday, it already felt like a lifetime ago. After meeting Dominick, it was hard to imagine that I'd put up with so much bullshit from Christopher. Never once had my ex made me feel the rush of exhilaration that

I experienced from the mere touch from Dominick. I could run down a laundry list of the things Christopher never did for me that Dominick already had, but it would only make me angrier that I'd wasted so much time with a guy who clearly didn't care about me.

"No use crying over spilled milk," I said aloud. Or shitty ex-boyfriends. Not when I was currently in a luxurious, Venetian palazzo with a drop-dead gorgeous man who was loaded and who seemed to like me a lot.

My fingers tingled as I thought back to the kiss he'd given me on the plane. Running up the stairs and into the jet had been such a rush that the dominant kiss hadn't even felt out of place. The heart-pounding thrill of his lips moving hard and fast against mine, pushing me back into the plush seat as we'd roared into the sky, had taken my breath away—and left me wanting more.

My gaze went to the bed and the crisp, ivory duvet that was topped with fluffy pillows. I swallowed hard, trying not to imagine Dominick stretched out naked across it.

"Geez, Ella." I scowled at myself, glad no one could read my mind or how quickly my mind had undressed Dominick Vicario.

Turning away from the bed, I walked to a tall, gilded wardrobe and pulled open one of the doors. How the hell? All my clothes were already hanging on wooden hangers, and my shoes were lined up neatly at the bottom. The luggage from the plane must have been sent ahead on its own boat, but still, it was an impressive trick. Dominick's people were very good.

I stifled a yawn as I opened a drawer to one side of the hanging clothes. Even my underwear was neatly folded, which made my cheeks flush. I hadn't seen anyone in Dominick's employ who wasn't a big, muscular guy. Then again, I doubted this was the first woman who'd been brought back to the palazzo, so maybe they were used to folding bras and panties.

I grabbed an oversized sleep shirt, wishing for a moment that I'd packed some sexy lingerie. But to pack it, I'd have to own it. Since Christopher had always told me I looked like I was playing dress-up when I'd tried to wear silky nightgowns, I'd gotten rid of them and stuck to big T-shirts. Now I felt ridiculous as I slipped out of my sundress and into a giant Columbia University tee, but there was nothing I could do about it.

Besides, the day was catching up to me and my eyes were heavy as I eyed the bed. I didn't know how late it was, but it felt like the middle of the night. I crossed to the bed, pulled back the duvet, and tossed half the pillows onto a satin tufted chair next to the bed. I didn't want to fall asleep before Dominick joined me—I wanted to be awake for that—but it wouldn't hurt to rest my eyes while I waited for him. My head sank into the downy pillows, and I groaned as my bare legs slid against the incredibly soft sheets.

Just a short nap, I told myself, as my eyelids fluttered and I drifted into sleep.

When my eyes flew open, the fire had burned down to a pile of smoldering, black char, and I was still alone in the huge bed. Light didn't stream through the windows and quiet hung over the room. I sat up; glad I hadn't slept through to morning, but curious why Dominick hadn't joined me. Had he changed his mind about sharing a room? Had he changed his mind about me?

My pulse fluttered as I got out of bed, the floor cool beneath my feet. I glanced down at the T-shirt that hung to the top of my thighs. I couldn't very well run around a Venetian palace half dressed, but it felt like overkill to put on an outfit in the middle of the night.

I spotted a door I hadn't noticed earlier. Maybe it was Dominick's closet, and I could snag something from there. I hurried over and opened it, startled when I saw that it led to a stunning bathroom. The bedroom might be filled with antiques, but the bathroom was completely modern, with a glass shower big enough for a crowd, and a sunken tub underneath an arched window. But it was the robe hanging on a wall hook that made me smile.

I pulled it off the hook, slipping into the beige garment that was as silky soft as the sheets, but lined with terrycloth. Tying it tightly around my waist, I padded back out to the bedroom and across to the door, breathing a sigh of relief when it opened easily. At least I wasn't locked in.

The hallway was quiet and dark as I tiptoed down it, retracing my steps from earlier. When I reached the bannister overlooking the main foyer, I peered down. The only light came from faintly glowing wall sconces and there was no sound.

I probably should have gone back to my room, but I wanted to find Dominick. Where was he? Come to think of it, where was anyone? A whisper of fear made my heart stutter, but I crept on silent feet down the wide marble stairs.

When I reached the enormous hall, I tipped my head back. In the shadows, the angels in the ceiling fresco looked more fierce than beautiful, their faces wild and their wings as pointy as blades, and a shiver went through me.

A soft, crackling noise drew me to the back of the building, although I paused outside the open, arched doorway to gape at the stone angels that appeared to be guarding the massive double doors. Like the figures in the fresco, these were no cherubic angels, and their faces were twisted in as they stretched stone arms toward the floor.

"What are you doing up?"

Dominick's deep voice slid through my bones and curled around my belly, and I put a hand to my heart when he appeared in the doorway from inside the room. "Don't sneak up on me like that!"

He cocked his head. "I'm not the one creeping around in the dark." His gaze drifted down my body. "Wearing my robe."

"Sorry. I didn't think you'd want me wandering around half naked."

His eyes flashed dark. "Since we are not alone here, no, I would not."

My heartbeat steadied itself, even though being near Dominick meant it couldn't go back to its normal rhythm. Not when he was looking at me in that brooding and possessive way of his.

"Are you okay?" His dark shirt was unbuttoned at the top, revealing the swell of his chest muscles, and his sleeves were rolled up to display bronzed forearms. As he lifted a hand to brush an errant curl off his forehead, I glimpsed the wings tattooed across the back of his hand, the ink almost appearing iridescent in the dim lighting.

I nodded; my mouth too dry to speak as my thighs clenched.

He stepped closer, his penetrating gaze raking shamelessly over me. Then he took my hand in his. "Come with me."

I had no choice to follow him as he pulled me back through the foyer, his fingers threaded tightly through mine as sinful heat tingled over my body. Maybe searching for Dominick hadn't been the best idea after all.

13

Ella

"Here?" I asked when he stopped walking. "This is where you wanted to bring me?"

He peered down at me. "You must be hungry."

I almost laughed as I took in the large kitchen, copper pots and pans hanging from the ceiling over what I could only assume was a professional-grade stove with half a dozen burners. Ambient light from the recessed ceiling lit the room enough so I could see that it was seriously tricked out—a double gas stovetop, a massive, chrome refrigerator, and side-by-side ovens. I'd thought he was dragging me off to bed, and he was bringing me to get a midnight snack?

My stomach growled, as if on cue. "I guess I am."

Dominick led me to one of the tall barstools that flanked the white and gray marble island. "Sit. I'll make you something."

I hopped up onto the stool, tracking him as he walked around to the other side and pushed his sleeves even farther up his arms. "You cook?"

He gave me a slow smile that made my heart lurch. "That surprises you?"

I looked at him, with his dark, tousled hair and his perfect five o'clock shadow. There was nothing domestic or commonplace about him. "A little bit."

His laugh was low and deep, rumbling through me. "Surprises are good." He pulled a skillet down from overhead, then locked his whiskey-colored eyes on me. "What are you hungry for?"

My mind went blank as I got lost in his gaze. Finally, I blinked and sat up straighter. "Can you make a grilled cheese?"

He inclined his head at me in a shadow of a bow. "If that is what you truly crave."

My pulse quickened, and my face warmed. His hint of an accent made everything he said sound both sensual and forbidden. "It's my comfort food. My mom used to make it for me when I had a bad day at school, then later, I made it for myself when I had a crappy day at work."

Dominick glided between the refrigerator and the bread box on the counter, pulling out a crusty loaf of bread and a block of cheese. This was clearly not going to be a Wonder Bread and Kraft Singles type of grilled cheese. I'd never expected it to be such a turn on to watch a man who knew his way around a kitchen, but watching him work made my heart beat faster, and I shifted on my stool.

"Tonight is one of the times you need comfort food?" he asked, as he deftly cut thick slices of bread, the yeasty scent telling me the bread was freshly baked.

I thought back over the whirlwind of the past twenty-four hours. I didn't want to insult him, but I also didn't want to lie. "It's been a lot."

"For me, as well," he said, slathering the bread with butter before placing it in the skillet and cutting into the block of cheese.

I choked out a laugh. "I have a hard time believing someone like you doesn't pick up women and jet them off to your palace all the time."

The butter sizzled in the pan as he looked up, his expression solemn. "Actually, I don't."

The laugh died on my lips. "Oh." My face burned as I dropped my gaze to the counter. "I didn't mean—"

"It's fine. You don't know me yet. It's understandable that my actions would raise suspicions."

That was putting it mildly.

"It's not that I don't appreciate...everything. You have no idea how it feels not to have all that debt hanging over my head anymore." I let out a breath as I raised my eyes. "But it's too much."

Dominick flipped the sandwich in the pan. "I assure you it isn't. Not to me."

I knew he was wealthy. That was evident from the hotel suite and the private jet, but if over a hundred grand in debt was nothing to him, then he must be seriously loaded. "Are you a billionaire?"

He glanced up and gave me a knowing smile as he slid the grilled cheese from the pan onto a plate, slicing it on the diagonal before handing the plate to me. So that was a yes. I picked up one of the golden-brown triangles, the cheese barely oozing out the sides. A billionaire who made a perfect grilled cheese.

"Money isn't something I worry about," he said.

"Spoken like someone who has a lot of it."

"Perhaps." He nodded at the plate, waiting for me to eat.

I took a bite and almost moaned. Even my memories of my mom's grilled cheese couldn't measure up. I dabbed at the corner of my mouth. "Where did you learn to cook like this?"

It wasn't like grilled cheese was a complicated dish, but getting the ideal ratio of bread and cheese, with the bread grilled just enough but not burned, and the cheese melted perfectly, wasn't always easy.

"I've had a lot of time to practice."

I eyed the gorgeous, thirty-something, hotel mogul/mob boss. "Yeah, right."

He shrugged. "I'm glad you like it. Next time I'll make you a Venetian specialty."

Next time? I took another bite, savoring the buttery richness. I wanted to pinch myself to see if it was real—if he was real—but I also didn't want to break the spell. It wasn't everyday a gorgeous man made me a grilled cheese in the middle of the night.

Dominick pulled two wine glasses from a cabinet and took a bottle of white wine from a wine cooler built into the lower cabinets. As I easily polished off the grilled cheese, he opened the bottle and poured two glasses, placing one in front of me as he came around to my side of the island.

"Wine and grilled cheese?" I asked after I swallowed the last bite.

"It's Italy. We drink wine with everything here." He lifted his glass as if to toast.

I picked up mine and tapped it against his. "Cheers."

He held my gaze as he lifted his own glass to his lips. "*Salute.*"

I took a big gulp, the wine a cool, crisp contrast to the savory sandwich. Dominick's eyes never left me as he sipped his wine slowly, and I downed almost my entire glass as my heart hammered in my chest and heat arrowed through me.

When I lowered my glass, he took it from me and set it aside. "Do I make you nervous, Ella?" He spun the stool around so that I faced him. "I promise you; you have nothing to fear from me."

That, I did not believe. The cold, hard truth was that he'd paid for me to be with him, and I'd learned early on that nothing came for free. Even if he intended to be a perfect gentleman, I didn't know if I wanted him to be.

He feathered his fingers through my hair, his gaze traveling from my eyes to my lips. "I can't figure you out."

"Me?" I managed to say, my voice breathy. How could I be hard to figure out? He was the dark, unknowable mystery who was both terrifying and baffling.

He nodded, moving his hand from my hair to cup my jaw. "You're so much more than you think you are. It's amazing that you don't see it."

My mind was in a fog as his touch sent jolts of desire skittering across my skin. I sucked in a quick breath when he tipped my head back. "I'm pretty normal."

"You are hardly normal." He rubbed the pad of his thumb across my cheek. "You're incredible and intoxicating."

No guy had ever called me intoxicating before. Pretty, yes. Hot, a couple of times. But never intoxicating. Then again, it might just be a European thing. Dominick didn't talk like any American man I'd ever met. Or any *man* I'd met—ever.

He wound a hand around my back and lifted me off the stool, turning and setting me on the counter as if I weighed nothing. Then he nudged my knees apart and positioned himself between them, using the hand at the small of my back to jerk me flush to him. I gasped as something hard and big pressed against me. Holy hell!

"Dominick." I grabbed a fistful of his shirt to steady myself and whispered his name as a plea, but I didn't know if I was pleading with him to stop or to keep going.

Power radiated off his body and into mine, holding me in a trance. He lowered his head to my neck, inhaling deeply and emitting a rumble that sent tremors down my spine. His lips brushed over my skin as he kissed his way from my neck to the hollow of my throat and then up to the curve of my jaw.

I tangled my hands in his hair as he lifted his face to mine, his eyes fathomless pools of darkness that burned raw into me. Desire and fear made the breath catch in my chest, even as heat coiled impatiently in my core. I didn't just want him, my body *ached* for him, although I knew I shouldn't want someone like him.

"Ella," he husked out my name, his voice teetering on the edge of control. His warm breath mingled with my desperate gasps, his lips hovering over mine. Then he pulled back, tearing his gaze from my lips. He stepped away from me, heaving in ragged breath, his expression tortured. "Not yet. Not until you know."

Know what?

14

Dominick

Even though my heart thundered in my chest and my cock ached, I forced myself to back away from her. As desperately as I wanted to claim her, and as much as my body craved the feel of her skin, I couldn't. Not until she knew the truth about me.

"Know what?" Ella asked, hitching in her breath. Her legs were still open, revealing so much creamy flesh I almost lost all control.

I took jerky steps around the island, bracing my hands on the smooth countertop once I'd reached the other side. I needed to put some distance between us—and some marble.

Why did I care so much about telling this human? I'd never told one before, having fucked thousands of women over the centuries who had no clue about my identity. It had always been better that way. Their minds couldn't comprehend what I really was, even though they all suspected I was different than mortal men. They just didn't know how different, or that my entrancing touch was courtesy of my divine immortality.

But this was different. *She* was different. Ella might have been a human woman I craved to dominate and make my own, but she also carried the trace of angelic power. I not only desired to claim her, but I also needed to possess her, to meld her divinity with my own, to bind her to my forbidden soul. And if the prophecy was true...? I forced that thought from my mind. I couldn't deal with the possibility, yet. It was too remote to allow it to creep into my thoughts and torture me.

"You don't know everything about me yet," I said.

"I didn't think I did. We still haven't known each other very long." She closed her knees and tugged the sides of the robe together. "You don't know everything about me, either."

This was true, but from what I could tell, she wasn't harboring a secret like mine. I already knew her life had been either started or saved by an angelic intervention. The only thing I didn't know was why, but if it had to do with the archangels, there was always a long game. The pressing question was if I was intended to be part of it, or if I'd truly stumbled across Ella and started the chain reaction that made her a target of demon vengeance.

"You deserve the truth. Once I have claimed you, there will be no turning back."

"Claimed me? I agreed to spend the summer with you, nothing more." The flush had faded from her cheeks, and she slipped down off the counter. "Is this the part where you tell me you're looking for another wife for your sister-wife stable or like to wear women's underwear?"

"No. Nothing like that." I straightened and narrowed my eyes at her. "You think I would wear women's underwear?"

She twitched one shoulder. "You never know, but whatever you want to tell me sounds like a big deal, so I figured maybe it was something like that."

I almost laughed out loud. She truly was an innocent, if these were the worst secrets she could imagine of me. "It is nothing like that. I promise you, I have never been married or worn women's lingerie, although I do not judge those who do."

Ella laughed. "Old world, but not old school." Then her laugh died on her lips. "Don't tell me you have some kind of underground sex dungeon here. Is that what you want to show me?"

"There are no dungeons here. It's Venice. They would flood."

She bit her bottom lip. "Right. Of course."

"Sex dungeons are also not what I prefer, although I've seen my fair share of them. Like I mentioned before, many of my holdings are places where people can indulge in their fantasies. You could say my business is in indulgence, sometimes forbidden ones."

"I'm guessing what you want to tell me has to do with that?"

I walked around the kitchen island and took her hand. "It will be easier to show you."

She followed me back to the main foyer, where I stopped in the center and craned my neck up to look at the fresco stretching across the ceiling. Even in the dim lighting, it was possible to make out the figures with white wings painted overhead.

"There." I waved a hand at the artwork adorning the ceiling.

She followed my gaze. "It's beautiful, but I'm not sure what I'm supposed to be taking away from it, aside from the fact that Italians don't do plain ceilings."

"The artwork throughout the palazzo is not here just because it's beautiful. It's here because it's a reminder."

Ella spent a few moments peering up, then looked at me. "I still don't get it."

Of course, she didn't. I was being too obtuse. I was skirting around the truth because I feared her reaction. But I also felt compelled to tell her, even though I doubted my fellow Fallen would have approved. We'd existed in the shadows for centuries, moving around the world so as not to draw too much attention to the fact that we didn't age or die. It was why we used shell companies and assumed names. Revealing the truth never went well.

Still, if Ella was now in danger because of us—because of me—she needed to know why. She would have to know about the demon hunting her and those who would protect her. And she needed to know what it would mean to be with me—and to submit to my desire.

"My family is not a traditional family, although we are brethren. We are bonded over a pact we made long ago, and the collective punishment it has brought upon us." I took her hands in mine. "We disobeyed our father's wishes and were cast out."

"That's pretty harsh." She looked back up at the mural, squinting. "So, this art is a depiction of angels being cast from heaven like you were kicked out of your family? And the stone angels above the doors in the back are the same thing?"

I nodded, rubbing the backs of her hands with my thumbs.

"Why would you want art to remind you of being kicked out of your home?" She asked when her gaze returned to me. "That seems like something you'd want to forget."

"Unfortunately, we can never forget. It's at the core of who we are, and has determined the course of our existence."

Her forehead wrinkled as she touched my arm. "I'm really sorry that happened to you, Dominick. To all of you. But I'm not sure why you felt you needed to tell me. It doesn't make me think any less of you. If anything, your dad sounds like an unforgiving ass."

I twitched at her touch, unaccustomed to sympathy and flinching at it. She still didn't understand. "There are those of us who believe that, but for the most part we accept our fate. We will not be redeemed, and it is our fate to punish the evil that has arisen because of our deception."

She tilted her head at me. "It sounds like you've got a lot of guilt over what happened, but I doubt punishing evil falls completely on you."

"Not entirely on me, but it is up to the Fallen to keep evil in check since we unleashed it on the world. And the demon prince is little help."

Her hands slipped from mine. "Demon prince? The Fallen?"

Fear iced my skin, and I hesitated. Did I really need to tell her? Once I did there was no going back—and she would not be able to leave. But I couldn't protect her the way I needed to without her understanding. And I also *needed* her to know. It had been so long since a human had known the truth about me, and I longed to see desire in her eyes that was not based on my deceptive enchantment.

"The art is not a metaphor for what happened to me and my brothers," I said, the words rushing from me before I could stop them. “It *is* what happened to us. We are the fallen who were cast out of heaven for eternity.”

She stepped back, her eyebrows lifting. “I’m sorry, what?”

“I am not the head of a mob family, Ella. I’m the leader of the Fallen.”

“The Fallen?” she asked, her blue eyes wide. “The Fallen what?”

“Angels.” I met her innocent gaze, knowing she might never look at me the same way again. “I am not mortal. I am divine and immortal, created at the beginning of time and then cast from heaven and cursed to exist on the human plane.”

Regret and pain ripped fiery talons through my soul as her lips parted in shock, but it was too late to recant my confession. “I am a fallen angel.”

15

Ella

Well, this was just great.

I clamped my gaping mouth shut and stared at him. I'd finally found a gorgeous, wealthy man who could even cook, and he turns out to be delusional.

"A fallen angel?" I asked, the disbelief dripping from my voice. "As in, from the Bible?"

He bobbled his head slightly. "That depends on which Bible you're reading. There is much that was left out of the book your religions use today."

"But you're telling me that you and the other guys I've met like Rami, are all former angels from heaven who were kicked out?"

"Yes." He stepped closer to me. "I know it sounds unbelievable, but it's the truth."

I put my hand over my mouth to stifle the hysterical laugh that burbled up. Then I peered up at the fresco of angels and clouds. What at first glance had seemed like an idyllic scene I now realized was a battle. The angels were not holding hands, they were pushing each other, with some remaining above the fluffy clouds and others falling below. I had to give Dominick credit. He went all-in on his delusions.

"And if I ask Rami about this?"

Dominick flinched. "He would be angry at me for revealing the truth to you, but he would not be able to deny it."

"So, it's not only you with a God complex, so to speak," I muttered under my breath.

"Believe me, Ella, the last thing the Fallen have are God complexes. Not after what our father did to us."

I held up my hands and took a step back. "Okay. I could handle your control issues, and even your mob connections, but this is not normal."

"I never claimed to be normal." The rich timbre of his voice rumbled through me and seemed to reverberate off the walls. "Or mortal."

The reality of the past couple of days rushed over me, almost bringing me to my knees. Had I seriously quit my job, dumped my boyfriend, and ditched my entire life to run off with a man who now claimed to be an immortal, fallen angel? I bent over and braced my hands on my thighs as the insanity of my actions hit me full force. What had I been thinking?

"Ella?" His hand rested lightly on my back, his voice a caress.

I shook my head hard. This was all wrong. Sure, I'd sensed something powerful and captivating about him, but it was his sexual magnetism. After all, the man was beyond stunning. Hadn't I thought he was the most beautiful man I'd ever seen?

I remembered the woman in the underground cistern and the fire in her eyes then how strangely the water had flown up around her and how Dominick had run us out so fast it had felt like we were flying. Just like his associates as they followed us into the plane, their feet hardly seeming to touch the ground as the swirling storm cloud had raced toward the tarmac.

Fear prickled the nape of my neck, and I forced the thoughts from my mind. There was no way he was what he said he was. No. Fucking. Way. And if he wasn't an angel, then he was certifiable. It was one thing to spend the summer with a billionaire. It was quite another to do it with a crazy billionaire.

I straightened quickly, knocking his hand back. "I'm sorry. I know we had a deal and all, but I need to get out of here."

I pushed past him and ran toward the stairs leading down to the massive, arched entrance of the palazzo. Even though I could hear the water of the canal lapping at the stone, an iron gate now blocked the exit. Grabbing the curling latticework, I pushed on the gate and then shook it. It rattled but didn't budge.

"The palazzo is locked down for your safety."

Dominick's dark purr was measured and calm as he walked down the steps behind me, but that only made me shake the gate harder.

Finally, I pressed my forehead against the cool metal and drew in a shaky breath. "What do you think you're keeping me safe from?"

"We are not the only unearthly beings roaming the earth," he said. "Although the others did not fall from the celestial realm like we did, and they have no desire to rid the world of evil."

I twisted around slowly to face him. "So, you think that I'm in danger from...?"

"Demons." He paused on the second to last step and put his hands casually in his pants pockets, as if we were talking about the weather.

A laugh escaped my lips, but its loud echo jangled in my ears. Now there were demons as well as fallen angels? This was getting better and better. My heart was pounding, but I attempted to take deep breaths. "Why would demons have any reason to come after me?"

Dominick's face, which already appeared fierce in the shadows, contorted into a mask of rage. "It's my fault. There is one demon who would love to destroy everything I hold dear as punishment for being rejected. Until now, that was not an issue."

"You're saying that I'm in danger from some deranged demon because I'm hanging out with you?"

Dominick cocked his head as he descended the last two steps. "We are doing more than 'hanging out,' wouldn't you say? And the demon is not a he. It's a she."

My stomach clenched. "The woman in the underground basilica?"

He didn't answer, but his furrowed brow told me what I needed to know. "I never intended for her to see you, but now that she has, I can only assume that you are also a target. She will want to get to me through you."

I took a step back and bumped against the iron gate as Dominick loomed over me. "Fallen angels? Demons? You don't honestly expect me to believe all this, do you?"

He loosed a mournful breath. "I hoped you might. It would make things easier."

"Sorry to inconvenience you," I said, the snark a little less potent since my voice trembled as I spoke.

He shrugged. "Your belief does not alter the reality. You are still mine to protect, and I will use all my power to do so."

I curled my hands into fists by my side. "I guess that means you aren't unlocking the doors?"

Dominick Vicario put a hand on my hip, rooting me in place as he stroked the back of his fingers down the side of my face. "No, I'm not. Letting you out of my sight would be irresponsible."

I gulped, the gravity of my situation crashing over me. I was halfway across the world from my home and everyone I knew, and I was locked up by a man who not only had as much power and money to do anything he wanted with me, but he was also convinced he was an immortal fallen angel.

"After all." Dominick bent over and his lips buzzed my cheek, a simmering heat making my thighs clench. "You might not have made a deal with the devil, but you did make one with a fallen angel. And some people consider that the same thing."

16

Ella

A deal with the devil?

Panic gripped me like a vise, even as his hushed words made heat pool in my core. As gorgeous as he was, I had to get away from him. I brought my knee up hard between his legs, contacting with something and causing him to stagger back and let out a string of words in a language I'd never heard.

Taking advantage of his momentary distraction, I ducked around him and ran up the stairs, glancing furtively to both sides. I knew the kitchen was to the left, and I didn't remember seeing a door leading outside, so I took off to the right. I'd barely made it across the foyer when I heard his footsteps behind me.

Shit, shit, shit. I guess I hadn't slowed him down much, although he was still cursing in a foreign language, so I'd done some damage.

Great, Ella. You just pissed him off.

I passed the sweeping staircase and ran through a doorway beyond it that led to a dark hallway. Holding my hands out to both sides, I rushed down it until I reached another door. Thankfully, it opened, and I burst through it and into a room that made me stop short. Although it wasn't a large space, the walls were covered with bronze shields and long swords, glittering crossbows and glinting daggers. It was like I'd stepped into what looked like a medieval armory.

Before I could process what I was seeing, a thick arm hooked around my waist. "I wish you hadn't done that, Ella."

I slapped at his arm as he pulled me backward and out of the room. "Let me go. You can't keep me here."

"Actually, I can."

I struggled against him for a moment before going limp. "Please let me go. I'll pay you back every cent. I promise."

He moved us back through the hallway even quicker than I'd run down it. "I don't want your money. I told you that your debts were nothing to me."

At the bottom of the stairs, he spun me around so I faced him. He seemed even taller and more menacing than he had before, his eyes completely black as they glittered like obsidian.

I forced myself not to drop my gaze. "I'm sorry if I hurt you. I just want to go home."

"I can't let you go, Ella. Not when you're in danger."

"The only person who's a danger to me is you."

He flinched almost imperceptibly. "I hope you'll come to realize that isn't true."

I wanted to cry, but then I thought about my best friend and tried my best to channel my inner Sara. "You can't keep me as your captive. I'll scream."

He moved so swiftly, I didn't know what he was doing until I was hanging over his shoulder and down his back. "You can scream all you want. The walls in the palazzo are stone and our nearest neighbor is deaf."

I smacked my palms on his back as he carried me up the stairs. "What happened to me being your guest?"

"You kicked me in the balls and ran."

I couldn't argue with that, although I kept beating his back as he reached the second floor and strode to the bedroom that we were supposed to share. He didn't let me down until he'd walked across the room, and then he deposited me onto the bed so hard I bounced. Before I could sit up and argue, Dominick was leaning over the bed and practically hovering on top of me.

"Why are you making it so hard for me to keep you safe?"

I trembled beneath him, but I didn't know if it was from fear or desire. His elbows were braced on either side of me, pinning my arms to my sides, and his body pressed hard into mine. His gaze was predatory as it raked over my face, and primal fear left me breathless.

"You're dangerous," I whispered.

"Yes, I am." A muscle ticked in his jaw. "But not to you. To you, I'm salvation."

Even as my mind told me to resist him, my back arched up, the tight points of my nipples straining against him. "I don't believe you."

"What scares you, Ella?" The velvet hum of his voice skimmed over my flesh. "That you believe I'm deadly or that it excites you?"

I opened my mouth to tell him just how wrong he was, but then I stopped. Even now—my chest heaving from running away from him and my palms burning from hitting his back—unwanted tremors of desire shook me.

"I think you know that I'm telling you the truth," he whispered. "I think you feel it in your core. You know I'm what I say I am, and it both scares you and thrills you."

I shook my head. "That's not true."

"Oh, I think it very much *is* true. You sense the same connection that I do—something you've never experienced before and something you can't explain away by mere physical desire. It's something deeper, isn't it? Something in your soul."

I wiggled underneath him, desperate to get away. As bizarre as his words were, they were also true, and it made no sense. I had just met the man and barely knew anything about him, but there was something so familiar about him—and so intoxicating about his touch.

"That's crazy." My words were barely audible, but he let out a deep laugh that echoed in my bones.

"But true." He dipped his head and inhaled at my neck, then groaned low. "You're right about one thing, though. You should be scared."

My heart stuttered in my chest, fresh fear blooming inside me even as his silky and seductive words curled across my skin.

"When you surrender to me—and you will—there will be no going back. Not for either of us. We will be bound together for more than the two months you promised me." He feathered a kiss across my lips, the soft brush of his skin electric. "It will be for life."

17

Dominick

"What do you mean you told her?" Rami sat sprawled on a leather armchair, but his expression was anything but relaxed.

I paced a small circle in front of the fire. Even though light had started to spill into the room from the arched windows, the fire still cast a golden glow across the floor that had not been matched by the sluggish rays of the rising sun. "I had no choice."

"Dominick Vicario, leader of the Fallen and head of the notorious Vicario family, was boxed into a corner by a human female?"

I shot him a look. "I needed her to know the truth so she could understand the danger."

Rami sat up. "You *wanted* her to know."

Sometimes I hated that Rami knew me so well.

"Maybe I did," I snapped back, fury bubbling up from my molten depths. "Maybe I wanted to claim a human who wasn't just entranced by my divinity."

Rami stood and faced off against me. "You've never cared what human females thought before. It isn't like we cast a spell on them. They all submit to us willingly." He gave me a wolfish grin. "Eagerly."

He was right. I'd never cared before. Like all my fallen brethren, I'd relished in the lust of humans and their unwitting desire for the forbidden. They'd never known why they were so drawn to us, but humans loved what they shouldn't, and that included fallen angels. It had been easy to indulge myself in the pleasures of the flesh with countless women over the millennia. They had been all too eager, and I hadn't cared why. Until now.

"She's making you weak, Dom." His words were low, but I felt them like daggers slicing my skin.

I growled as I spun around and gazed into the spitting fire, the writhing flames mirroring my own tortured soul. Ella had awakened a part of me that had been lying dormant for eons, but I couldn't believe that it made me weak. Not when I finally felt alive.

"Do not make the mistake of thinking I have gone soft." I slid my gaze to him, pinning him with it for several beats.

Understanding flickered in his eyes, and he gave me a knowing smile. "I am glad to hear it. So, have you claimed her? Is it done?"

I thought of Ella's face when I told her she'd made a deal with a fallen angel. All the heat I'd seen earlier when we'd been in the kitchen had been replaced by fear and horror. She didn't know what to think about my story, but it was no longer arousal that made her eyes flash dark. It was terror.

"No." I ground out the words. "And I doubt it ever will be now."

I thought of her kneeing me, the dull ache barely a memory, and one of my hands moved instinctively to my crotch. As unpleasant as it had been, I admired her fight. Of course, I couldn't let her leave. Not only would she be at risk, but I also couldn't let her go. Not when I'd just found her. Not when she might be the answer to my redemption.

I'd hoped she would believe me, although I realized now that I'd been woefully naïve. Her screams as I'd carried her upstairs over my shoulder had devolved into cries that had rung throughout the palazzo, but no one had come to her rescue. No one would. She was mine, and all the Fallen would respect my need to keep her, even if they didn't fully understand it. Even if *I* didn't.

Rami clapped a heavy hand on my shoulder as he joined me at the fireplace. "You underestimate your powers of persuasion. You have never been denied a woman you desired."

"None have ever known what I am. They spread their legs for Dominick Vicario, mafia don."

Silence lingered between us I thought about one who had known who I was, although she wasn't human. Jaya. Fucking a demon hadn't seemed worse than anything else we'd done, especially when our banishment was fresh, and our pain simmered just under the surface. I'd been fueled by rage and vengeance, and a demon lover had been just the way to retaliate for eternal punishment. But it had been my soul that had been tormented by Jaya's evil.

"You haven't always been who you are today," Rami said, as if reading my mind.

This was true. Through the millennia, we'd been different incarnations of ourselves. We'd fought in the battle for Troy and in the

Crusades, and we'd been confidantes of sultans and lovers of queens.

"But you have always been a loyal soldier," I told Rami. "One I haven't always deserved."

"I told you I would follow you into hell."

I let out a dark laugh. "An eternity of banishment with humanity is close enough, my friend."

He shrugged. "I don't know. I've never lost my taste for human women."

I cut my eyes to him. His appetite for carnal pleasures rivaled even my own. "Did I take you from your distraction in Istanbul too quickly?"

He waved my comment away. "There is plenty in Venice to amuse me. I thought we were talking about your distraction."

I blew out a long breath. "I wish that was all she was. Then I could release her, and our troubles would go away."

"Hardly. Jaya was trouble before she spotted the human. She was already mobilizing against us and using a rival family to do it."

"Arturo Solano cannot be foolish enough to let his stupid son start a war." And I had not built up our current empire to let it be toppled by one demon bent on revenge. "We should initiate a dialogue. Perhaps there is a way to diffuse the conflict Jaya has stirred up."

"Demons are gifted at rousing human anger, and Jaya's skills are unsurpassed. She will have spun a web of lies so thick they might never escape."

I gripped the marble mantle, my knuckles going white. "Then they will pay."

Rami turned to me. "If we take out the don or his son, we will have to take out the entire family. Do you really want to draw so much attention to ourselves?"

I swiveled my head to him. "Then find me another way."

"Dan is already meeting with one of their captains, but you know they will want to hear from you. Especially if Mateo Solano is behind this."

I grunted in response. "I will meet with Mateo Solano—and show him the full power of the Fallen."

A rumble of laughter escaped Rami. "That would be effective, but unwise."

"I already have a reputation for being the devil, although we both know that Samiel fell before we did."

"Yes, but the devil stays in hell. We roam the earth freely."

I inclined my head at him. "Which makes us the fallen angels the world should truly fear."

His eyes shone red from the reflected firelight. "If only they knew."

"Indeed." I stared into the dancing flames once more. "Regardless of Jaya or the Solanos, I need to exert my dominance in our city. I cannot hide out here, as much as I might wish to."

"A trip to *Epicurus Venice* is overdue," Rami said. "It might send the right message to the demons if they see you out and unafraid."

"And with my future mate on my arm."

Rami opened his mouth as if to protest, then clamped it shut. "You think she will appreciate *Epicurus*?"

I met his gaze. He meant to ask if Ella would be able to handle the hedonism on wanton display at our Venetian nightclub. My cock twitched at the thought of her surrounded by so much abandoned inhibition and embraced pleasure. "It will be a good test."

"To see how she handles the embodiment of so many dark desires?"

I spun and jammed my hands in my pockets. "To see how she handles *my* dark desires."

18

Ella

"We're going where?" I gaped at Rami as he stood in the bedroom doorway holding out a garment bag.

Although the man was gorgeous and imposing in his own right, he didn't send shivers through me like his boss did. "Dominick would like you to join him at his nightclub this evening—*Epicurus Venice*."

I eyed the garment bag. I knew about the Epicurus clubs, and I'd actually been to the one in New York, though I'd only gone once and my memory of the night was fuzzy. Located in cities throughout the world, they were upscale, luxurious, and known as the places to go if you wanted to indulge in just about anything. I'd heard whispers about the wildly attractive owners before, which made sense if the clubs were owned by Dominick and his "family."

Folding my arms over my chest, I narrowed my gaze at Rami. "I thought I was being held in the palazzo for my own protection."

He shifted from one foot to the other. "Dominick believes you'll be safe at Epicurus since it's guarded and staffed by our guards and members of the..." he hesitated for a beat, "our family."

"You mean the Fallen, right?" I couldn't keep the disbelief out of my voice. "*Epicurus Venice* is run by fallen angels like you and Dom?"

His jaw tensed as he clearly picked up on my derisive tone. "He shouldn't have told you."

"No." I snatched the garment bag from him. "What he shouldn't have done was throw me over his shoulder and refuse to let me go."

"I assure you that Dominick is only trying to protect you."

I sighed. If this guy was as delusional as his boss, I wasn't going to make any headway with him. "From the demons, right?"

Now he let out a weary breath. "I sincerely hope you don't learn the truth of our world the hard way."

I didn't have a smart-ass comment for that, and my skin prickled as I contemplated what he meant by "the hard way." Then I thought about everything Dominick had told me the night before and everything he'd done to me.

My cheeks warmed as memories rushed over me—his hard body on top of mine, my heart pounding as he whispered to me, the touch of his lips making heat pulse between my legs. I huffed out an impatient breath.

Ugh. Dominick was impossible and infuriating—and irresistible. And now he was requesting I accompany him to one of his wild nightclubs.

My first instinct was to refuse. He might have bartered for my company for the next two months but that didn't mean he could order me around. Then I thought of the alternative—staying inside the palazzo for who knew how long. At least if I agreed to go to *Epicurus Venice* there was a chance I could get away.

"You can tell Dominick that I'll go," I snapped.

Rami's eyes widened.

I softened my tone. "I mean, I accept his kind invitation."

Rami didn't look like he was buying my contrite change in tone, but he nodded. "We'll leave in an hour."

After closing the door behind him, I strode across the room and hooked the top of the garment bag hanger on the front of the ornate wooden wardrobe. I unzipped it impatiently, eager to see what kind of outfit Dominick wanted me to wear to the club. Aside from the black dress I'd met him in, I didn't own anything that was *Epicurus*-level chic.

I pulled back the sides of the bag and inhaled a quick breath. Although the dress inside was white and silky, there was nothing innocent about it. Thin spaghetti straps hung from the padded hanger and the neckline draped low. I pulled the hanger from the bag and twisted it so I could see the back of the dress—what there was of it. The back also draped dangerously low, and I could tell that it would reveal most of my back.

"I guess I'm not wearing a bra," I whispered, glad for once that I didn't have huge breasts.

The dress looked like it fell above the knee but there was a high slit up one side. I ran my fingers over the soft fabric, slightly stunned that Dominick had selected such a provocative dress. Then again, Epicurus clubs were known for being provocative.

"Then I'll fit right in," I said to myself, swallowing hard as I stepped out of Dominick's robe.

19

Dominick

I glanced over at Ella as the speedboat powered through the canal and sent water spraying behind us. Lights shone from buildings one either side of us, the reflections like smears of gold across the black canvas of the water at night.

She wore my dark jacket draped over her shoulders to protect her from the cool evening air and the wind from the boat ride, but I was seriously considering making her wear the oversized jacket when we reached the club.

I'd wanted to ask her what she'd been thinking when she'd put on that dress, but she wasn't the one I needed to confront. I'd put Gadriel in charge of selecting an appropriate dress for her, which had obviously been a serious delegation error on my part.

I shook my head, scolding myself for not remembering that Gad loved nothing more than a woman falling out of her clothes. For him, less was much, much more.

Although Ella looked stunning in the slip of a dress and sparkly, high-heeled sandals that made her long legs look even leaner, I hated the idea of so much of her on display. Especially at *Epicurus Venice*.

The boat slowed to a stop as Rami steered us to the dock attached to the back of the nightclub. At least we'd be entering from a secret entrance and not from the front. It would be easier to slip in unnoticed that way.

Taking Ella's hand in mine, I helped her onto the dock then leapt up after her, wrapping an arm around her waist. She flinched slightly, but I didn't take it too personally. I hadn't seen her since the previous night when I'd had to chase her down and drag her back to her room, and I suspected she hadn't forgiven me for that. Not to mention the fact that we hadn't discussed my revelation or that she didn't believe a word I'd told her.

I couldn't blame her for thinking I was either a liar or a lunatic. That had always been the human reaction to the truth about the Fallen. It was why we rarely revealed our true nature anymore. The modern world had all but abandoned the assumption that angels and demons walked freely among humans, despite the ample evidence.

One of our broad-shouldered human guards approached as we walked toward the stone building that shone with flashing, colored lights from the inside. "We reserved your usual table, Don Vicario."

"Good." My usual table was in the upper level of the club, overlooking the dancing. From there I had the perfect vantage point to watch the guests and assess any threats.

Ella moved closer to me as we stepped through the backdoor and were enveloped with the throbbing beat of the club music. We weren't yet in the main part of the club since we were approaching from the back, but already the energy pulsed into me.

I guided us into a sleek, silver elevator, and Rami joined us, along with two thick-necked guards, their skin as dark as their perfectly tailored suits. When the doors slid closed, Elle slipped my jacket off her shoulders and handed it back to me.

Seeing how much of her creamy cleavage was exposed, I wanted to wrap her back up in it, but I fought the urge and instead shrugged on the jacket and coiled my arm around her waist. "We don't need to stay long."

"I didn't get all dressed up for nothing," she said, flipping her auburn waves off her shoulder. "I want to have some fun."

Rami didn't turn his head, but his flinch was noticeable. I let out a tortured breath as the elevator opened, and we were met with blue lights that undulated over the crowd like waves. Ella hesitated at the sight of the crush of people, but I propelled her forward behind Rami, who cleared a path to an elevated, roped-off area with several curved banquettes facing the dance floor.

The table fronting the tufted banquette was low, so when Ella sat next to me and her skirt rode up exposing even more thigh, it was not hidden beneath a tabletop. I put a hand possessively on her leg, holding her to me as Rami sat on the other side of her and angled his body toward the crowd. The two guards positioned themselves at either end of the banquette, their arms crossed in front of them.

"It's different," she said loudly over the pounding music.

I tilted my head at her, not sure if I'd heard her correctly. "Different?"

"From the one in New York."

I nodded in understanding. "Each Epicurus is designed to fit in with the city where it's located and features art from local creators."

She swiveled her head to take in the particularly Venetian décor—stone bridges arching across the dance floor at several points, striped poles rising from the crowd for guests to swing around as they danced, and a fresco covering the ceiling that depicted the pinnacle of Venetian power and was original to the building.

"You definitely don't have that in New York." She stared pointedly at one of the stone bridges where women hung over the side, exposing and shaking their breasts at the men below.

"That's modeled after the Bridge of Tits." It was late enough in the evening that the female guests were sufficiently lubricated enough to take part in the well-known *Epicurus Venice* tradition, laughing as they flashed their tits to the crowd.

She gaped at me. "I'm sorry, the what?"

I grinned at the blush suffusing her cheeks. "In the 13th century, at the height of Venetian power, there was a bridge near several brothels from where the prostitutes would hang out of the balconies and show the goods to passersby."

She jerked a thumb at the women on the bridge as they flashed their tits. "You're telling me all these women know their Venetian history?"

My grin widened. "Doubtful, but when something catches on it's hard to stop it."

"From what I hear, nothing is stopped in an Epicurus club."

"You might be right," I admitted, watching a couple on the bridge as he fondled her exposed breasts from behind and the crowd below cheered them on. "Although all the truly forbidden takes place in Hell."

Her head swung back to me. "Hell?"

"The lower-level VIP room." I leaned close to her. "I don't recommend it for novices."

Before she could do more than splutter at me, a cocktail waitress approached, flashing me a smile and bending over our table to deposit thick coasters and flash me a lot of cleavage. She wore the black, fitted Epicurus T-shirt with our gold winged logo emblazoned across the front and a short black skirt. Rami circumvented her, drawing her eager smile with a seductive one of his own and ordering Champagne for the table along with two glasses of our usual single malt.

"More wings," Ella said after the woman walked away.

I glanced down at the wings tattooed across the back of my hand then around to see if any of the Fallen had unfurled their own wings before realizing she meant the waitress's top. "You mean the Epicurus logo?"

"I just made the connection. Fallen angels must have wings, right?" She flicked her gaze to my back. "Or you used to."

I wasn't sure if she was mocking me or asking seriously, but I decided to answer her honestly. "We have wings. They only appear at will."

She blinked at me a few times before looking away and muttering, "Convenient."

"You wish to see my wings?" Her doubt made my ire flare, but Rami pinned me with a sharp gaze from across Ella and a hard shake of his head. I relaxed back against the tufted furniture. He was right. I couldn't reveal myself to Ella, especially not in a crowded nightclub. At least not where it was so brightly lit.

I stood and grabbed Ella's hand, pulling her with me. "Come on."

"We're going already?"

I gave her a dark grin as I tightened my grip on her hand. "I'm taking you to Hell."

20

Ella

I hoped Dominick was being metaphorical again, although I was having a hard time keeping up with all the innuendos and celestial references. For a delusion, it was quite thorough.

We snaked through the crowd so quickly that the guards had to run to keep up, and soon Dominick was leading me down a staircase to a lower level. As we descended, the lighting grew dimmer, and the music shifted from thumping to sultry. Whereas the walls upstairs had been stone to mimic the look of the city's palazzos, the walls on the lower level were draped with scarlet fabric.

The corridor wasn't wide—giving me the sense of being swathed in red—and soon we reached a door flanked by two more enormous guards. They nodded at Dominick and opened the wooden door. Stepping inside, I realized that there was a curtain dividing us from the actual room, which Dominick swept aside with one arm.

I followed him but stopped once we were inside. The room was so dark that I could barely make out shapes, although the noises were distinct. Moans and heavy breathing were audible over the slow, sultry music, and as my eyes adjusted to the glow provided by a handful of candles, I knew why.

The stories I'd heard about the VIP rooms at Epicurus clubs hadn't been exaggerated. I might not be able to make out everything, but I could see enough to know that nothing was forbidden in the room Dom referred to as Hell. My pulse fluttered and my mouth went dry as my eyes adjusted even more to the darkness.

"Do you like what you see?" Dominick whispered in my ear, his sinfully rich voice sizzling down my spine.

Dominick's question made my cheeks burn, even though no one could see them. Did I like it? Heat rushed between my legs and my nipples hardened as I watched a woman straddle a man on a low ottoman, bouncing up and down as he slapped her ass to urge her on. On the banquette that appeared to line the walls, couples embraced with hands roaming freely over bodies that were barely clothed. I bit my bottom lip as heat coiled in my core. Maybe I did like it. There was something about the forbidden that was intoxicating, and I felt lightheaded just watching.

I did a doubletake when a man grinned from across the room as a woman knelt between his legs, her head bobbing up and down and leaving me in no doubt as to what she was doing. He arched an eyebrow and licked his lips, locking eyes with me. Had his eyes just flashed red?

Shaking my head and convincing myself that I was seeing things, I let Dominick lead me to a section of the fabric-draped wall.

When he pressed my back to the wall and lifted my hands over my head, I drew in a sharp breath.

"What are you doing?"

He pinned his body against mine and lowered his head so that his lips buzzed against my ear. "You like to watch, right?"

I twitched at this, straining slightly against his large hand that was holding my wrists together over my head. "I never said—"

"You didn't have to say," Dominick cut me off. "I heard your breathing change and can feel the heat coming off your body."

"That's impossible," I spluttered, wiggling in his grasp. "You can't hear my breathing over the music or feel if my body gets hotter."

"That's where you're wrong," he purred, moving his lips down the length of my neck.

A traitorous shiver of pleasure went through me, and I bit back a moan.

"So, you don't like this?" He feathered a kiss over the hollow of my throat. "Being taken where people can see you? Watching couples fuck?"

My head fell back, and I instinctively arched my breasts toward him, his words arrowing through me like fire. "I didn't say that."

He let out a dark laugh that rumbled through my body. "There is a lot you don't want to say." He nipped at my skin. "What *do* you want to say, Ella?"

Don't stop, I thought. Then just as quickly I thought that I should definitely stop. Making out in a kinky sex room wasn't the kind of thing I did, even if it was getting me so worked up that heat throbbed between my legs.

Dominick ran his free hand up the side of my leg, his fingers teasing the slit in my dress. "Are you wet just from watching?"

I knew I was, but I was afraid to answer him. Already, his scorching touch was melting my resolve and making me forget that I was trying to escape from the dangerous mob boss, not fall in deeper with him.

His fingers slipped just under the slit in the dress, caressing my skin. He lifted his head, so his dominant gaze held mine. "I promised you I wouldn't do anything you didn't want. But I think you want me to touch you." He lowered his voice. "I think you want me to spread your legs right here against this wall."

I let out a whimper, my body betraying me as my hips rocked into him.

He smiled, his eyes dark pools of desire. "Tell me to stop."

The sounds surrounding us grew in intensity, flesh slapping against flesh and moans becoming deep and throaty. Dominick's own desire pulsed off him in waves as his body pressed harder into me and his fingers teased even closer to the slickness between my thighs.

Despite my rational mind knowing that it was crazy to want him, I didn't want him to stop. I hadn't had a sip of alcohol, but I felt drunk with need, any inhibitions I had about being fucked up against a wall crumbling and falling away. My body craved his touch even as fear curled its claws around my heart.

"I don't want you to stop," I said, lifting my chin and meeting his hot gaze.

"What do you want?" It was more of a snarl than anything, the words barely a question.

"I want you." The confession spilled out of me in a breathy rush. "All of you."

There was a strange rustling and something large and dark unfurled behind Dominick on both sides, blocking out what light there was and cocooning me in pitch blackness as his mouth crashed onto mine.

21

Dominick

It was impossible to resist her when her eyes were dark with desire and her chest was heaving. Despite being as close to an innocent as I'd encountered in a long while, Ella wasn't repelled by the couples in Hell. Her own arousal as she'd watched them had been palpable, even if she didn't know that many of the beautiful bodies belonged to pleasure demons.

I spread my wings and enveloped both of us as I crushed my mouth to hers, my body humming with need. She might be aroused by watching others, but I also knew that my angelic power caused humans to lose whatever shred of inhibitions they had, and I didn't want Ella to regret anything. It was dark enough in Hell—and guests were so preoccupied with their own wanton activities—that no one would notice my black wings as I pressed us both against the wall.

I parted her lips with a hard sweep of my tongue, tangling my tongue with hers and savoring the taste of her. Desire unfurled as dark and powerful as my wings, wrapping me in an erotic daze as the need to possess her stormed through me. I couldn't think, and I could barely breathe as her body yielded to me, her soft moans making my rigid cock ache.

"Dom."

The sound of my name stoked my desire even more, until I realized it was coming from behind us, and the voice wasn't female. I quickly retracted my wings and disentangled myself from Ella, tearing my mouth from hers.

She gasped up at me, panting with obvious desire—and confusion—as I released her hands and slipped my hand from under her dress. "What's—"

I stopped her with a finger to her lips then spun around to face Rami. My second-in-command would not have interrupted me without a good reason, but I hoped for his sake that the world was on fire, or the final reckoning had begun. "You need me?"

My friend shifted, his eyes flitting around the room and then back to me. None of the other couples in the room had stopped, and a few of the incubi had been spurred on by the interruption, the red glow of their eyes unmistakable as the presence of two fallen angels obviously stoked their demonic lust.

"Don Solano and his crew are here."

This made me snap to attention. The old don was at *Epicurus*? This was hardly the type of place he frequented, even more so since it was controlled by his rival.

I gave Rami a single nod before striding out of Hell with Ella's hand firmly in mine. When we'd left the VIP room and were in the hallway, I paused and turned to her. "I need to meet with a business associate, and I need you to go back to the palazzo."

I did not want Don Solano to see me with Ella, even if I didn't believe the old man would dare make our business personal. Besides, I couldn't be sure his eldest son wasn't with him. So far, there was no indication that Jaya had tracked us to Venice, but I didn't want to make it easy for her, especially if the rumors were true and she was working with Mateo.

"I'm leaving?" Ella peered up at me, the dazed look on her face fading and her eyes hardening. "Just like that?"

"Change in plans." I put a hand on her hip, rubbing the silky fabric of her dress, the memory of slipping my fingers under the garment making me harden again. I wasn't used to restraining myself or having to go slow, so my cock ached.

Her gaze darted around the hallway, taking in the guards at the door to Hell and the two Fallen who accompanied Rami. "But we just got here."

"And it's no longer safe for you to be here," I said tightly. "Not when I need to conduct business."

"I guess I'm still your prisoner. Taking me out was all for show?"

I steeled my reaction. "It was not for show, but I can't allow you to be put at risk."

She took a step back from me and put her hands on her hips. "Because of the demons chasing me?"

I didn't answer her right away, but I noticed that Rami and the other Fallen exchanged glances. I folded my arms over my chest and pinned her with a stern gaze. "Partly. But it doesn't matter why. It's my responsibility to keep you safe—even if that makes you angry."

She muttered something and shot me a murderous glance. If I'd thought her arousal inside Hell had meant that she'd forgiven me for tossing her over my shoulder, I'd been wrong.

"You don't own me," she snapped.

I let my eyes roam down her body, my fingers tingling at the recollection of her velvety softness. "Not yet."

Her lips parted in surprise and her blue eyes flashed before I turned on my heel, murmuring to myself as I strode off to deal with the Solanos. "But soon."

22

Ella

I sat up and rubbed my eyes. Sunlight streamed through the tall windows—dust motes floating lazily in the beams—the bright light evidence that it wasn't early morning. Or maybe not morning at all.

The fluffy white duvet covered me, but the robe I'd been wearing the night before—Dominick's robe—was draped across the nearby chair. I didn't remember taking it off. My last memory was stomping back to my room after being forced to leave the club.

Two of Dominick's sizable guards had returned me to the palazzo, not giving me even the smallest chance of escaping as we'd taken the powerboat through the canals, and they'd bustled me quickly inside the mansion. I'd been more upset that Dominick had sent me home than I had been about not being able to escape.

How could he work me up like that and then send me away? I'd been seconds away from letting him fuck me up against a fall when Rami had interrupted us. Even thinking about Dominick's hard body pressed against mine and how he'd dominated me with that kiss made my pulse quicken and my stomach do a flip.

I put a hand to my temple. And what had happened right before he'd kissed me? I closed my eyes and tried to place the strange fluttering I'd heard before everything had gone dark and he'd kissed me, but the memory of the kiss made my head swim even now.

"Come on, Ella," I muttered to myself as opened my eyes and swung my feet over the side of the bed, the tightly woven rug rough under my toes. "He's not *that* hot."

Okay, that was a lie. He was that hot and more. But that wasn't the point. I'd made a deal to spend the summer with him, not the rest of my life, and I'd certainly never signed on to be his prisoner.

I spotted a tray on the low gilded table in the sitting area and rolled my eyes. There was a silver coffee service along with a wrapped basket. Of course, Dominick had thought to have breakfast waiting for me when I woke up.

"Infuriating," I said, casting a dark look at the tray and walking instead to the door. I paused with my hand on the knob, holding my breath as I twisted it. I expected it to be locked, but the door opened easily. I released a breath. At least I wasn't locked in my room. That was something.

I closed the door and hurried back to the bathroom. After barely waiting for the water to warm and taking the world's fastest shower, I finger combed my hair and applied my version of a full face—tinted moisturizer, lip gloss, and mascara. Padding back into the bedroom in a towel, I snatched a pink sleeveless shift from the wardrobe, tugged it over my head, and headed for the door. I was not standing off against Dominick Vicario again in nothing but a bathrobe or a skimpy dress.

The palazzo was still quiet, but the ominous shadows that dominated the interior at night were gone. Light from high windows I hadn't even noticed filled the foyer as I walked down the stairs, my bare feet silent on the marble steps. A quick glance at the entrance told me that the iron gate was still in place. Not that I suspected it would be standing open, but my heart sank a little.

I peered up at the fresco as I walked to the middle of the enormous hall. Even in the daylight, the angel battle painted in pastels and framed in gilded swirls made goose bumps prickle my arms. Tiny fissures in the paint told me that it was old, but I didn't want to know *how* old.

"You're awake."

I should have been steeled to the low rumble and exotic lilt of Dominick's voice, but it startled me each time. I didn't jerk, though, instead pivoting slowly to face him, my arms crossed over my chest.

Seeing him again made my breath catch in my throat. It didn't matter how much sunlight surrounded him, Dominick Vicario looked dark and dangerous. He'd changed into a midnight-blue suit that looked like it was molded to him, with a crisp white shirt that he wore open at the neck. Stubble still shadowed his cheeks, although he appeared rested.

"Did you eat the rolls I left?"

"I'm not hungry." The words sounded petty the moment they left my mouth, but he only shrugged. I wanted to continue glaring at him, but my curiosity got the best of me. "How late did I sleep?"

"It's afternoon." He didn't glance at a watch or pull out a phone. "You were tired."

I bit back a smart-ass response about being held captive really taking it out of me. As irritated as I was, I'd seen enough glimpses of the man's anger that I didn't want to see it again anytime soon.

"I'm glad you're awake," he continued, his tone as light and conversational as if he hadn't chased me down and thrown me over his shoulder, kicking and screaming. Or as if he hadn't almost screwed me up against a wall in the VIP room of his club. "We should talk."

This guy was the king of understatement. "You mean about your mob business last night or maybe about you being immortal?"

Something dark flashed behind his eyes, but he merely smiled as if I were a child who'd said something amusing. "Not necessarily." He held out his hand. "Come. I want to show you more of the palazzo."

It was clear that the word "come" was not a request, and since I didn't want to end up being thrown over his shoulder and carried through the place, I took his outstretched hand. As soon as our skin touched, warmth radiated up my arm, along with a faint hum of excitement. I frowned at myself. It wasn't easy to remain furious at the man when he had such a physical effect on me.

Dominick shifted his grip so that our fingers were interlocked, letting out his own sigh as he glanced at our joined hands, although I doubted such a scary, powerful man would feel the same kind of tingles I did.

I followed him silently through the expansive entry hall, making sure not to glance up at the painted ceiling again. Instead of turning to walk toward the double doors where I'd found him the night before, he continued straight until we reached a wall of glass French doors. He opened the one in the center and led me outside.

But we weren't outside the house. We were inside an open-air courtyard. Constructed from weathered, ivory stone, it was every bit as ornate as the inside, with a colonnaded, covered walkway featuring intricately carved columns. A small fountain sat in the center of the inner courtyard—an angel spouting water that splashed down into the circular pool beneath—and marble statues were tucked into recessed alcoves along all four walls. Stone urns were positioned at the base of each column, with colorful flowers spilling out.

I breathed in the fresh air and the perfume of the flowers, tipping my head up to look at the stone walls rising high on all sides and the windows peering down. "How big is this place?"

"It serves as our headquarters in Italy, so it's large." He pulled me toward the center, and a small, round table I'd only just noticed.

Even if I didn't believe he was an angel, I did believe he was the head of a powerful family—one that might or might not be involved in criminal enterprise. "How many are in your...family?"

When we reached the table that was set with a white, linen cloth that brushed the floor, Dominick dropped my hand and pulled out my chair. "There were two hundred of us who were appointed as holy watchers of humanity. Not all who fell remained with me, and we've brought on mortals to help with certain tasks."

We were back to the angels again. I sat and allowed him to push my chair in, trying to enjoy the fact that he could be quite the gentleman when he wasn't throwing me over his shoulder or talking crazy. "Do they all live here?"

He gave a quick shake of his head. "We have other headquarters throughout the world that require staffing—, not to mention all our clubs—although headquarters this is one of my personal favorites."

I glanced at the embellished columns and the classical sculptures flanking us. I'd seen a lot of company headquarters and none of them looked like this. Then again, I'd never been in a mob boss's headquarters. Maybe they *did* all look like this.

A man appeared from a side door, holding a bottle in one hand. Without a word, he filled both the champagne flutes on the table then melted away again.

Dominick raised his own flute as the bubbles that had teased the top rim of the glass receded. "To your visit to Venice. May it be the first of many."

I could drink to that. I lifted my own glass and met his eyes. Sitting outside surrounded by art and flowers, leaning back and smiling as he sipped expensive champagne, Dominick Vicario appeared almost tame. His whiskey-brown eyes were warm, and there was almost no trace of the fury I'd seen in him the night before—or the unbridled desire. But I knew it was there. I knew the smooth, beautiful man hid the heart of a beast.

I drank slowly, letting the bubbles tickle the roof of my mouth as I swallowed the delicious sparkling wine. "This is good. Is it Italian?"

"French. After all this time, they still make the best wine."

Dominick placed his glass back on the table, lifting his hand and flicking two fingers toward us. The man who'd poured the champagne returned, this time with two plates that he set in front of us before backing away.

"I know you said you aren't hungry, but you cannot come to Italy and not eat." He held up a finger before I could speak. "And grilled cheese does not count."

The three rounds of crusty bread on my plate were topped with a something fluffy and white with diced tomatoes as garnish.

"*Baccala Montecarlo.*" Dominick took a bite of one of his, closing his eyes for a moment before swallowing. "A Venetian specialty."

When in Rome, I thought, lifting one of the rounds of bread to my mouth. Or in this case, Venice. I took a bite, chewing thoughtfully. Okay, so it was fish. Not normally my favorite, but I had to admit this was pretty good. And I was hungry.

"Well?" Dominick asked, resting his forearms against the edge of the table.

"I like it."

"Good." He sat back and grinned. "I was afraid you might be one of those Americans who only likes hamburgers."

I tilted my head at him. "Or grilled cheese?"

His grin widened, his eyes sparkling. For a moment, I wondered if I'd imagined the terrifying side of him that had pinned me against the wall and whispered dark words into my ears. He seemed so relaxed and charming as we dined together in the courtyard with blue skies overhead and bright sunlight shining down, that it seemed impossible that he'd been the same man I'd run from.

"And you have never been to Italy before?" He sipped his champagne while he watched me eat.

I shook my head and swallowed another crunchy, savory mouthful. "I haven't been much of anywhere. Cancun once, and London for work, but I was so booked with meetings that I barely saw anything."

"Like Istanbul?"

"Exactly." I took a drink of champagne to wash down the food and wash away memories of my sad past. "Pretty pathetic, right?"

He twitched one shoulder as he watched me. "I would never call you pathetic. You were lost."

My breath hitched in my throat. Lost was exactly how I'd felt since my parents had died. Unmoored and drifting, allowing my life to be steered by everyone but me. I met his gaze. "Was it a coincidence you found me, or do you have a talent for saving lost souls?"

He barked out a laugh. "I hardly save lost souls, Ella. I am very good at entertaining fallen ones though."

A shudder passed through me. "So, you paying off my debts and taking me all over the world with you isn't saving me?"

His pupils flared, making his eyes appear black. "I believe it is you who is saving me."

Before I could respond to that or assure him that he was sadly mistaken, muffled voices from inside reached us through the glass doors. Dominick's back stiffened as he stood, pivoting to face the man who burst through the doors.

Although the man was about Dominick's age, he had nothing on him in build or magnetism. While Dominick Vicario was clearly a powerful person to be feared, this dark-haired man looked almost baby-faced in comparison—clean-shaven, and too slickly dressed.

His eyes locked on me immediately, a curious smile crossing his face. "So, this is the reason you sent a deputy to meet with me?"

Dominick widened his stance, so he was blocking the man's view of me as Rami and several other dark-suited men appeared behind the intruder. The air crackled with tension, but the man who'd walked in unannounced only laughed.

"I never thought the famous Dominick Vicario would risk his empire for a woman, but I have to admit that she is beautiful. I only wonder if you'll be able to keep this one, my friend."

Dominick twisted his neck slightly to one side and it cracked. "Why don't we take this inside, Mateo?"

23

Dominick

I pinned Rami with a menacing look as I left the courtyard and followed Mateo Solano and my fellow Fallen into the palazzo. How had my rival's overeager son managed to waltz into our headquarters and interrupt my late lunch with Ella?

Rami slowed his pace to match mine so that we were out of earshot of the intruder. "I was leaving to meet him, like you asked me to. As I pulled our boat away, I heard his arriving behind me. He was off his boat and running inside before the gates could close." He scraped a hand through his hair. "I circled back as quickly as I could."

I clapped a heavy hand on my friend's shoulder. "You are not to blame. This must have been the plan all along."

Rami scowled at Mateo's back. "You think he came up with it?"

I almost rolled my eyes at the suggestion. "He might have the bravado, but not the brains."

"To what end?" Rami asked, his voice nearly a whisper as we followed our guards into the main hall.

I paused underneath the sprawling fresco. "That, I do not yet know."

The men ahead of me stopped when they realized I had, spinning to face me. Mateo was the last to turn. Although his shoulders were squared, he no longer hummed with the brash energy he'd had when he'd arrived. If he was being advised by demons, their frenetic energy was wearing off, leaving only the impulsive, foolish son of the Don in its place.

I folded my arms over my chest and widened my stance, knowing how imposing I looked to the less-powerful man. "What reason could you possibly have for barging into my family's home?"

"We had a meeting scheduled," Mateo Solano said, his voice higher -pitched than it had been.

I cut my eyes to Rami, who stood in solidarity with me, his arms also crossed over his broad chest and his gaze menacing. "I know. I made it with your father last night. You were to meet with my second."

Mateo's own eyes flashed anger. "You should not have pawned me off to a subordinate. I am the heir to the Solano empire."

I would hardly have called the Solano's petty crime organization an empire, especially when compared to the vast holdings of the Vicario family, most of them now legitimate. I cocked my head at the man, who appeared to me just a boy. "You're one of them."

Mateo's lip curled up. "My brother has no interest in the family business. In the future, you'll be dealing with me, not Anthony."

Despite my irritation, I almost grinned. So, there was some sibling rivalry I could use to my own advantage.

I managed a casual shrug. "But you are not yet don. I showed you respect by sending my second in command."

This did not calm him. "You've never shown our family the proper respect. My father might be fine to accept your scraps, but I'm not."

"Like I pointed out before," I said, my voice modulated. "You are not yet the head of your family. When you are in charge, we will talk. Until then—"

"You're making a big mistake." Spittle flew from his mouth as his voice rose. "I'm going to be bigger than my father ever was. I was going to offer to cut you in—work together—but maybe you don't have the vision people say you do."

If this child thought his clumsy tricks were going to work on me, he was sadly mistaken. "What ventures did you want to work together on? More of the women you're kidnapping and whoring out against their will?" I narrowed my eyes at him. "Does your father know about that?"

"He knows how much money I'm bringing in," Mateo spat out. "What does he care how I make it?"

He could be lying, but he could also be telling the truth. Arturo Solano had never struck me as a man with morals, although he'd never been as impetuous as his son.

I rocked back on my heels. "The Vicario family does not sully itself with trafficking in humans. We do well enough profiting off their secret pleasures."

Mateo's gaze swept across me and the Fallen who flanked me. "Don't pretend you're better than me. Not when you've done the same thing. Not when you're the same as me."

I couldn't stop the laugh from escaping my lips. "In what way am I the same as you?"

His gaze flitted behind me. "That woman you brought here from Istanbul."

I flinched infinitesimally. How did he know Ella had come with me from Istanbul? We'd passed through private customs when our plane had arrived in the dead of night.

I tempered the flash of anger that flared within me. "What does my guest have to do with you?"

"You're keeping a woman in your headquarters under lock and key? How is that different from what I and many other families do?"

I unfolded my arms and spread them wide. "I'm afraid you're mistaken, *friend*. There is no woman being held against her will." I made a *tsk*-ing noise at him even as guilt stabbed at me. "You really think I need to lock up women for them to want to stay with me? I'm surprised you didn't hear that she was with me at *Epicurus* last night."

His face reddened. "I know what I've heard. The great Don Vicario is losing his head over a woman. That he's obsessed." The last word was a hiss that lingered in the air like acrid smoke.

Rami twitched next to me. Not enough for anyone but a celestial to notice, but enough for it to register with me. Is this what my Fallen thought, as well? That I was losing my edge over my fascination with Ella? Had I let it so quickly become an obsession?

I jammed my hands in my pockets. "You've said what you came here to say. I think it's time you left."

"She must be incredible for you to risk everything," Mateo said, taking a step back toward the steps leading down to the arched door and the dock beyond. "I can only imagine what a spectacular cunt she must have to tame the notorious Dominick Vicario."

"Do not speak of her," I growled. "Ever."

His eyes popped wide, but not in fear—in malicious delight. "That good? Maybe I'll have to get me a taste of it someday. It would be something to fuck Don Vicario's obsession."

Without thinking, I strode forward, blinded by a crimson rage and rendered deaf by the rushing of blood in my ears. I grabbed the man by the shirt and blasted him back with a single flick of my wrist. He flew down the stairs and across the dock, missing his own boat and even the water, as his body slammed into the stone building across the canal.

There was a flurry of screams as Mateo Solano's own guards jumped into the water to fish him out. With another flick, I slammed the iron gates shut and spun on my heel. The Fallen stood unmoving, their expressions betraying nothing but disdain for the human. My own gaze still burned hot, only faltering when I spotted Ella at the far end of the room, her hand over her mouth. From the look in her eyes, she'd seen everything.

"Ella," I said, the simmer of wrath fading from me as I crossed to her.

She backed away, shaking her head. "You barely touched him, and he flew all the way..."

This was not the way I'd hoped to prove my supernatural origins. Not if I wanted her to believe I was an angel and not a demon.

I pulled her into my arms, smoothing her hair as I whispered, "It only looked that way from where you're standing. Trust me, it took some effort."

A lie, but one she needed to hear.

"Who was that, and why was he saying those things?"

My muscles tensed. "He is a business rival you don't need to worry about. He was trying to get under my skin."

She drew in a shuddering breath. "I think it worked."

I had to laugh at that. "You're right. I won't let anyone talk about you like that."

She tipped her head up. "I've never seen anyone so angry, and I've never had anyone defend me like that."

I feathered my lips over her forehead. "There is nothing I won't protect you from, Ella."

Rami cleared his throat behind me, forcing me to glance back at him. He held his phone in one hand, his brow furrowed. I could not have expected to attack a rival's son without answering for it, and I should not have been shocked by how quickly challenges would be issued. Especially since Mateo had come to my headquarters looking for a fight.

The cold realization settled in my gut like a stone. He'd known exactly how to provoke me and which buttons to push, and I knew precisely which demon had told him.

24

Dominick

"Before you tell me that I was rash and impulsive and shouldn't have done that," I said, pacing in front of the fireplace as Rami, Dan, and Gad stood across from me. "I know."

"Saved us some time," Gadriel muttered, his jet-black eyes sparking as he shrugged off his jacket and tossed it over the back of a chair. "Although you did take all the fun out of this."

"He's a punk, Dom." Dan shook his head. "Since when do you let humans barely out of infancy get to you like that?"

Gad cocked his head at me. "Since the punk insulted *her*."

"You talk like she's some random human I picked up for my amusement," I stopped pacing and stared him down. "You know she's more than that."

Dan held up his palms. "We know. Have you learned anything about her or why she carries an angel's mark?"

"Or what it means for you?" Gadriel added. "Or us?"

"There are no records of her ever being in an accident or having a serious illness," Rami said, reclining in one of the leather chairs and appearing unconcerned by what had happened and the impending repercussions, although I knew that was an illusion.

I shook my head in frustration. "She knows nothing about it. Her parents are dead, so I'm not sure how I'll be able to find out without..."

Gad choked out a laugh. "Asking the archangels? You know that's not going to happen. You can't ask and they won't tell, especially if it's no accident she's here with you."

"It doesn't matter why," Rami said, his sharp voice silencing the other two. "Nor does it matter why Dom attacked the Solano boy. It's done, and now we need to make sure it doesn't blow up into something we can't control."

"Rami's right." Dan leveled his gaze at my second. "What do we know so far?"

"Don Solano is furious that his son was attacked." Rami cut his eyes to me quickly. "And almost drowned in the canal. Even so, he's also aware that his son came here uninvited and issued threats. I think even Arturo knows his son is a fool."

"Do I need to leave Venice?" I asked.

We'd only just arrived, but I didn't want to stay in a city if there was a target on my back. It wasn't that I feared the Solano family for my sake, but Ella wasn't immortal, and I wasn't pleased that she'd been seen by Mateo and piqued his interest. That was two of my enemies who now knew of her existence. I pivoted toward the fire and gripped the marble mantle, squeezing until a tiny fissure formed from the pressure. So far, I was doing a poor job of keeping her a secret and ensuring her safety.

"The don has agreed to a truce." Rami shifted forward. "In exchange for our discretion."

"Discretion?"

"It seems his son doesn't want word getting out that he broke his ribs by being tossed across the canal by Don Vicario."

Dan shook his head in disgust. "That's all they want?"

Rami shrugged. "I've already offered my sincerest apologies."

"Then you offered too much," I growled.

Before Rami could speak again, I waved a hand. "I agree to their request for discretion. No one will ever hear about it from my lips. But we have a larger problem than a don's son with his nose bent out of shape."

Dan clasped his hands behind his back. "That he isn't smart enough to do any of this on his own?"

I gave him a single, slow nod. "We already heard rumors that he was being advised by Jaya. I saw her in Istanbul, and now he barges in here spouting just the right things to set me off."

"She's never forgiven you, Dom." Rami said.

I rubbed a hand across my forehead. "I haven't fucked her for ages. Did she really expect a tryst between an angel and a demon to end any other way?"

"Demons," Gadriel said, with a sigh.

I stepped away from the fire, flopping down in one of the leather chairs and stretching my long legs out in front of me. "I know she's behind what Mateo said when he was here. That I'm obsessed over Ella. That I'm losing my touch because of her. Those are Jaya's words."

It wasn't lost on me than Dan and Gad exchanged a glance.

"This is not obsession," I bit out. "You know me better than that. In all this time, when have I ever chosen a woman over our empire?"

"I think that's the point," Gadriel said, pushing up his shirt sleeves to expose his dark, muscled forearms. "You've never bothered with a woman for more than a night, and it's always been about the carnal pleasures they could provide. Believe me, I'm not judging. Women have never failed to entice me either. But have you fucked her yet?"

I bristled, glaring up at him.

He waved a finger at me. "And since when do you get offended when I ask you if you've had a woman? You're usually willing to share the especially tempting ones."

I fixed him with an icy stare. "This one I will never share."

"Enough about this," Rami said. "It is not an impossibility that one of us would someday wish to take a human mate again."

"Because that went so well the first time."

I ignored the truth of Gad's half-whispered statement, as did Rami who crossed his arms and drummed his fingers on his biceps. None of us mentioned the prophecy again, and I knew it was something they didn't consider a realistic possibility. I didn't blame them. Even the thought it could be possible had raised hopes in me I hadn't known existed. Hopes that would be crushed if the prophecy was a myth.

"Aside from seeing you with Ella, how could Jaya know anything about her?" Rami cut into my mental wanderings. "It's only been a matter of days since you met the woman. Jaya can't know about her angelic connections. She shouldn't even know you brought her to Venice."

"Maybe she's watching," I said, my skin going cold at the thought of the demon stalking Ella. A rival crime boss and his son's wounded pride were the least of my concerns.

25

Ella

It was another day before I saw Dominick again, and the mood in the palazzo was strained, as broad-shouldered men came and went, speaking in furtive voices. Although I'd been returned to my room, the door was not locked, and I poked my head out frequently enough to know that something was going on. When I crept to the balcony overlooking the main hall, there was always a steady stream of imposing men coming and going, their expressions grim.

If Dominick slept, it wasn't in the room he claimed we would share, although I wasn't complaining. The thought of sleeping next to a man who could do what he'd done scared me. The possessed look in his eyes had scared me even more. It was true that a part of me loved that he'd defended me, but I couldn't ignore that his violent temper had sent a man flying into a wall.

Each time I thought about the guy being propelled from the house and hitting the building across the canal, my brain hurt from trying to figure out how Dominick had done it. The man might be built, but even muscles of iron couldn't do *that*.

His earnest claims that he was a divine being—a fallen angel—echoed in my head, but my logical brain couldn't believe that. Angels, demons, divine curses? Those were ancient metaphors used to explain the unexplainable. They weren't real. Besides, fallen angels—if they'd ever actually existed—certainly weren't walking around looking like Dominick Vicario.

After yet another meal tray had been delivered to my room, I finally got bored enough to venture downstairs. If nothing else, I could raid the kitchen and scrounge up a decent grilled cheese. His staff might be busy, but I could *not* eat another bowl of minestrone.

I kept to my tiptoes as I descended the staircase. The palazzo was quiet, and the light streaming in from high windows told me it was afternoon, although I'd been unable to locate a clock in the place. I paused on the last marble stair to listen. Deep voices came from somewhere, but I couldn't tell if Dominick was among the men speaking.

It didn't matter. I wasn't even sure if I was ready to see him yet. Not only could I not explain what he'd done, I couldn't figure out if the glimpses I'd seen of kindness and warmth meant he was a tortured soul or if he was masking a violent criminal.

"Wandering again?"

My foot hadn't touched down on the floor when his voice made me freeze, my toes hovering in mid-air as if immobilized. "I wondered if I would ever see you again."

The laugh that echoed across the spacious hall was genuine and relaxed. "Has it been so long?" He walked toward me with an easy gait, as if nothing had happened. When he reached me, he put a hand on my hip and smiled. "Did you miss me?"

Again, even through the fabric of my dress, his touch sent heat shooting through me. "I...I..."

Had I missed him?

He laughed again, sliding his hand around to the small of my back. "Regardless, I have missed you." The purr of his voice eased across my skin, making me tremble with unwanted pleasure. He took in my outfit, nodding. "I'm glad you're dressed. I thought we could go out today."

"Out?"

He inclined his head to me, obviously amused that I was having such a hard time speaking. "I thought you should see some of Venice aside from my club. Besides, your sleeping attire needs an upgrade if you're going to remain with me."

My cheeks warmed. He'd seen me in my oversized T-shirts, which meant he'd watched me sleeping. "You're going to let me out to buy nightgowns?"

He gave me a charming smile that reminded me of the man I'd first met in Istanbul. "You're not my prisoner, Ella, and we will do more than shop for nightclothes."

I took a step back, which meant going up a stair. "But I can't just walk out the door, right?"

"That would be unsafe."

I narrowed my eyes at him. "So, this outing will be with you?"

Dominick closed the distance between us and looped an arm around my waist before I could back up again. "Naturally. I'm an excellent tour guide."

"And I'm sure you know the best places to buy women's lingerie, right?"

He shrugged, giving me a wicked smile.

"You aren't afraid something horrible will happen to me out there or that I'll make a run for it?" I half-teased.

"I will be by your side to keep you safe as will some of my Fallen. No one would dare attack you when you're surrounded by us." His eyes hardened, but his smile didn't falter. "And running would not be in your best interest."

I lifted an eyebrow. "Because of your enemies and the demons?"

He ran a finger slowly up my throat to my chin, tipping it so that I couldn't avoid his gaze. "Because of me. If you run, I'll be forced to hunt you down and never let you out again."

I waited for him to laugh, but he didn't. Instead, he dropped my chin and stepped back, extending his bent arm for me to take. "Shall we?"

My only other option was to stay inside all day again, so I nodded. "Why not? I've never seen Venice."

Rami materialized from the side of the house I'd run to a couple of nights before, and my mind flashed back to the room filled with weapons that were not from this time. Then again, the entire palazzo was a mix of the old and new. Should I be surprised that they kept old-style weapons? They probably had guns as well, but I hadn't happened upon those yet. I shifted my gaze back to the devastatingly handsome man I'd made a deal with. Not that he needed weapons to inflict damage.

I swallowed hard, reminded that whatever Dominick Vicario and his friends were, they were part of the criminal underworld. I should probably be way more worried about that than the fact that Dominick had delusions of celestial grandeur.

Rami walked ahead, opening the gate with an ancient key and pushing the creaking latticework apart. Dominick led me to the boat we'd taken the night before, jumping down and then holding his hand out to help me. It had been so dark when we'd traveled the canal previously that I hadn't gotten a good look at the boat, but now I shielded my eyes at the gleaming wood hull that shone in the sun.

Everything was bright and gleaming now that the sun was high in the sky. Light bounced off the water and shone on the ivory buildings lining the canal. A gondola skimmed by. The gondolier in a black and white striped shirt, nodded at us as he passed, although the two occupants only had eyes for each other. I couldn't help smiling. The city of canals was just as romantic as I'd imagined with the sound of water replacing the noise of cars, and the scent of brine hanging in the air.

Dominick circled an arm around my waist as the boat accelerated away from the dock, his grip keeping me from stumbling back. As Rami steered us through the waterways, my gaze was drawn to the stone balconies, some crumbling and others boasting greenery or flowers that spilled down like waterfalls. Wooden docks were not as common as simple arched doors that sat barely above the waterline, the stone foundation green below.

Venice was unlike any place I'd ever seen—a combination of the broken and the beautiful, the imperfections part of what took my breath away. There was nothing shiny or new about the old city submerged in water, and that made it even more appealing. I longed to run my fingers along the cracking stone walls and dip my hand in the glimmering canal, but I contented myself with touching the glossy wood of our boat as we cut through the water and sent a wake unfurling behind us.

When Rami slowed the motorboat and brought it alongside a red and white striped pole, Dominick jumped out and secured us, then held his hand to me again so I could disembark the bobbing vessel without falling. Even the firm, warm grip of his hand was like a silent current, snapping me from the trance Venice had lulled me into and reminding me of his powerful presence.

The canal we'd stopped in was flanked by red brick buildings that jutted from the water beside yellow stone ones with an ironwork bridge arching across and connecting them. One side of the canal had a walkway lined with tables in front of a restaurant that boasted a green awning. The scent of freshly baked bread and simmering tomatoes that spilled from the restaurant reminded me that I'd ignored the food delivered to my room.

"You are sure you aren't hungry?" Dominick asked, still holding my hand as we passed the outdoor diners.

I was, but I was more interested in seeing Venice than in stopping to eat so soon. I waved him off. "I'm fine."

Even though we were off the boat, Dominick slipped an arm securely around my waist as we continued down the walkway and through an arch. Rami walked behind us, but not by much, and I got the distinct feeling that both men were on the lookout for something. After winding through a few streets, Dominick paused in front of a nondescript opening in the wall that boasted an ice cream case.

"You cannot say no to Italian gelato." He loosened his grip on my waist as he beckoned the gray-haired man behind the glass counter.

I peered down at the mounds of ice cream swirling up from the rectangular metal compartments and the small name plates poking from each one—*stracciatella, baccio, fragola.* I wouldn't say no to ice cream in any language.

"What is your favorite flavor?" Dominick asked.

"I like chocolate." That sounded a bit lame, considering all the different colors on display.

He nodded, his voice dropping to a whisper. "Do you trust me?"

Well, that was a loaded question. Maybe because he realized how it sounded, he choked back a laugh. "When it comes to gelato."

I cut my eyes to the ice cream vendor then back to Dominick. "Maybe *only* when it comes to gelato."

A smile teased the edges of his mouth as he turned to the old man, speaking to him in lilting Italian that made my pulse flutter. The language really was beautiful to listen to, although it was clear when I now heard Dominick speaking it that Italian had not been the language he'd cursed in when I'd kneed him in the balls.

The ice cream vendor worked swiftly, scooping and smoothing piles of the cold confections onto pointy cones, then he handed them one at a time to Dominick. When Dominick tried to pay him, the man waved him off, lowering his eyes and speaking in fast Italian. He sounded both deferential and scared. Dominick gave the man a slight incline of his head as he thanked him.

"*Cioccolato fondente* and *bacio*," Dominick said, presenting a cone to me. "Or dark chocolate and chocolate hazelnut."

I tore my eyes from the ice cream vendor, who still wouldn't look up at us, and took a taste from the top, almost moaning at the rich, chocolate flavor and the velvety smoothness of the gelato. I'd tasted gelato before—the kind you could buy in the grocery store —but real gelato was so much better. "This is amazing."

Dominick licked the side of his own cone as he moved us farther down the sidewalk. I glanced back, but the ice cream vendor had disappeared behind his refrigerated case. "Did you know that guy?"

Dominick lifted one eyebrow and followed my line of sight. "The *gelataio*? No."

A small chill went through me. The old man might not have known Dominick, but he knew who he was. And he'd been terrified.

26

Ella

"Where are you taking me?" I pulled back on Dominick's hand as he walked toward a marble-fronted boutique with a cream-colored awning and the words "LA PERLA" tastefully printed in the center. Large, glass windows were filled with faceless mannequins in delicate lingerie.

He glanced back at me, his brow furrowing in confusion. "You have nothing to sleep in but old T-shirts."

This was true, but I hesitated. Not only was I still bristling at being kept cooped up in Dominick's palazzo, but I also couldn't stop my ex-boyfriend's words from ringing in my ears, and I found myself repeating them. "I look silly in fancy lingerie."

Dominick's gaze traveled slowly down my body, his eyes unrepentant as they devoured me. "I doubt that very much."

I stood my ground, frowning at him. "If you're trying to make up for—"

"For keeping you safe?" He lowered his voice as a few passersby turned. "I won't apologize for that."

I wanted to argue with him, but I also didn't want to make a scene. Part of me was just happy to be out of the palazzo and exploring Venice, even if so far I'd just eaten gelato and walked along the canal.

Dominick's shoulders relaxed as he stepped closer to me. "Consider this an early birthday present."

"How do you know my birthday's coming up?"

"You mentioned it when we first met," he said. "You don't think I remember everything you've told me?"

I flushed at this. None of my exes had ever remembered my birthday without plenty of reminders.

"You object to me getting you a birthday present?"

I was going to tell him that lingerie was a pretty intimate birthday present, but then again, he had paid off all my debts so that I'd spend the summer with him. And I wasn't kidding myself into thinking it was out of the goodness of his heart.

"Fine," I sighed as he pulled me inside the boutique, and a bell rang softly to announce our arrival. I guess this was happening.

Although the façade of the shop fit in with the other marble and stone buildings on the Venetian street, the interior was sleek and modern. Lavender carpet cushioned our footsteps, and a darker purple armless couch was flanked by two curved chairs. Glass and gold display cases were interspersed with waist-high tables, all holding carefully arranged lace and silk panties and bras.

"*Buongiorno.*" A willowy woman with dark hair pulled into a high bun approached us, her spike heels sinking into the plush carpet. She allowed her gaze to linger on Dominick, her pupils darkening, before cutting her eyes to me and switching to English. "How may I help you?"

Dominick smiled at the woman politely and returned her greeting before turning to me. "What do you see that you like?"

Despite the soft background music and the hush of the store, I was overwhelmed by the silky robes draped over clear hangers and satin nighties adorning headless mannequins on Plexiglass shelves. I didn't dare lift one of the price tags, but I knew everything in the shop was more expensive than anything I owned. This was definitely a case of "if you had the ask the price, you couldn't afford it."

"It's all beautiful," I said, but my voice quavered.

Dominick gave my hand a small squeeze before dropping it and walking over to a display case and nodding to a sheer black bra and panty set. "We'll take this—and also in the pale pink."

The store clerk followed him around the store as he nodded to nightgowns, shorty robes, teddies, and more matching bra and panty sets. I glanced over my shoulder, curious where Rami had gone during our detour into the lingerie shop, and spotted him standing outside the glass doors, his hands clasped behind his back as his head swiveled to take in the pedestrians passing by. Part of me wished I was standing outside with him instead of being surrounded by luxury underwear that was way out of my league.

"Ella?"

Dominick's deep voice made me look away from the door and back to him.

"Sorry."

The corners of Dominick's mouth twitched. "The signorina needs your sizes."

The woman eyed me quickly as she shook her head. "I can tell her sizes by looking at her." Then she turned and bustled off to the back of the store, leaving me standing with Dominick and a lot of pricey panties.

"I really don't need all this," I whispered, since the shop seemed like the kind of place where you kept your voice low.

He closed the small distance between us, capturing my face in one hand. "The best things in life are not about need. They're about want."

My breath hitched in my chest as I peered up into his eyes.

"And I want you to have beautiful things." He stroked his thumb down the length of my jaw. "I want to see you in things that are as beautiful as you."

My cheeks warmed. "You don't have to do all this. I already agreed to your deal."

He tilted his head slightly. "This isn't about our deal, and I expect nothing in return."

Now I cocked an eyebrow at him. When had a man ever gifted underwear to a woman without expecting something in return?

He allowed himself a small smile. "Not that I can't hope to one day see you in them, but as I've told you before, Ella, I will never force myself on you." He bent his head so that his words hummed at my ear. "I won't have to."

A jolt of forbidden pleasure sizzled down my spine, as he straightened and rested a hand on my hip, holding my body to his and reminding me how much bigger he was than me.

You are in so much trouble. I could almost hear Sara's voice in the back of my head, but I tried to ignore it. It was starting to get hard to determine what was most alarming about my new reality —the fact that I'd basically sold myself to a billionaire mob boss for the summer, the fact that said mob boss also thought he was a fallen angel, or the fact that I was having a hard time fighting my attraction to the man.

The saleswoman returned with a pair of large white *La Perla* shopping bags with ribbon handles. She beamed at Dominick as she handed the bags to him. "I hope you enjoy your purchases." She glanced at me with a less enthusiastic smile. "*Signorina*."

Dominick gave her a respectful nod before steering me from the shop. When we emerged on the sidewalk, Rami glanced over at us. Then he allowed his gaze to drift past us into the boutique to where the saleswoman bent over a display facing us, her blouse draping open slightly.

"We can continue to St. Mark's without you," Dominick said, tracking his friend's line of sight.

Rami shook his head, pivoting back to face us and taking the shopping bags. "You know I never indulge when I'm on duty."

Dominick shrugged. "As you wish."

Rami's eyes widened for a moment as he looked past us, but he shook his head.

"You saw something?" Dominick asked, the merriment quickly leaving his eyes. His grip on my waist tightened, and he shifted himself in front of me.

Rami squinted down the stone-paved street toward a bridge that arched over the canal. “I’m seeing things that aren’t there.”

Dominick stared down the sparsely trafficked street. “You’re sure?”

Rami nodded. “The Solanos aren’t known for their stealth. If they’re here, we would see them.”

“It’s who we can’t see that worries me,” Dominick said under his breath.

27

Dominick

Venice seemed to get hotter and stickier as we walked toward St. Mark's Square. But even crowded and humid, the city was an assault of pleasures—the sound of the water slapping against the stone houses, the songs of the gondoliers drifting through the narrow canals, the richness of the gelato that dripped down your fingers. I'd known it for centuries, and unlike many places, change was slow for the city that was gradually slipping into the sea—a true comfort for those of us who were immortal.

The crush of people grew thicker as we approached the popular square, and I wondered for a moment if this had been wise. Although no trip to Venice would be complete without seeing the iconic tower and the wide square where pigeons flocked to tourists who eagerly fed them by hand, it was also a chaotic jumble. So far, people had moved out of our path as we approached—some because they were locals and knew me by sight and others sensed the energy field I projected around me. If Ella noticed that the crowds seemed to part miraculously for us, she didn't comment.

I cast a glance at Rami who prowled behind us, his gaze sweeping the waterways, sidewalks, and skies for any threats. Although his head barely moved, I knew he was aware of every person who passed, and every gondola gliding by. I also knew there were other Fallen following and watching unseen from a distance. Still, I couldn't relax my iron grip on Ella's waist.

"I can't believe it," she said, as we crossed a small bridge and entered the square. "It looks just like the pictures. Except there are way more people."

"Always."

The ruddy stone tower rose at one side, the green top like a pointy bishop's hat. Next to it sat St. Mark's Basilica, its many Byzantine domes topped with ornate crosses and arching across the skyline. Long, grey-tone buildings flanked the piazza with open-arched columns running along the ground level. The square itself opened onto the water, guarded by two stone columns, *Colonna di Marco* and *Colonna di Teodoro.* I knew the history of each of these buildings and monuments, and some I'd even witnessed being built.

"Would you like to go inside the basilica?" I asked Ella as she stood taking in the square.

She eyed me warily. "Don't tell me you bought out all the tours for this one as well?"

I grinned at her. "No, but that would have been a good idea." I slipped my arm from her waist and took her hand in mine. "Next time."

From the corner of my eye, I tracked Rami as he tracked us. Even though he moved silently, his dark, good looks attracted stares from both women and men. Especially since he walked close to me. Two Fallen so close always drew attention, whether we wanted it or not.

We crossed the square, dodging laughing tourists and swooping pigeons. Ella's small hand tightened in mine as I pulled her away from a photographer backing up without looking, lifting us both off the ground for the briefest moment to avoid being hit.

Her gaze swung to me, but I kept moving forward toward the cathedral. Despite being a fallen angel, I had no problem with churches or holy sites. Most of them weren't as holy as people thought they were, and those that truly carried the spirit of the divine within their walls reminded me of meeting an old friend after years apart—a pleasant encounter, but not overly consequential.

I passed the red stanchions outside the basilica, nodding to one of the guards. I had not bought out all the tours because the cathedral was open to the public, which meant it was usually crowded, with lines to get inside that could linger for hours. I was, however, known to the people manning the doors. The name and face of Dominick Vicario was not one anyone in Venice wished to disappoint, and they waved me quickly inside.

Once we passed the main doors, the hum of the square dissipated, and a hush enveloped us as I led Ella into the narthex. The air was cool and held the aroma of dust and burning candles. Windows high in the cupolas let in light, but candlelight flickered across the gilded ceilings and walls.

Ella inhaled sharply as her head fell back, and she took in the glittering, gold mosaics that covered the domes towering overhead.

Even my breath slowed at the depictions of saints and angels peering down from arches and naves.

Ella's hand slid from mine as she walked forward as if in a trance, her head tipped up. The basilica's beauty had this effect on people the first time they saw it, and my eyes moved over her as her chest rose and fell. She hadn't struck me as a religious person, but even I couldn't deny the power of the ancient holy site. I swiveled my head as I took in the shining mosaics that told various Biblical tales, narratives that were as familiar to me as my own past stretched around the inside of domes.

"Is that Greek?" Ella whispered as she pointed to the writing above a saint painted into a gilded alcove.

I came up behind her and wrapped my arms around her, leaning my head down so my lips nearly touched her ear. "Much of this cathedral is Byzantine, and was inspired by the Hagia Sophia in Constantinople, I mean, Istanbul. Many of the relics were even plundered from Hagia in the fourth crusade." I moved her forward and nodded to some Latin inscriptions. "But much is also in Latin."

"You know a lot about this place," she whispered.

I shrugged. "I've lived in Venice a long time." I didn't tell her that I'd witnessed the structure being built over hundreds of years, from a church to house the body of St. Mark that burned to the ground, to all the later churches and their lavish additions that had finally become the imposing cathedral in which she stood.

She nodded, and I wondered what she was thinking. Did she still think I was insane—a madman claiming to be an angel, or were inklings that I spoke the truth niggling at the back of her brain?

We moved underneath a series of arches and hanging ottoman-style lanterns suspended between marble columns. She twisted to face me; her face shadowed in the soft light.

"So." She fluttered a hand overhead. "If you're some sort of fallen angel, all these guys would be your friends, right?"

I eyed the saints she indicated with the flourish of her fingers. "I would not call these saints friends, no." I lowered my voice as people walked by us. "I fell long before these men walked the earth, and we didn't exactly run in the same circles."

"Right." Her tone told me she found my explanation to be weak. "Since you were cast out?"

"Correct. If you want, I could tell you about the fires and earthquakes that ravaged the church at the beginning of the former millennium, or how Napoleon separated the church from the Ducal Palace when he arrived, and the Republic fell."

She narrowed her eyes at me. "Anyone can be a history buff."

"You wish for evidence?" I glanced around me again, spotting Rami standing with his arms folded at the base of a black marble column.

"I don't go off blind faith."

I studied her. How had this practical American woman been marked by angelic forces? Not only was she not a religious zealot, but she also didn't seem to be one of the faithful. Not that I blamed her. As a fallen angel, I could relate wholeheartedly to her resistance to religion. Rules and false moral strictures had always made me bristle. But then why her? Angels so rarely interfered on Earth, and so infrequently left their mark on humans. Yet one of them had been compelled to either save or bring about the existence of Ella. Not knowing was driving me mad, but there was only one way to discover the answer, and I wasn't willing to do it.

People flowed steadily around us, most peering up and recording with their phones or taking selfies. I curled a possessive arm around her waist and yanked her flush to me. "For now, you'll just have to take my word for it."

"That you're a fallen angel who's been cast out of heaven for eternity?" Her voice was quietly mocking. "No problem."

Rami cleared his throat, pulling my gaze to him and reminding me that there was more of the city I wished to show Ella before night fell.

"Come," I said, taking long strides from the basilica. "There is still much of Venice to see."

Ella didn't complain as we walked back into the piazza, retracing our steps across the vast, open area. When we reached the far side, I ducked between the arches of the *Procuratie*, skirting us underneath the grey buildings that framed the square.

Rami's urgent voice made me stop and turn. He'd paused, his phone pressed to his ear and his face stricken.

"What?" I asked, knowing already that it was bad.

He approached quickly, his gaze darting to Ella before he decided to speak anyway. "There's been an attack at the palazzo."

A knot formed in my gut. "Who?"

"Unknown as of yet." Barely suppressed fury crackled off him, his shoulders bunched with tension.

"Go," I told him. "Find who did this." I didn't need to tell him to punish them accordingly. That much was understood.

His eyes flicked between Ella and me. "You are sure?"

I gave a curt nod. "She will be safe with me." Especially since the attack had come when we'd left the palazzo. "Go."

The last word was an order, and Rami spun on his heel and vanished into the crowd. Anger prickled the back of my neck as I watched him go. No one had dared attack our home in a hundred years. The boldness both shocked me and filled me with rage.

I held Ella tighter. If the palazzo of the Fallen was not safe for her, we would need to leave Venice. I pulled out my phone and made a call.

28

Ella

"I don't understand," I said, as Dominick bustled me from the square. "Where are we going? Who did you just call?"

"No time," he muttered as he pulled me along behind him. We hurried over an arched bridge and then down a narrow street with houses rising on both sides and blocking the sun.

I'd seen the anger on his friend's face and heard the furtiveness in Dominick's voice as he'd told the person on the other end of his phone call to prepare for our arrival. Were we seriously leaving Venice when we'd just arrived? I might have made a stupid deal with the man, but I had not signed up for *this.*

I wrenched my hand from his and stopped in the middle of the sidewalk. "I'm not going anywhere else with you."

Dominick whirled around, his expression both terrified and terrifying. "Ella, I do *not* have time for this."

Even though my heart hammered in my chest as he glowered down at me, I backed away when he made a grab for my hand. "I mean it. You can't just drag me wherever you want at the drop of a hat."

"I can, if it keeps you safe," he growled, his gaze moving quickly around the quiet street, as if he expected someone to leap out at any moment.

"Just because your house got broken into doesn't mean you need to freak out," I said. "It doesn't mean we need to run off to who knows where. I thought Venice was your city. I thought no one here would dare cross you. How can it suddenly be unsafe?"

"It is not the Venetians who are targeting you." He held out his hand with the palm up. "I can't tell you where we're going here in the middle of the street, but I promise I will tell you. Just please come with me, Ella."

The way he said my name—the pleading tone and the outstretched palm—made my resolve crumble. Just when I was convinced he was a monster, he would show me a glimpse of something beneath his fierce exterior. His softened expression and patiently waiting hand was the grilled cheese all over again.

I huffed out a breath. "Okay, but only because I have no idea where I am, and these winding streets confuse me. This doesn't mean I'm letting you off the hook."

"Understood."

I placed my hand in his, feeling the usual tingles when his skin contacted mine. He threaded our fingers as he led us through another street, tilting his head up. I followed his gaze, seeing the dark clouds moving fast to darken the sky. The temperature around us seemed to plummet several degrees as the sun was shrouded, and fat raindrops splattered the stone beneath our feet.

Dominick's fast walk turned into a run as he darted into a small square. I tried to keep up, but my sandals skidded on the slick stones, and for once, I was grateful that his grip on my hand was so firm. I spotted an ivory-stone church through the falling rain, the peaked roof boasting a series of small statues, and the edifice covered in ornate carvings. Somehow, it appeared to glow even as the darkness of the storm descended around us.

"Inside there," I cried out as the heavy rain became faster, the sharp drops stinging my skin.

Dominick didn't yell back over the pounding rain, but we both ran for the church, pushing through the center doors made of heavy, gray iron. We burst inside, panting for breath and dripping water all over the marble floors.

After I caught my breath and the doors slammed shut behind us, I swiped my wet hair off my face and looked around. The church was significantly smaller than the basilica and boasted no gold mosaics, but the interior didn't suffer from a lack of soaring columns or dramatic frescos. Both sides of the church were lined with recessed alcoves, flanked with columns and marble sculptures. Even though it was a bit tucked away, I was surprised to find that we were the only people inside. Collections of red candles glowed behind the two rows of dark-wood chairs, but aside from our labored breathing and the dripping of water from our drenched clothes onto the floor, the church was almost ominously quiet.

I turned to watch Dominick drag a hand through his dark hair. How did the man get soaked to the bone and look even better than before? He shrugged off his dripping suit jacket, and his white shirt was plastered to his damp skin, showing every hard curve of his muscles. I sighed. There had to be some rule against looking this hot inside a church. I clenched my legs together as heat pulsed between them. And there definitely had to be a rule about getting turned on in a church.

"Are you okay?" he asked, folding his jacket over his arm.

I glanced down at the pink dress that stuck to my skin. "I'm sure look like a drowned rat, but I'm fine."

He put a hand to my arm and rubbed my bare flesh. "You hardly look like a rat, but you do look cold."

A voice came from behind the church's altar and echoed off the arched ceiling above it, the Italian words unfamiliar to me. A Catholic priest in a black cassock walked toward us from between two marble columns, his thick, brown hair shot through with silver.

Beside me, Dominick flinched and stepped closer, responding in what I assumed was perfect Italian. When the priest saw me, his smile widened, and his soft, brown eyes sparkled with curiosity. "You are not Italian?"

"No, American," I said, almost apologetically. It felt like I should apologize for not being Italian in a city as beautiful as this one.

"You are very welcome here." The priest beamed at both of us as he spoke in heavily accented English, his gaze lingering for a moment on Dominick.

"As soon as the rain stops, we will not need to drip onto your floors, Father." Dominick gave him a deferential bow.

The man shook his head. "Do not worry about that. The church is here for all those who need sanctuary—even if it is only from the rain."

Dominick backed away and returned to the door, opening it to check on the storm. When I met the priest's eyes again, they were searching. I cut my eyes to the mafia don at the door. What would happen if I asked this priest to give me sanctuary from Dominick? Could he hide me away or would Dominick drag me out anyway?

As soon as the thought entered my mind, I dismissed it. I knew the answer to my own questions. A man like Dominick would not be thwarted by a priest, especially not an older man by himself. If the head of the Vicario family was as deadly as he claimed, and as powerful as the people in Venice seemed to think he was, a single man—priest or not—couldn't stop him from getting what he wanted. And now, what he wanted was me.

"Is something troubling you?" The priest's accent was thick, but his English was surprisingly good. I guessed the constant influx of English-speaking tourists made learning the language an advantage, even in a small church.

I smiled at the holy man, hesitating before shaking my head. "Nothing."

His gaze slid to Dominick and then back to me. He reached out and touched my hand. "Are you sure?"

I wondered if he knew who Dominick Vicario was by sight, or if he could sense the ominous power radiating off the man like I could. Even though thunder boomed outside, it wasn't the storm that sent energy humming through the air inside the church. It was Dominick.

The priest's brow furrowed as he locked eyes with me. "The church is salvation for many lost souls."

A claiming hand rested on the small of my back as Dominick joined us again. "You do not need to worry about our souls, Father."

My heart sank as I felt the slim hope of escape slipping away from me. Even though the possibility had been small, I now knew that

Dominick would not be so easily outmaneuvered. Nor would he be intimidated by the church, even as stone angels with alabaster wings sounded silent trumpets from above the altar.

The priest did not drop his gaze, but he gave a single nod. "Stay for as long as you wish."

A gust of cold air blasted my legs as the tall doors opened, then closed again, with a shuddering thud. Dominick stiffened before he turned, whispering a single word like a death knell. "Jaya."

Before I could turn, Dominick had pivoted and tucked me behind him and in front of the priest.

A woman's laugh reverberated off the marble interior. "You think you can hide her from me?"

Dominick squared his shoulders, making himself look enormous even from my vantage point behind him. "She isn't your concern."

"The question is, why is she yours? You rarely linger over a female for longer than it takes you to roll off them. But not this one." The flirty tone hardened. "Why?"

The priest shifted behind me; no doubt unused to hearing talk like this in his church.

"She amuses me." Dominick's voice was so easy, I almost believed his feigned disinterest. But his shoulders were tensed, and the veins in his neck throbbed.

"Does she amuse you enough for you to risk your empire?"

"The only risk to my empire is you, Jaya." Dominick pivoted, keeping me behind him—and I could only assume away from the woman's sight—as he turned. "Your thirst for revenge will be your downfall."

"You would know all about downfalls, wouldn't you?" The words were a low hiss as sharp footsteps tapped the floor, bringing her closer.

My heart raced. Who was this woman? I didn't buy the story that she was a demon, but she clearly made the powerful and deadly Dominick Vicario nervous, although I suspected he was holding himself back in front of me.

"If you persist in this, I will retaliate." Dominick's warning carried so much menace even I shivered. "And all of your kind will pay."

"As usual, you're blinded by your own self-indulgence. It isn't us you should fear. *We* aren't the reason she's here."

Dominick emitted a dark growl. "You know nothing, Jaya."

She laughed, the sound containing no humor. "It's clear I know more than you do."

"Leave now." Dominick spat out the words, curling his hands into fists. Heat roiled off his body, evaporating the last remaining droplets of water from my skin as I huddled behind him.

"Or what? You wouldn't dare show your true self."

A flash of black overhead caught my eye—the woman I'd seen in Istanbul was spiraling through the air and landing on the other side of me, her ebony hair flying around her face. Dominick spun almost as quickly as she moved, but a blade flashed in her hand and darted forward.

In an instant, a wall of black surrounded me and the priest, shielding us from the blade's thrust. I screamed as all light was drowned by the pitch-darkness of the cocoon. Even Jaya's scream of rage was muffled as the priest stumbled into me. A pulse of energy throbbed off Dominick that was so strong it brought me to my knees, the marble hard as my legs buckled and I hit the floor.

Then as quickly as darkness had enveloped me, it was gone again. I blinked a few times as my eyes adjusted to the light of the church, then I turned to see Dominick behind me with dark wings unfurled and the woman named Jaya staggering from the church, her blade gone. I suspected she'd gotten the worst end of the energy pulse that had blasted me off my feet. I barely had time to comprehend Dominick's enormous, feathered wingspan before he'd pivoted to face me and retracted them.

My mind whirled as I stood, trying to come up with logical explanations for what I'd seen. It wasn't possible. There was no such thing as angels, and certainly not fallen ones with breathtaking wings, masquerading as mob bosses. But I hadn't imagined it. Dominick had wings. Huge black ones with feathers so dark and glossy-black they shimmered an almost inky, iridescent blue.

"You're..." my voice cracked.

"An angel," the priest squeaked, reminding me that he was still there and had been witness to everything I had.

"I did try to tell you." Dominick reached behind me and caught the priest before the man hit the marble floor in a dead faint.

I sank down beside the crumpled priest. If Dominick had been telling the truth about being an angel, then that meant everything else he'd told me was probably true. Which meant that for some reason, I was being hunted by demons.

29

Dominick

"It couldn't be helped," I told Rami as he poured me a drink, the liquor splashing in the glass over the smooth rumble of the yacht's engine.

Rami handed me the glass, taking a seat on the beige sofa across from me, and stretching one arm across the low back as he swirled the whiskey in his own glass with the other. "You revealed yourself to a priest, Dom."

And to Ella, I thought, as I remembered her wide eyes as I'd hurried her from the church and to the Venice yacht pier, where the Vicario yacht was anchored and waiting for our arrival. She'd barely said a word as I'd rushed her up the gangway and onto the gleaming white ship that spanned over fifty meters.

"Think of it this way," I said. "He'll never doubt again."

Rami snorted a laugh before slugging back his own drink. "After seeing a Fallen unfurl enormous, black wings? Oh, I suspect he's going to have quite a few questions."

I swallowed a generous gulp of my favorite single malt, welcoming the burn as it rolled down my throat. Not as many as Ella probably had. Even though a part of me was glad she'd seen my wings, I hadn't wanted to give her such a shock. Then again, I'd had no choice.

"The attack on the palazzo was a ruse." I leaned forward and braced my elbows on my knees. "It was never the target. We were."

Rami scowled, no doubt furious that he'd been distracted and pulled away from us. "The damage to the palazzo was minimal and nothing was taken."

"Demons?"

My friend's lip curled up in distaste. "Humans. We killed two of them."

"Solano?" I clenched my fingers around the sharp etchings in the rocks glass. If our rival don had ordered an attack on the Vicario headquarters it would mean war.

Rami shook his head brusquely. "Amateurs. Hired muscle. If it was the Solano family, we've never seen these soldiers before."

I stared down into the amber liquid in my glass. I wasn't willing to discount my rival. Mateo Solano was just brash and undisciplined enough to attempt an attack on our headquarters, with only enough intelligence not to use soldiers we would know. Still, unless we could prove it, I couldn't make a retaliatory move. Especially since I had more important things to worry about.

"How's the woman?" Rami asked, as if sensing the shift in my thoughts.

"Ella?" She'd followed me to the master suite on the top of the ship, barely registering the windows curving around the room giving a one hundred and eighty degree view of the water from the king-sized bed. Of course, the shades had been drawn, and it had been dark.

And she was in shock from seeing proof that you're a fallen angel.

"She's worn out from the whole thing, but she'll be fine," I said.

Rami nodded but his dark brows pressed together. "She said nothing after she saw your wings?"

"Nothing of consequence."

"It's a lot for humans to process. Their minds perform all kinds of gymnastics to explain away the supernatural. She's probably convinced herself that she was hallucinating or that it was a trick of the light."

The last thing I wanted was for Ella to convince herself that my wings weren't real and that I wasn't a fallen angel. I wanted her to know what I was. I *needed* her to know the truth.

"At least she's safe now." I swallowed the last of my whiskey and savored the heat as it pooled in my stomach. A yacht sailing the Adriatic Sea and crewed by fallen angels wasn't an easy target.

Rami leaned forward, mirroring my stance with his elbows resting on his knees. "Not that we can stay out here forever."

"Not forever," I said, thinking about the woman asleep in bed. "But long enough."

Rami tilted his head at me. "Long enough for what?"

I didn't answer him, instead, placing my empty glass on the blonde wood coffee table and standing. Moving on silent feet across the plush, cream-colored carpet, I crossed the spacious lounge and up the spiral staircase to the master suite, closing the door behind me after I entered.

The lights were off, but my eyes quickly adjusted, helped by the one window shade that wasn't closed all the way and the moonlight slipping beneath it. I sat on the edge of the bed, the mattress sinking slightly from my weight and hovered a hand over Ella's sleeping body. The pale gray duvet was pulled up around her shoulders, but her hair spilled across the pillow, strands of red glinting in the faint light.

Even now, with her safe on my ship and away from Venice, my heart squeezed as I remembered the sight of the blade slashing dangerously close to her. It had been pure instinct that had caused me to unfurl my wings—a primal need to keep her safe that eclipsed all reason and all vows I'd taken to keep my identity hidden from humans.

I wasn't worried about the priest. His newly discovered religious fervor would be an attribute in his line of work and would not be completely unusual in Italy. He would also not be the only Venetian who could claim to have seen an angel with wings as black as night, although most who'd glimpsed our divinity over the years were dead. It was Ella's reaction I feared. It was one thing to be the girlfriend of Dominick Vicario, mafia don. It was another to be the mate of a fallen angel.

Ella shifted in her sleep, turning over and blinking up at me. "Dominick?" She pushed herself up on her elbows, her gaze sweeping the dark room. "Where...?"

"We left Venice," I reminded her, resting a hand on her bare shoulder. "We're on my yacht, remember?"

Her brow wrinkled as she nodded. "I remember." She sat up all the way. "I remember everything."

My stomach tightened as I braced myself for hysterics or anger, but she raised a hand to the side of my face, her fingers soft against my stubble. "You saved me."

"Of course, I saved you." I sank into her caress. "I told you I would protect you."

"You also told me who you really were, and I didn't believe you." Her gaze searched mine. "But I saw your wings. I couldn't have imagined those."

No, not many could envision the magnificent and terrible sight of a fallen angel's wings, so dark they seemed to suck in the light, and so powerful they could break a knife's blade. "I'm sorry if I frightened you. I didn't have much choice."

"No." She shook her head and put her other hand on the other side of my face. "I wasn't frightened. Well, okay, I was a little bit, but it was incredible. *You* were incredible."

"It doesn't upset you that I'm a fallen angel?" I husked out. "That I'm cursed?"

"At least I don't feel like I'm crazy." She gave me a shy smile. "And I don't think *you're* crazy anymore. That's a good thing. Besides, my guardian angel had been doing a crappy job lately. I was due an upgrade."

I laughed. "You think I'm an upgrade from a guardian angel?"

"Oh, yeah." She bit her bottom lip as she let her gaze rake over me. "A big one."

30

Ella

Maybe I was the crazy one now, but the realization that Dominick Vicario was an angel—and a fallen one, according to him—didn't make me want to run. It made me want him even more. After spending my life doing what was supposed to be right, what I apparently craved was what was forbidden.

I slid one hand down the side of his face, my fingernails rasping against his dusky stubble and trailing around to the nape of his neck.

A shudder wracked his body, and he grasped the hand that remained on his cheek. "Ella. You shouldn't."

His skin buzzed warm under my fingertips, as I locked my gaze on his. "Why not?"

The warm brown of his eyes had been swallowed up by molten pools of darkness that threatened to consume me. "There's a reason I'm one of the Fallen."

The husk of his voice made my fingers curl around the base of his neck, instinctively grasping him to steady me. "That was a long time ago."

The laugh that escaped his lips held no mirth. "I have spent more lifetimes than you can imagine indulging myself in humanity's carnal pleasures and meting out punishment to the wicked. I make no apologies for what and who I am, but I am not the heavenly creature my wings might make you think I am." His grip on my hand tightened. "Do not try to redeem me, Ella. I am no angel."

The dim light of the room kept his face in shadows, his handsome features contorted by the dark that masked them, but it didn't give me pause. He was wrong about one thing, though. There had been nothing about his magnificently ferocious wings, the glossy feathers as hard and glittering as black steel, that had led me to believe he was anything but what he said he was—a fallen angel who was cast out for his lust for the forbidden. And I didn't care.

"I don't want to redeem you." My pulse trembled beneath his fierce grip as the dark truth spilled from me. "I want you just as you are."

He bit back a groan, his body stiffening as if he was trying to restrain himself.

If he wouldn't believe my words, I thought, he would have to believe my actions. I slid my fingers up through his thick hair and yanked his mouth to mine.

If I'd thought he would hesitate or continue to protest, I was wrong. Dominick's lips moved hard and fast against mine, opening my mouth to him and caressing my tongue with his. As he tangled a hand in my hair, he pressed me back onto the bed, pinning me in place even as he braced his elbows on the bed to keep from crushing me.

Not that I wanted to be anywhere but underneath him. My heart raced, my skin burning from his hardness and the need to feel more of him. I arched my back, the hard points of my nipples aching for contact.

As if sensing my need, he tore his mouth from mine, kissing his way across one cheek and then sucking on my earlobe until my thighs clenched, and I raked my fingernails through his hair. Lifting his head so I glimpsed the dark flash of his eyes, he growled and nipped down my neck, tracing the tip of his tongue along the hollow of my throat.

“Dominick,” I rasped, not sure if I was actually begging for more of his delicious torture.

He made a low noise in his throat that hummed across my flesh, sending a shiver of desire arrowing down my spine as his lips worked across my collarbone. His hands moved from my hair, skimming down my shoulders and arms, leaving a scorching trail. When he reached the neckline of the dress I’d collapsed into bed wearing, he reared back, tearing off the duvet.

I sucked in a breath as the cool air hit me, and he eyed my clothing.

“Do you want to take it off or should I?” he asked.

My breaths were shallow, arousal fogging my brain. Before I could think of an answer, he’d grasped the hem of the dress that had ridden up to my waist and ripped. I let out a surprised yelp as the thin fabric tore apart in his powerful hands, falling away from me and leaving me only in my ivory lace bra and panties.

His intensity should have scared me, as should the way he loomed above me dark and dangerous, but it only stoked my desire. I loved that I could drive him to release his wrath, and that I was at the mercy of his barely contained lust. I glanced down at the bulge in his pants—the fabric straining and pressed my hand to it.

He hissed out a breath, his eyes holding mine as he tore off his own shirt, the buttons scattering across the room. I sat up and dragged my fingernails down the iron curves of his chest muscles and the hard ridges of his stomach. When I reached the waistband of his pants, I stopped and peered up at him, licking my lips.

With a menacing growl, Dominick pushed me back on the bed. As his dominant gaze raked across me, I saw a flash of the dark angel behind his burning eyes—wanton desire shrouded in immortal beauty. As tormented as he was and as much as his touch provoked forbidden desires in me, I didn't care. I wanted to embrace the dark side of the sinful angel, even if it meant falling hard.

Dominick's hands moved over my body hungrily, across my breasts and bare belly, hesitating at the strip of lace between my legs. His movements stilled as did his breath. He teased one fingertip along the lace edge and then slipped it underneath.

I fluttered my eyes closed and arched my back as his featherlight touch made fire simmer in my core. Then his mouth was on me again, moving hot across the swell of my breasts and sucking the tight points of my nipples through the lace of my bra. Burying my fingers in his hair, I gasped as he swirled his tongue around one nipple and then the other, sucking until my breath was ragged. He brought me to the edge again and again with his punishing mouth until I was writhing, my body burning.

"You're torturing me," I managed to say as I panted beneath him.

His voice was a rumble that shook my bones. "Torment is what I know."

I fisted my hands in his hair and jerked his head up so my eyes were on his. "I want more."

"You are sure?" His warm breath tingled over my skin.

I nodded. "I've never been more sure about anything."

With a single, lightning-fast movement, Dominick knifed up, moving to the foot of the bed. He grasped my ankles and tugged me down, spreading my legs and dropping down between them. When he moved my panties to the side and dragged his tongue through my folds, I grasped handfuls of the sheet beneath me.

I was already so close and so wet that my body trembled the moment his tongue circled my clit. In the past, it had taken me a while to come, but somehow Dominick knew exactly how to touch me. His tongue moved deftly, flicking and sucking until my body quivered, the simmering heat exploding in waves that consumed me. I cried out, jerking up and clenching my thighs around his head until I finally sagged back onto the bed.

Instead of being sated, though, I wanted more. I gazed up at him as he stood and undid his pants, letting them drop to the floor. Fresh desire throbbed between my legs as I stared at the cock that stood out ramrod straight from his body—thick and long and perfect.

Lifting my legs into the air, Dominick slid my panties up and off then he opened my legs and ran his hands down the length of them until his palms were under my ass. I twitched my hips, holding my breath when he dragged his broad crown through my wet folds and then notched himself at my opening. He pushed himself in just enough that I could feel the delicious burn as he stretched me, but then he stopped.

His jaw was tight as he stared down at me, as if he was fighting a battle within himself.

I closed my hands over his large ones clutching my hips. “Take me, Dominick. I’m yours.”

Then darkness shuttered his eyes, his defenses crumbled, and he plunged his cock deep inside me.

31

Dominick

My control shattered as I thrust my cock deep, her tight heat sheathing me as if her body was made for me. I forced the thought that maybe it *had* been from my mind. None of that mattered now. All that existed were our two bodies forged together, our slick flesh entwined.

Ella arched up, letting out breathy moans as I held my cock all the way inside her, letting her adjust to me. Angels might be like humans, but there was nothing about us that was average.

"You don't have to stop," she said between uneven breaths. "I promise I can take all of you."

That did nothing to help my self-control. "You do not know what you're promising."

Her lips twitched. "Try me."

I bent over her, crushing my mouth to hers. I had to taste her again and feel her sweet tongue moving against mine. Anything to keep myself from unleashing my punishing desires on the woman I so desperately wanted.

Ella kissed me back hard, her tongue thrashing with mine and her fingers scraping through my hair, tugging my head closer to hers. As she kissed me with desperate wanting, my hips jerked out and then in again. I lodged myself all the way inside her with a hard thrust, savoring the delicious tightness of her and the sharp inhalation of breath that caught in her chest.

Wrapping her arms around my back, she dug her nails into my flesh. "More," she commanded, after ripping her mouth from mine.

She was so small compared to me, but she'd taken all of me and wanted more. I should go slow for her, but I couldn't. Not when she was begging for it, and not after I'd imagined how she'd feel around my cock since the moment I'd seen her on that rooftop in Istanbul. Her human body was like none I'd ever felt before, and her breathy cries made it impossible for me not to respond.

"We should go slow," I said between gritted teeth as I dragged myself out, instantly missing the velvet tightness of her.

"You're one of the Fallen, aren't you?" she purred. "Then show me how a fallen angel fucks."

My body jolted. For the briefest moment, I wondered if Ella was a demon in disguise. Her rough, seductive words and her sultry movements were not what I'd expected from her. It was what I'd expect from a practiced temptress. Not a sheltered woman who'd seemed conflicted about me and had bristled at being under my control. But now she was submitting to me eagerly, taking everything I gave her and begging for more.

I slid my hands to her hips, my fingers biting into her flesh as I thrust myself again. My body buzzed with a million sensations at once as I stroked my cock into her tight heat, feeling every tremor as she ran her hands down my back, her touch branding me. If she was a demon, I didn't care. I would gladly surrender my soul to her for endless nights like this.

But I knew she was no demon. No amount of dirty talk and eager fucking could erase the angelic trace that hummed across her skin. Now that our bodies were locked together, our shared angelic bond sent vibrations ricocheting through me. Everything I'd suspected about Ella had been right. She was the perfect mate for a fallen angel. The only human who could be my ideal match. The only mortal who could stoke such fire within me and fill the hole of my tortured soul.

And if my forbidden lust dragged her into eternal torment with me? If I was the reason another angel fell?

A roar of rage tore from my chest as my tenuous control incinerated. I thrust hard, unable to slow my savage rhythm as her gasps became screams. Rearing up, I scooped my hands under her ass without pausing, lifting her hips and hooking her legs over my shoulders.

Her breathing became faster and her cries more desperate. I wouldn't have been surprised if the entire yacht was filled with the sounds of her pleasure. I didn't care. The only thing that mattered was savoring the exquisite feel of her. There was nothing else. Nothing.

Holding myself inside her for a beat, I stared down at where our bodies met. The look of her pale skin being split by my cock, the curl of heat almost a visible shimmer of gold on my skin, made a possessive growl escape my throat.

"You really aren't human, are you?" she managed to gasp out.

I looked up to see her eyes wide in the moonlight. But she wasn't scared, she was aroused. Heat flared in my core, but I couldn't speak. I lifted her hips higher and plunged deeper, desperate to claim her. With every hard stroke of my cock, I was branding her as mine forever.

And pulling her in deeper to your dark realm, a dark voice whispered. I ignored it, telling myself that she wanted this. Ella knew, and she still chose me.

Her eyelids fluttered and her fingers gripped my shoulders as I braced myself over her with both hands. She arched back, her teeth biting at her lower lip and her fingers digging fiercely into my skin, golden light sparking from the contact.

The pain barely registered as her body begin to ripple again, and her husky moans became cries. I thrust harder as her muscles clamped around my cock so tightly, I had to press my eyes together, the euphoria nearly blinding me. White light glowed behind my eyelids as I lost all control, my release a searing inferno of heat as I threw my head back and roared, emptying into her.

Ella gripped my slick shoulders, trembling and panting. My heart thundered in my chest as I slipped her shaky legs back down and rested my forehead on hers, the skin glowing where we touched and our warm air mingling until I didn't know which angel breaths were mine and which were hers.

32

Ella

Dominick rolled over to lay beside me, his chest heaving. After a few deep breaths, I twisted so that I was tucked up against him, my cheek pressed to his side and an arm draped across his taut stomach. I'd never literally glowed during sex like that, but I guessed it was a fallen angel thing. I could definitely get used to more of that.

It made no sense that being with someone like Dominick felt so right, but even when he'd been claiming me with ravenous hunger that stole my breath and spiked fear within me, it had felt inevitable. I'd actually glowed for fuck's sake.

I bumped one finger down his corded stomach. "If you'd told me last week that I'd end up in bed with someone like you, I never would have believed you."

He stroked a hand over my hair and rested it on my back, pulling me closer. "Trust me; this is as much of a surprise to me as it is to you."

"Because you don't stay with any woman longer than a night?" He stilled, and I continued, my words rushing from me. "I hear things, and your friends aren't all that quiet." I lifted my head and rested it on his chest. "I'm not judging. You're the type of man I'd expect to have a different woman in his bed every night."

His throaty laugh rumbled through me. "What type of man is that?"

My face warmed, and even though it was dark, I pressed my cheek back to his bare chest to hide my embarrassment. "Gorgeous, powerful, dangerous."

His fingers trailed lazily across the small of my back again. "You think I'm dangerous?"

"I know you are," I said before I thought better of it. "Not that I think you'd hurt me, but you have a scary, mob-boss vibe that probably makes most people pee their pants a little. And that's even without you whipping out your wings."

He laughed so hard that I couldn't help laughing myself. "It isn't my goal for people to pee on themselves at my approach."

"You can't help it. You're a tortured soul and tortured souls are always the most dangerous."

"Hmmm." He pressed a kiss to the top of my head. "You are wiser than most mortals, especially for one so young."

"I'm not that young," I said. "I turn thirty in a few days."

He let out a low whistle. "That *is* old."

I smacked his chest. "Very funny. Maybe it isn't old to you because you're..." It was hard to comprehend what he was, much less admit it out loud.

"Immortal?"

"I was going to say ancient, but immortal is nicer." I propped my chin up on his chest again and looked at him. "But thirty feels old when you're right back to square one and you haven't done any of the things you thought you'd do before you hit the big three-O."

He shifted his head to meet my gaze. "And what did you think you should have already done?"

I let out a sigh. "Well, I definitely thought I'd be married by now. That didn't really work out so well."

"That boy you were with was never going to marry you," Dominick said, with a certainty that stung.

"I know that now, but it's hard to see things like that when you're in the middle of them. I thought all men needed time, and Christopher was just a typical guy who was nervous about commitment and would eventually realize that I was the perfect woman for him." Even as I said it, I felt my throat tightening. "Sara was right all along. I was an idiot, and I wasted years on a guy who was never going to be ready."

"It wasn't wasted if it brought you to me."

A laugh burbled up as I blinked away tears. "You really are smooth, you know that?"

"I'm not trying to be smooth, but I have had a little bit longer to gain some perspective on time." He rolled me over so that we were both on our sides, facing each other. "And you are neither old, nor have you wasted your life."

"But if you're really an immortal, then a human lifespan must feel like the blink of an eye to you."

"Not always." He shifted down so that our faces were even. "Right now, I'm savoring every breath with you."

"I don't even care that that sounds like a really good line," I said, brushing my fingers through the short hair at his temples.

"How can I convince you that these aren't lines?" He flipped me onto my back so that he was on top of me again, then he swiftly parted my legs and settled himself between them. "How can I prove that you're different?"

I wanted to believe him, but he was still an immortal, and I was human woman. As much as I desired him, this could never be more than a fling. A two-month fling, according to our deal, but still a fling. Not that I was complaining. I was seriously due for something hot and fun that didn't even have the possibility of a future. That thought made my heart squeeze a little, but then I was distracted my Dominick moving between my legs.

I sucked in a quick inhalation. "I guess fallen angels don't have to wait for long before going again?"

"Wait?" He kissed me, his lips dominating me as he took both of my hands and pressed them over my head, interlocking our fingers. "Why would we wait?"

"No reason," I mumbled, feeling how hard he was already. He really wasn't like a normal man, not that the wings hadn't been a big tip-off.

"I have no desire to wait."

"I believe you," I whimpered, as his rigid length pressed against my inner thighs, my juices already making his cock slick. "That you mean what you say."

"You don't." His gaze was darkening. "But you will."

Dominick's voice, like everything else about him, radiated certainty. As insane as it was, when he looked at me like that—predatory power rolling off him in waves and with me the object of his desire—I couldn't help but believe him. I needed to believe him.

This time when he entered me, he moved with such exquisite slowness that I twitched my hips to pull him deeper. But Dominick only tightened his grip on my hands and locked his gaze on me as he stretched me inch by inch. "Like I said, I'm savoring you."

Closing my eyes, I bowed my head back, straining my arms against his iron grip. I wrapped my legs around his waist in a desperate attempt to take more of him. "I think you enjoy torturing me."

When he'd filled me to the hilt, I opened my eyes to see him hovering over me, the muscles in his shoulders tight, and the pulse in the side of his neck throbbing.

"Torture isn't my specialty. I much prefer indulging in the pleasures of the flesh." He dropped his head, and his lips were soft as they tickled my ear. "But I do like to hear you scream for me."

33

Dominick

When I woke again, light peeked in from under the window shades. Ella lay curled up beside me, so I got up quietly, covering her with the rumpled duvet before padding across the carpet to the master bathroom. The wide window was shaded, but the room was still brighter than the dim bedroom, making me squint as my eyes adjusted. Walking past the huge, round whirlpool tub that sat on a raised white marble platform, I stepped into the glass shower and flicked on the water.

The first blast was cold, which I welcomed to wake me up, but as it warmed, I rolled my head back and let the water cascade over my face and down my body. Turning, I flattened my palms against the wall as the jets pounded my back and uncoiled all the tension from my muscles that hadn't been released the night before. I moaned as my shoulders relaxed, and I remembered being inside Ella—the snug heat of her as she'd taken all of me.

My cock twitched to life, but I did not slide my hand down to grasp it. If I did, I would be tempted to crawl back in bed and bury myself beneath Ella's legs, and I might never leave the bedroom. As appealing as that was, there were things I needed to discuss with my fellow Fallen.

I finished my shower, toweling off and walking naked to the bedroom where I pulled a pair of black drawstring pants from a drawer and tugged them on, tying a loose knot at my waist. Giving one more longing look at Ella in bed, I left the room and hurried down the spiral stairs.

When I reached the ship's main lounge, I paused. I'd expected to see Rami on one of the armless beige sofas or maybe Gad and Dan perched on upholstered ottomans. Instead, I was greeted by a host of the Fallen. Like me, they were tall and broad-shouldered, hiding ebony wings beneath dark suits or crisp, tailored shirts.

Spotting coffee on the sideboard built into one wall, I crossed to it and poured myself a cup, keeping my voice intentionally measured. "It's good to see you all."

"It seemed appropriate we should come." One of the original Fallen I knew as Asbeel sat on one of the long sofas, his arms resting on his knees. "Considering."

"The incidents with the demon in Istanbul, and the rival family in Venice?" I stirred a cube of sugar into my coffee and took a sip, not turning back toward them.

"That surely requires discussion," another said, entering the lounge from the glass doors leading outside to one of the yacht's many covered terraces. "But we're here because of the woman you've taken."

Although my back stiffened, I remained facing the wall. "You must have heard wrong. I have taken no one against their will."

"I told you that Dominick is not holding any human captive," Rami said.

I turned and saw my friend leaning against the wall, his arms folded tightly across his chest. "Rami is right. A woman is with me, but she is by no means a captive."

"If the noises last night were any indication of her willingness to be here," Gadriel said from his position at the end of one of the sofas, "then I can confirm Dom's claims."

A flush of heat bloomed inside me at both the memory and the thought that we'd been heard. "I'm used to rumors about me, but I am not used to the rumors coming from my own brothers."

"We are here out of concern," Asbeel said. "Is it true she's not fully human?"

I swept a disdainful glance across the gathered Fallen. "She might have an angelic trace on her, but she is human."

Eyebrows lifted and looks were exchanged.

Asbeel gave a snort of laughter. "Why am I not surprised that our leader found himself a celestial?"

"She is not a celestial," Rami said, before I could. "Humans have carried angelic marks before."

"You're sure you're not trying to restore yourself by taking an angel, Dominick?" Asbeel gave me a cold smile. "Leading us isn't enough for you?"

Rage simmered under my skin, but I attempted to quell it as I took another sip of coffee, barely registering the taste as I locked eyes with Asbeel over the rim of my cup.

"You mean the prophecy?" I asked.

Murmurs passed through the group and Asbeel grinned and shrugged. "Well?"

"That prophecy has never been confirmed," I said, "nor does it provide redemption only to the fallen mate."

"That's right." Gad sat forward and set his shoulders wide as he rested his hands on his knees. "A true union with a Fallen and an angelic human means the path to restoration for all the Fallen."

Dan crossed one leg over the other, a move that conveyed ease, although his neck muscles were bunched. "If you believe in unconfirmed prophecies."

Asbeel stood and spread his arms open wide. "Who are we to know what deals Dominick might have made without our knowledge? Maybe he knows more about the prophecy than we do."

"Deals?" I cocked my head at him in disbelief as I set the coffee cup back on the sideboard. "With whom? The archangels? They guard against our return to grace. They have no bargains to make. And how could I know more about a prophecy that has only ever been a whisper?"

Asbeel narrowed his eyes like he didn't believe me. "Then what is your need for the human? You've never bothered with one for more than a night before this, but suddenly you're jetting one around and installing her in our headquarters? And then you're starting a war against one of our rivals over her? If her angelic mark doesn't make her more valuable, why do you risk so much for her?" His scowl morphed into a sly smile. "Don't tell me the angelic mark makes her that much of a better fuck, Dom."

Within an instant I'd flown across the room and lifted him off his feet by the throat, propelling him to the wall and slamming him into it. “I’ve already had to teach another not to talk about her like that. I didn’t think I would need to school one of the Fallen as well.”

Asbeel’s chiseled features had morphed into a contorted mask of rage. “You are the one who needs to be schooled. Do you not remember? Every single heavenly watcher signed your pact and defied the rules with you, and we have all paid the price.”

My grip on his neck loosened as the truth of his words hit me like ice. “I remember.”

“Then you know we would follow you into hell.” Rami’s voice was low and steady, and I realized he stood next to me.

Asbeel’s face was still mottled pink, but his flashing eyes lowered. “I meant no insult. You have never cared about a human like this.”

I uncurled my fingers and released him. “It is not because she has some angelic connection.” I raked a hand through my hair. “Or maybe it is. I don’t know. There is something about her I need.” I backed away from Asbeel. “But I promise you it has nothing to do with our penance. I will serve it alongside you until the final judgment.”

“That is enough for me.” Dan stood. “We have stood together too long to let something as insignificant as this drive us apart.”

“How many thousands of women have we all bedded?” Gadriel asked, his wicked smile wide. “If Dominick wants to indulge himself in this mortal a little longer than usual, is that such a crime?”

“And if he needs our help to protect her from Jaya?” Rami scanned the group.

Several of the Fallen flinched at mention of the demon, but Gad stood, the mischievous grin gone from his face. “I pledged to you before, and I do it here again."

I inclined my head to him as the others stood and gave me their reassurances of loyalty, while Asbeel slipped out the glass doors, unfurled his wings, and lifted into the sky.

34

Ella

I opened my eyes at the sound of ice rattling in the silver bucket and tipped my head back as Dominick placed a fresh bottle of champagne in the melting ice. The dark glass glinted in the afternoon sun, the pale gold label like a shield inscribed with delicate flourishes.

"You only drink French Champagne?" I asked, taking a final sip from my flute, even though it was warm.

He shrugged one shoulder as he lowered himself into the hot tub next to me, and I tried to avoid staring at his hard-to-miss package nearly bulging out of his black, spandex swim trucks. "It's the best. Besides, any monk like Pérignon who devotes himself to wine is a holy man after my own heart."

"Since you enjoy your wine and women so much?" I teased, peering over the top of my sunglasses at him.

He stretched his arms out along the edge of the hot tub, wrapping one hand around my shoulder. "Now I'm only enjoying the pleasures of one woman."

"Sweet talker," I said under my breath, but so he could hear me.

Dominick grinned lazily and closed his own eyes, leaning his head back and letting the sun beat down on his golden, tanned skin. "I already told you that I speak the truth. Has anything I said to you yet been a lie?"

I thought about that for a moment. No, nothing he'd told me—even the craziest bits—had been lies. He'd been honest with me from the beginning, even if I hadn't wanted to hear it. Even so, believing that a gorgeous fallen angel who was also the head of a powerful mafia family wanted me was hard to buy. He could have any woman he wanted—and probably already had, come to think of it—so what made me so special?

I cut my eyes to him as he relaxed in the bubbling water next to me, his perfect profile silhouetted against the blue sky. The dark hair at the nape of his neck was wet and the errant curls that usually fell over his forehead were joined with a few others. My fingers tingled with the urge to touch them, but I didn't want to break the spell of quiet, especially since we'd spent most of the morning tangled up together in bed. I'd admit we had some scorching chemistry, but anyone would, with a man as smoking hot as Dominick, right?

I allowed myself to stare at the tattoo that marked the back of one hand, the wings outstretched from the base of his thumb to the beginning of his pinky. Now that I'd seen his actual wings, I realized that his tattoo was a recreation of them, the ink somehow as black and shimmery as the ebony feathers themselves. I wondered if it was a real tattoo or a celestial marking of some kind. Then I thought about the look on his face as he'd unfurled his wings around me in the church. His fury had been both intoxicating and terrifying.

My thighs clenched, and I sank lower in the water, letting the bubbles tickle my nose. Trying to decipher a fallen angel was a losing proposition, and one I should probably give up before I made myself crazy. Besides, despite the unusual circumstances and the even more bizarre deal we'd made, I was enjoying being with Dominick Vicario. To everyone else he might be a notorious don, but to me he was sweet. Not to mention, very attentive. My cheeks warmed as I thought about our morning and the previous night. Still, I was curious.

"So, you'll tell me the truth?" I asked. "No matter what I ask you?"

He rolled his head toward me without sitting up and opened one eye. "Of course."

"You told me before that you were holy Watchers. That's a kind of angel?"

He nodded, closing his eyes again. "We were angels tasked with watching over early humans, but we became too involved. We shared knowledge that was forbidden, and we ultimately found human females too tempting to resist."

"All of you?"

His expression twisted for a moment. "We signed a pact with each other to disobey as one. Maybe we thought it would protect us. Maybe we thought that we wouldn't all be banished if we stood united."

"But that didn't work," I said.

"It didn't." Dominick opened his eyes again. "We were cast out of heaven and cursed to live on Earth until the final reckoning."

"Then what?" My voice was hushed.

"We'll be cast into eternal damnation."

My breath caught in my throat. He said it so casually, but I knew it haunted him. "So that's why you chase pleasure."

He shrugged. "There seems no reason to deny ourselves. Why not enjoy all the delicious indulgences earth has to offer while we can?"

That made sense, but there was one more thing I needed to know. "If you could go back and choose all over again, would you fall or would you remain a heavenly Watcher?"

He didn't hesitate. "I would fall a million times if it brought me to this point right here and right now with you."

A laugh burbled up in my throat even as a flush of pleasure warmed my cheeks. "So smooth."

He slid his hand down from my shoulder to my back then used it to tug me over so that I was straddling his waist. Smiling up at me, he opened one eye as my body blocked his face from the sun. "It's the truth, Ella."

"The water wasn't warming you up enough?" I asked, returning his smile.

"I missed your touch." He shifted me on his lap so that the bulge I'd had such a hard time not gaping at earlier was pressed between my legs.

My eyelids fluttered in response. "Now I know why you've never kept a woman for more than one night before. None of them could survive it."

His wicked grin faltered, and his gaze flicked south. "Are you sore? Have I hurt you?"

I was sore, but not painfully so. "A little, but it's not bad. It's a good kind of sore." I hesitated before admitting the rest. "It's just been a while for me, so I'm adjusting."

Dominick's brow creased. "I thought you had a boyfriend?"

"We'd stopped having sex very often." My face reddened as I was reminded of the humiliation of Christopher rebuffing me because he "wasn't in the mood," or I was "too needy." "He said he didn't have a high sex drive."

A muscle twitched in his jaw. "How long had it been?"

"Months," I said, not meeting his eyes. "I lost track. Maybe that's why I threw myself into work so much."

"Another reason that boy wasn't good enough for you." He rubbed his warm hands up my back as his scowl softened. "I cannot imagine a man not wanting to live inside your tight, little—"

I swatted his chest, and he smiled, moving his hands so they spanned my waist.

"If it's too much, you can tell me." He dipped his fingers under the fabric of my bikini bottom. "The last thing I want to do is hurt you."

I bent forward, strands of my wet hair dripping on his chest. "I don't mind the way you hurt me, Dominick."

He growled, the hardness beneath me growing as he rocked his hips up. Then he lifted me and spun me around so that I was still in his lap but facing the other way.

"What—?" I started to say, but when he slipped one hand into my bikini bottom and his wet fingers parted me, the question died on my lips.

"There are ways to make you scream that won't make you more sore."

My body was already wet and hot, so the sensation of his finger circling my clit made me arch back against him and moan. He slid his free hand under one side of my bikini top, thumbing my nipple as he worked his hand expertly between my legs.

There was no one else on the top deck with us, but we were still out in the open. "Anyone could see us."

"No one can see anything I don't want them to see," he whispered hot in my ear as his large hand caressed my breast. "No one will see what is mine."

He readjusted his hand below so that his thumb flicked my clit while he slid a thick finger inside me. "But let them hear me make you come."

I bucked against him as he held me tight, his hands moving on me with the skill of a thousand lifetimes. I was already so close, quivering around his finger inside me while the hard peak of my nipple sent jolts down my spine as he squeezed it. Rocking my hips forward, I took him deeper as my quivers became spasms and my entire body jerked wildly while he held me flush to him.

Even though my release came quickly, it was no less intense. I choked out a scream as pleasure blazed through me hard and fast, my own hands gripping his and holding him prisoner to my desire.

When I went limp on him, he eased his hands out of my bikini and wrapped his arms around me. "Better?"

"If it was even possible," I managed to say between stolen breaths, "yes."

A clearing throat from behind us made me sit up swiftly and readjust my bathing suit as I slid off his lap. Dominick sighed but waved the steward forward.

"Rami asked me to convey the message that we will be in Split by nightfall," the young man in the white uniform said, his eyes anywhere but on the hot tub. "And he requires your input on a business matter."

The corner of Dominick's mouth quirked up. "Rami sent you? Very well. Tell him I'll join him shortly."

When the steward disappeared down the spiral staircase, I glanced at Dominick. "Split?"

"Croatia. Have you been?" he asked so casually it made me laugh.

I hated to admit I'd never heard of it. "No. I didn't know that's where we were going." I hadn't known we were going anywhere in particular. I'd thought we were sailing around so we'd be harder to reach.

He stood and stepped from the hot tub, grabbing a towel from a nearby lounge chair and drying himself. "There's a charity event I should attend. I thought we could go together."

Again, my gaze was drawn to his now rock-hard cock that threatened to burst out of his spandex trunks. What kind of spell did he have me under that I was already getting aroused again? Then I realized he was addressing me directly.

"Ella?" His expression was amused, as he hooked the towel around his shoulders.

"Sorry. A charity event in Croatia. Right." My mind went to the clothes I'd packed. The only new items I'd procured in Venice weren't appropriate to wear outside of the bedroom. "Unless the event calls for business-casual attire, sundresses, or fancy lingerie, I don't have anything to wear."

"You would look breathtaking in anything." Dominick leveled a sinful gaze at me. "Especially the lingerie. But don't worry. I've arranged for something more appropriate for you to wear." He held out a hand. "You should probably get out of the water before you get lightheaded."

I took his hand and let him help me out. He was right. Between the heat, champagne, and mind-blowing orgasm, my legs were wobbly.

Without a word, he scooped me into his arms. "You need some time away from the sun." He managed to carry me down the winding staircase and placed me gingerly on an upholstered lounge chair on the covered deck below. Then he nodded to the side table where a glass of water sat next to my phone. "And I thought you might want to talk to your friend Sara. The one I seem to agree with often."

My heart leapt as I picked up the phone. "Thank you. I have so much to tell her."

He smiled at me. "Not everything, I hope."

"Don't worry," I said. If I told my best friend that the hot guy I'd shacked up with was actually a fallen angel, she'd definitely have me committed.

35

Ella

After Dominick went inside to dress and meet with Rami, I speed-dialed Sara's number and leaned back on the lounge chair, stretching my legs out in front of me. For the first time in as long as I could remember, I was relaxed. My shoulders weren't tight with stress from the seemingly millions of work projects I'd taken on to impress my boss, and my stomach wasn't in knots because my boyfriend had picked a fight with me, and I'd been the one to end up apologizing. Again.

It was almost hard to believe that before a few days ago, that had been my life, and I'd been content to settle for such meager scraps. And now I was on a luxury yacht with a billionaire who was unbelievable in bed. Oh, and he also happened to be immortal.

"Suck on that, Christopher," I whispered as the phone rang.

"Oh, my God," Sara said when she answered, her voice thin and breathy. "I've been wondering where you were."

Using my shoulder to hold the phone in place, I took a sip of ice-cold water. "Here I am."

"And where is that exactly? The last time we talked, you were on your way to Venice."

"Now I'm on my way to Split."

"Croatia? What happened to seeing Venice?"

"I did see Venice." I tried not to sound defensive. "But we needed to leave. Dominick has a charity event he needs to attend in Croatia."

My friend blew out a breath. "I feel like I should buy a wall map to track your movements."

"Ha ha." I peered at the horizon and the wake the ship was making in the blue waters of the Adriatic. "Where are you? You sound out of breath."

"Fifth floor walk-up." She sucked in a breath. "Remember?"

I'd trudged up the stairs of her charming, yet elevator-free, walk-up enough times to remember the breathless feeling. "Right. So, what's going on with you?"

Now she stifled a laugh. "More of the same—work, eat, sleep. It's starting to get hot, and I'm not looking forward to more of the city's sticky heat in July and August."

A pang of guilt gnawed at my gut. Usually, Sara and I came up with ways to escape the heat together, from pooling our funds to split a hotel room at a property with a pool, to sitting on one of our cramped balconies and soaking our feet in a plastic kiddie pool. "I'm sorry I won't be there this year."

"Yeah, me too, but you'll be back in a couple of months, right?"

My mind brushed over Dominick saying that our deal was now more than the original two months. He hadn't mentioned that again, and I was pretty sure it had been said in the heat of the moment. Besides, I couldn't exactly become the full-time girlfriend of a mafia don. "Definitely."

"Good." Sara fumbled with something in the background then opened and closed a door. "I kind of freaked out when I found out what happened to your old boss."

The tightness in my stomach returned, but this time it wasn't guilt, it was dread. "What do you mean?"

"You haven't heard?" Sara's voice took on the low tone she used when passing on a particularly good piece of celebrity gossip. "I was sure someone at the company would have texted you."

I couldn't tell her that I hadn't had access to my phone since the last time we'd spoken. Not that I'd missed it. I'd been too busy to want to check in with the real world.

I glanced at the screen. It *was* strange that I hadn't heard from any of the people I'd worked with. I hadn't been besties with anyone at work, but I would have expected at least one or two to reach out after I'd quit. "I haven't been checking messages much, and the signal hasn't been great here."

"Well, apparently your boss got caught up in some sort of mess while you all were in Istanbul. Something about hookers and drugs. I forget the details."

"In Istanbul?" I shook my head. That couldn't be right. "The entire team flew out the next morning."

"Then I guess it happened the night you called me. Didn't you say they were all going out to celebrate the guy getting promoted over you?"

Even though it felt like a lifetime had passed since then, my heart raced with fresh outrage. "They sure did."

"I don't know where they went, but they all ended up getting arrested. Your boss was a big enough deal that pictures of him even ended up in the paper here. Only the *Post*, but people saw it."

"Shit," I closed my eyes and drew the word out several syllables more than it required.

"Exactly. It was a shitstorm when they got back. Your boss got fired, and I heard his wife left him. Even Christopher got canned."

My eyes flew open. "Wait. Christopher got what?"

"Arrested and fired." Sara sounded pleased about this. "He was with all those guys. I say it serves him right for ditching you."

The niggling sense of dread had morphed into full-on anger. No way this was a coincidence. The same night I meet Dominick and tell him my sob story about my awful boss and traitorous boyfriend is the same night they both end up arrested?

"You said there were photos?" I asked.

"Even though they were in some exclusive club, someone took photos of them. And not just any phone photos. Telephoto ones." Sara blew out a breath. "It might not have blown up like it did if there hadn't been such wild pictures."

I didn't want to ask, but I needed to know. "Were there photos of Christopher?"

"He appeared in some of the ones of your boss, but he wasn't enough of a big shot to make the papers by himself." Sara's voice lost some of its excitement. "I'm just glad you'd already dumped him by then, El. He wasn't close to good enough for you."

I rubbed a hand across my forehead as I processed all this. As angry as I'd been at both my boss and rotten ex, I'd never wanted to blow up their lives.

"Listen," Sara said, her tone now all business. "I know you. You're going to put this on yourself somehow, but this had nothing to do with you. Those guys treated you—and I'm sure every woman they ever met—like crap. No one forced them to do lines of coke and hire hookers. They did this to themselves."

"I guess so." Somehow, I suspected there'd been someone pulling a few strings to get such high-quality photos to the media.

"Promise me you won't call Christopher because you feel bad for him. That douchebag does not deserve your pity. Spoiled pretty boys like him always land on their feet."

I laughed, even though my stomach was still roiling. "Admit it, you're going to miss him."

My best friend barked out a laugh. "Like a genital rash."

I put a hand over my mouth as giggles spilled from me. Sara always had a way of making me laugh, even over the worst things.

"I do miss you, though," she said. "I hate that you're so far away."

"Me too."

"Liar," she said, but in a teasing way. "You're jetting around Europe with some hot guy. I know you're not sitting around missing me."

"Truth?" I said, sweeping my eyes over the water as the sun dipped lower. "I don't miss my old life, but I do wish you were here with me. You would love it."

"Okay, that I'll believe." She hesitated for a beat. "And is this Dominick guy still treating you well?"

"Definitely," I said. "I'll have so many stories to tell you when I get back."

"I hope at least some of them will be dirty."

"Sara!"

"What? If any woman needed to get laid, it was you. And don't try to deny it. You were a hot mess of pent-up sexual energy. Just don't get knocked up or married."

"No danger of that."

"Good. Now, I've gotta run, but you'd better not wait days to call me again."

"I won't," I promised, disconnecting after saying goodbye and dropping the phone on the lounge chair as I stood. Although I'd loved talking to my best friend, she'd raised more questions than she'd answered, and I was pretty sure I knew who would have the answers I needed.

36

Dominick

When I walked into the office after showering and pulling on drawstring pants and a T-shirt, Rami sat in one of the boxy, cream-colored chairs across from my desk. Light from the sinking sun dappled the shelves behind the blonde wood desk, drawing my gaze to the wall of glass that overlooked the aft of the ship and the Adriatic Sea beyond.

"We'll be in Split soon," he said, not standing as I took a seat behind the desk and swiveled the beige, high-backed leather chair toward him.

"That isn't why you sent for me." I eyed my second-in-command, his tan pants and loose white button-down a contrast to his serious expression.

"I wouldn't have interrupted you if it wasn't important." He leaned forward, steepling his fingers together as he rested his arms on his knees.

I waved a hand at him. "It's fine. I'm being indulgent."

Rami shrugged, no stranger to a little hedonistic indulgence himself. "Unlike Asbeel, I have no issue with you and Ella."

I smiled at his use of her name, then frowned as I thought of our Fallen brother and his hurried departure. "Should I be worried about him?"

"Asbeel?" Rami tilted his head. "He has followed you for millennia. I doubt an argument over a woman would change such loyalty."

I grunted, hoping he was right. "If not Asbeel, then why did you summon me? You're a handsome man, but I would rather be looking at Ella in a bikini."

That got a smile from my friend. He stood, walking to the glass and peering at the sea as our yacht cut smoothly through the water. "It's the Solanos."

I blew out a breath. "Again? I thought we'd settled things, made amends, agreed to their request for discretion."

"We did." Rami slid his hands into his pants pockets as he turned. "This is about the don. He's requesting a meeting of the families."

The hairs on the back of my neck immediately stood on end. "No one's called one of those in years."

"He wants one now. He says he has new business ventures he wants to discuss."

"If this is the human trafficking his son is dabbling in, he won't find a friendly reception from me or most of the others." A cold fury rose in my chest. I wished I could punish Mateo Solano like he so richly deserved, but I could not afford to draw even more attention to the Vicario empire or the Fallen who ran it.

"Should I tell him we aren't interested?"

I put my head in my hands, scraping my fingers through my damp hair. It was customary to respect a meeting when it was called by one of the dons. It was done rarely, and with the understanding that it was a privilege not to be misused.

"Even if his son is a fool, Arturo is not. He would never risk what he's built—however paltry—to violate the traditions of the families. If he's requesting the meeting, I want to assume he's in earnest." I looked up. "Still, I'd like us to set the location."

"You want to take over Don Solano's meeting instead of returning to Venice for it?"

I rocked back in my chair. "Tell him we're unavailable to return to Venice, but we want to honor the don by hosting the gathering and covering all the expenses. Request the dons meet us in Croatia."

Rami's eyes widened. "You plan to bring them on the yacht?"

"No." I shook my head forcefully. I did not want those old-world thugs anywhere near Ella. "Don't tell them we're in Split. Arrange suites for them in The Palace in Šibenik."

The luxurious resort that we'd built around ancient Roman ruins was suitably impressive to intimidate the other dons, but was equipped with state-of-the-art security to ensure none of them stepped out of line. It was also located far enough away from where we'd be docked to be a threat.

"I assume Don Solano will agree once he's heard your offer," Rami said.

The Palace was also one of the most difficult luxury resorts to book in the country, favored by celebrities and the Uber-wealthy who enjoyed our unmatched security and unmatched privacy. Like all my properties, it provided refuge for those wishing to indulge their forbidden desires in secret.

"Be sure he understands that his son's presence is not required," I added, as Rami turned to leave, his phone already out of his pocket.

He hadn't made it to the door before Ella barreled inside, her gauzy cover-up hanging open, and barely covering anything at all. Rami stepped back, startled as she squared off in front of me with her hands on her hips.

"Dom," he started to say, no doubt wondering if I wanted help diffusing whatever situation had arisen.

"You can go." I met his eyes briefly. "I'll handle this."

He flicked his gaze to the fuming Ella, and then ducked out the glass door.

"Like you handled my boss and my ex-boyfriend?" Her eyes blazed as she glared at me, challenging me to argue with her.

Even though it wasn't hard to figure out what she meant, I wasn't going to make this easy on her. "You're going to have to be more specific."

She curled her small hands into fists, and I couldn't help flashing back to holding those same hands over her head as I'd entered her with exquisite slowness only hours earlier. "My friend Sara said that my boss and my ex both got arrested the last night they were in Istanbul, the night we met. Apparently, there were lurid pictures of them with prostitutes that ended up in the papers back home. Both lost their jobs, and my boss' wife left him."

"It sounds like they got themselves into serious trouble." I kept my voice calm as I stood and came around the desk. "You do know that prostitution is legal and regulated in Turkey. Of course, there are rules, which perhaps they broke, and unlicensed brothels, which maybe they visited."

She narrowed her eyes at me. "Did you do this?"

"Get them arrested? No." I put my hands on her arms. "My dealings with law enforcement are few by design."

"You expect me to believe it's just a crazy coincidence that the same night I complain to you about my boss and my boyfriend, they go to a brothel where there happens to be a photographer taking illicit photos of them?"

It was hard for me to keep my hands from wandering from her arms as Ella stood in front of me in her tiny, white bikini with her skin flushed such a pretty shade of pink.

"No, I don't. What surprises me is that you care so much about two men who treated you so badly."

Her mouth fell open as she shrugged off my grasp. "Are you saying you *did* have something to do with it?"

"No one forced them to snort lines or get their cocks sucked, Ella. Every one of your esteemed colleagues willingly partook of the services offered, and some of them have proclivities even I find distasteful. All my people did was steer them in the right direction and document every sordid moment for posterity."

She closed her mouth and blinked rapidly. "I can't believe this. I can't believe *you.*"

"Me? I held them accountable for their actions. I ensured they were punished for their deceit." I widened my stance. "You do know that not a single one of those men were single, don't you?"

"This wasn't about you punishing a bunch of cheating men," she spat out. "This was about you proving that the guy I was dating was no good. This was your way of making sure I'd never go back to him, right? If I ever had second thoughts, you could whip out some dirty picture that proved he never loved me. This was proof that the reason we hadn't had sex in forever wasn't that he had a low sex drive. It was that he didn't want to fuck me."

Her face had mottled a blotchy red, and she waved her hands as her voice rose to a shriek. "I'll bet you even have the pictures around here somewhere." She pushed by me and went to other side of my desk, yanking open drawers. "Your insurance policy, in case I ever decided that this whole deal was too nuts and wanted to go back to New York."

I watched her but didn't stop her or speak until she'd opened all the drawers and stood, her chest heaving across from me. "This was never about hurting you. This was always about punishing them." Rage simmered in my belly as I thought about how they'd treated her, and how easy they'd been to tempt. "The thought of them dismissing you and making you think you deserved less enraged me. I won't apologize for that. The fact that any man made you think you're undesirable makes me want to ruin his life a second time, so don't tempt me."

Aside from the rage, something else stoked hot in my core as I watched her scream and fume—carnal lust.

Her chest rose and fell as she sucked in ragged breaths. "You can't go around punishing everyone who hurts me."

"I don't see why not." I closed the distance between us so fast she backed up and bumped against the bookshelves. Her anger was like fuel to my libido. I wanted to feel her passion, even if it was raw and untamed. "They richly deserved what happened to them. You're mine now. I'll never let anyone treat you badly again."

She slapped my chest even as the heat from her skin seared into me. "You have to stop saying things like that. I'm not yours. I'm not anyone's property."

I grabbed her wrists to keep her from hitting me again. "You are mine. I may not own you, but your soul belongs to me."

She struggled against me. "You can't own someone's soul."

"I might not own it." I pinned her arms behind her. "But I possess it."

"Dominick." The way she said my name, desperate and pleading, made my cock thicken.

"You know I'm telling the truth. You are mine, whether you can admit it to yourself or not."

She wiggled in my grasp. "This isn't forever, remember. It's only for the summer. It may be normal for you to punish people by destroying their lives, but I don't live in that kind of a world. And in a couple of months, I have to go back to my world."

Her urgent movements only made my cock harder and provoked my desire beyond what I could control. I released her wrists and ran my hands down until I reached her ass, then I lifted her quickly and set her on the ledge behind my desk, spreading her legs and positioning myself between them. "I'm so sorry, Ella. I thought you understood." I bent and nipped the side of her neck, pressing my body hard against hers and feeling her arch into me, her body responding to me like it always did. "This is now not only my world. It is yours as well. It always has been."

Her heaving breaths had become breathy shallow ones as I tugged down the waistband of my pants, and my cock sprang up.

"What?"

"It's too dangerous for you to leave, even if I could bear to let you go." I used one finger to move aside her bikini bottom, dragging the head of my cock through her slickness. "You are the mate of a Fallen. There is no leaving."

"Dominick, please," she begged, her hands gripping my shoulders and her legs wrapping around my waist. But it was clear from the ravenous look in her eyes, she was *not* begging me to stop.

I let out a roar as I thrust deep.

37

Ella

I stepped out of the shower, wrapping a towel around me and letting the water stream down onto the fluffy, ivory floor mat. The cold water had helped cool me down, but every time I thought about what Dominick had done, irritation flashed fresh within me.

I strode to the mirror and swiped my fingers across the steamed surface. On the one hand, I thought that my boss and my ex got what they deserved. Dominick was right. No one had held a gun to their heads and forced them to snort lines and hire prostitutes. They were assholes who deserved to get called on their slimy behavior. On the other hand, I didn't need Dominick running around punishing everyone who wronged me, no matter how tempting the prospect.

At least I hadn't found any of the photos in his study. It did seem like he'd done it strictly to punish them and not to convince me to stay with him. He'd never mentioned what had happened or that Christopher had hooked up with a prostitute the same night we'd broken up. Not that he'd needed to. Christopher had done a bang-up job of alienating me all on his own.

I studied my reflection in the mirror. It was surprising how even a few days of relaxation and pampering—despite the moments of frustrations with Dominick—could make such a difference. The shadows under my eyes had vanished, along with the crease that had seemed to be a permanent fixture between my brows. My skin was lightly sun-kissed, and my cheeks had a healthy glow. Thinking about why my skin glowed made my cheeks flush pink. As infuriating as Dominick could be, I couldn't fight my attraction to him or how the man was working his way into my heart.

Sighing, I pulled my hair from its topknot and let it spill across my shoulders. The sun had added even more glints of red to the rich brown and even a few strands of gold. Much longer, and I wouldn't be able to recognize myself.

I put on just enough makeup to highlight my features, then went back out to the master bedroom. As promised, Dominick's people had procured a dress for me to wear to the charity reception, and it was draped across the bed. One look told me the dress cost more than my monthly rent.

"Seriously?" I ran my fingers across the black lace of the garment.

Although the dress was cocktail length, the shoulder straps were feathery wisps that plunged down to a V neckline edged in lace. It wasn't overly ornate—exquisitely delicate lace being the main design element—but it still took my breath away.

I dropped the towel and stepped into the dress. I knew there was no way I could wear a bra with it and once I'd zipped up the back, I realized that the snug fit of the fabric hugging my hips and ass would reveal any panty line—even a thong.

"I guess I'm going commando," I said to myself, tugging the hem of the dress down until it almost reached my knees.

I eyed the black heels on the floor, their red soles bright against the plush, ivory carpet. My pulse fluttered, and I pressed a palm to my stomach.

What was I doing, going to a party on the arm of Dominick Vicario? I was so out of my element it wasn't even funny. I might have achieved some success in business, but that didn't mean I knew anything about the world he moved in or the types of people who jetted to charity events. What would I even say to these people if they spoke English?

I rubbed my sweaty palms on the front of my dress, then groaned at my nervous habit. They might be able to put me in a designer dress, but that didn't mean I fit into this crazy world of yachts and mansions and private planes. I felt a pang of longing for my cramped apartment in New York. What I wouldn't give to be sitting on the floor of my living room and sharing a pizza—bacon, red onions, and extra cheese—with Sara.

"Are you ready?"

I'd been so lost in my own thoughts I hadn't heard Dominick come up the stairs or open the door. I spun around, backing up and almost stumbling over the shoes I still hadn't stepped into.

He caught me by the elbow, righting me and then taking a long look. "You look beautiful. The dress is perfect for you."

My sweaty palms were nothing compared to my hammering heart. In his black tuxedo, Dominick looked even more striking and handsome than usual. The black jacket fit him like second skin, showing the expanse of his shoulders and the taper of his waist. My eyes instinctively drifted down to the stomach that I knew boasted tightly corded muscles, and my mouth went dry as I remembered the feel of my fingertips bumping across them.

"Ella?"

The velvet hum of his voice brought my eyes back to his face.

"Thank you," I finally said.

He cocked his head.

"For the dress and shoes," I said, finding my voice again and steadying my pulse.

Dominick shook his head, scooping the shoes up and hooking them on two fingers. "It's my pleasure, but you don't need to thank me. You're doing me the honor by being my date this evening. I'm afraid the reception might be a bit boring."

He led me from the room and down to the lounge, the tightly winding stairs reminding me why he was carrying my shoes. Once we'd crossed the room and exited the ship, Dominick picked me up and carried me down the gangway.

"You know I can walk, right?"

He cut his eyes to the spike heels dangling from one hand. "I'd prefer you arrive at the reception without a broken ankle."

I glanced down at the dock and the gaps between the wood. Okay, he had a point. Designer heels were not made for navigating gangways and docks. Once we reached the end, he lowered me into a shiny, black sedan then joined me inside. After closing the door, he lifted my feet one at a time and slipped the shoes on them so slowly I stopped breathing for a few beats.

"Now you're ready," he said, taking my hand in his and squeezing.

As our car wound its way up from the shimmering, blue coastline into the Croatian hills, I hoped he was right.

38

Ella

Dominick extended the crook of his arm as I stepped from of the car, and I gladly took it. The building that towered in front of us looked more like a castle than a reception venue or hotel.

"The charity event is *here*?" I whispered as he led me through the massive front doors.

"Don't be too impressed," he whispered back. "The Croatian coast is covered with castles. This is one of many."

I stifled a laugh. Since I'd spent my entire life in the U.S., my experience with castles was limited, and it was hard to imagine a place covered in castles as imposing as this one.

My heels echoed on the stone floor as Dominick led me through the enormous foyer with vaulted ceilings and tapestries hanging on the walls. Even though there were no frescoes adorning the ceiling, the building was no less awe-inspiring than Dominick's Venetian palazzo.

The dimly lit interior soon gave way to another set of double doors that led us onto a stone terrace. The sun was setting, and the enclosed courtyard was illuminated with a canopy of draping string lights overhead and candles along a path that wound through the garden below. Lush palm trees burst up from the manicured lawn with lights shining up from the base of their trucks, giving them a warm glow. The sound of string music played in the background, overlaid with the buzz of conversation as guests stood in clusters sipping champagne.

My stomach clenched as I saw how put-together the women were with stunning dresses and perfectly coifed hair. For a moment, I almost forgot that I was also wearing a designer dress that could hold its own with anyone else's.

"Champagne?" Dominick offered me a flute as a waiter hovered by his side.

"Thank you." I took the glass, glad to have something to do with the hand that wasn't holding onto Dominick. This way, I wouldn't be tempted to wipe it on my dress.

After letting me take a sip, he steered me over to a couple, introducing them as the hosts of the evening and the patrons of the charity and introducing me as his girlfriend. The label startled me, although I had to admit I was pleased.

"It's nice to meet you," I said to them both, smiling and offering my hand.

The man glanced briefly at my hand then kissed me on both cheeks. "I'm too European for American handshakes."

I laughed, my cheeks warming at my gaffe.

Dominick only put his arm around my waist and laughed. "I will only allow the kisses because I know your wife so well, Ivan."

The wife laughed, also giving me kisses on both cheeks before we moved on.

"Should I kiss everyone I meet here?" I asked Dominick when we were out of earshot of the couple.

"I would prefer if you didn't," he said, his voice low as he leaned close to my ear. "But kissing on the cheek is a common greeting, so I doubt I can prevent it."

"You aren't seriously threatened by Ivan?" I asked, casting a quick glance back at the man with thinning, grey hair and a prominent belly. I then scanned the rest of the crowd—mostly older couples and lots of bald heads. "Or anyone here?"

"No, I'm not." His breath was warm on my neck. "I doubt any of these mortals could steal you away from me. That's one of the reasons I feel safe bringing you here. None of my business rivals will be in attendance. Only wealthy old couples and no demons. "

A waiter approached with a silver tray of crostini, rattling off an explanation in a language I didn't understand.

"Lobster," Dominick said, before I could ask him, plucking one of the small rounds of bread topped with lobster off the tray. Instead of handing it to me, he fed it to me, then plucked another off the tray and popped it into his own in his mouth.

The waiter seemed unfazed by this, even though I lowered my eyes as he moved on.

"Did you like that?" Dominick asked, leading me to the edge of the terrace.

"The hors d'oeuvre or being fed by you?"

He gave me a wolfish grin. "Both?"

I ignored his smile and glanced down at the people milling throughout the garden. "So, this is it? You just come here, eat and drink, and then leave?"

He twitched one shoulder. "I have already made a sizable donation, so yes. But it would have been a slight to the patrons if I didn't attend. The Vicario organization has been one of their largest donors for years, although we don't publicize our involvement. Still, I've known Ivan for ages through my legitimate business." His expression darkened, as he spotted someone or something below. "Of course, there is always the chance that I'll need to do some business while I'm here."

As if he'd materialized from thin air, Rami appeared at Dominick's side, nodding to both of us before saying something low in his ear. Dominick frowned.

"It's fine," I said, when I saw Rami's intense expression. "Go do your business. I'll mingle and kiss some more strangers."

Rami's eyebrows lifted, but Dominick only laughed. "You are sure you'll be all right?"

"I have been to parties before." Although, to be fair, I hadn't been to any quite like this one. "I'll find a table and enjoy the champagne while I wait for you."

Dominick glanced at Rami and then back at me.

"I don't need a babysitter." I gave him a gentle shove. "It's a party in a walled garden with lots of harmless old people. I think I'll survive."

After another moment of contemplation, Dominick nodded and leaned down, kissing me by the ear and whispering, "I'll be right back."

I watched Rami lead him away, then turned back to my view overlooking the beautifully manicured gardens with a smaller stone courtyard. Tables dotted the lower courtyard, and I spotted an empty one in the corner.

Walking carefully down the curved, stone stairs, I made my way over to the farthest cocktail table draped in white linen and sank down in one of the chairs. I'd only been standing for a few minutes, but already my feet ached. Expensive shoes did not mean more comfortable shoes.

Slipping my feet under the tablecloth pooling at the ground, I slid my feet out of my heels.

"Gotcha!"

I almost yelped in surprise as a man sat down next to me, grinning widely.

"Excuse me?" I said, fumbling as I tried to get my feet back into my shoes.

"I'm just joking." He glanced down at my feet hidden beneath the cloth. "Don't put your shoes back on on my account."

I eyed him. Unlike most of the other guests at this event, the man who'd taken the seat next to mine was young, probably close to my age if I had to guess. He had chocolate brown hair and hazel eyes, and an easy smile. But what was most noticeable was his accent, or lack of one to my ears.

"You're not from here," I said.

He shook his head and leaned back. "I was about to say the same about you."

I almost groaned. "Is it that obvious?"

"Only when you speak. I'd recognize an American accent anywhere."

Great. Just like I suspected. I stood out like a sore thumb.

"Don't get me wrong" the guy said quickly. "I love American accents. I went to university in New York."

"You did?" Now I was interested. "The city?"

Another nod and grin. "Columbia."

"I'm from New York," I said, thrilled to talk to someone who knew my city.

"Really?" He held out his hand. "I'm Anthony."

I shook his hand. "Ella."

"Okay, Ella. Where do you live in the city?"

"The Village," I said.

His eyebrows went up. "Not bad."

I didn't mention that the only reason I could afford a tiny apartment in the village was because I'd shared it with my ex-boyfriend who got regular and sizable cash infusions from his parents. "And you?"

"Upper West."

"Close to Zabar's?" I asked, my stomach rumbling just at the thought of the popular bagels.

He moaned and touched his own belly. "Not close enough." He gave me a conspiratorial grin. "Not that the food here isn't great, but there's nothing like a bagel from Zabar's."

"Agreed."

Anthony gave me another look as if we were sharing some deep dark secrets. “So, Ella from the Village who loves Upper West side bagels, what are you doing all the way over here at a stuffy charity reception?”

“That’s an excellent question.” And one I couldn’t really answer without a longwinded explanation that would make me seem crazy.

“Ella.”

Dominick’s voice made me snap my head up as he strode toward us. He barely acknowledged the man sitting with me when he reached the table, instead glowering down at me. “We need to leave.”

“Oh.” I hurriedly jammed my feet back in my shoes and stood. “Sorry, I guess—“ My farewell to the fellow New Yorker who’d stood when I had was cut short, as Dominick took me by the arm and practically dragged me away.

I tried to jerk my arm from his vise-like grip, but he was holding me too tightly and moving me too rapidly across the terrace and up the stairs. I cast a final glance at Anthony, whose eyes were wide as he watched me being led away.

When we reached the other side of the house where Rami stood next to the sedan, I ripped my arm from Dominick’s grip. “What the hell was that?”

His eyes burned as he towered over me. “I should be asking you the same thing.”

“Are you really angry because I was talking with a guy who happened to be from New York?” I jabbed a finger into his chest. “For your information, our illicit conversation was about bagels.”

Dominick’s glare didn’t fade. “That man is not from New York.”

39

Dominick

"What do you mean he's not from New York?" Her small hands were in fists by her side as she stared up at me, her eyes narrowed. "He goes to Columbia. He knows the best bagel place on the Upper West."

"Anthony Solano is the youngest son of my family's most prominent rival." My blood still boiled at the sight of the man laughing so easily with Ella, her face animated and her eyes dancing.

"Oh." Her fists uncurled. "He's part of a mob family?"

"Yes." I didn't tell her than Anthony was the only member of the family who wasn't involved in the family business—as far as we knew. "He did attend Columbia, but that does not make him a New Yorker. Nor does it make him safe."

Now her scowl returned. "You're telling me you think that guy is some kind of threat to me? He didn't have any clue who I was."

I didn't think Anthony Solano was a threat. Not in the usual way. The youngest son of the Solano family appeared to have little interest in his family's operations, which was why he'd gone so far away to school. From snippets I'd heard over the years, he was nothing like his brash and thick-headed brother Mateo, and he'd never gotten into the trouble his brother seemed to attract like a magnet. Still, he'd charmed Ella with apparent ease.

"I cannot be too careful." I waved her into the car. "He's still a part of a crime family."

"So are you," she snapped before getting inside.

I exchanged a glance with Rami, clenching the top of the car door. "How did he end up here? I thought I said no Solanos."

"You said to make sure Mateo Solano wasn't here. Anthony has never been on our radar, except to know that he exists and stays far away from the rest of his family."

I grunted. "If he stays so far away from his family, why is he here now?"

"I'll find out," Rami said before I ducked inside the car.

Ella's arms were crossed tightly when I settled myself next to her and the car accelerated away from the castle. "You can't freak out every time I speak to another man, Dominick."

"I can when the man is a Solano." Even saying the name left a bitter taste on my lips.

"I guess I should be glad you didn't throw him into a wall," she muttered, her face turned toward the car's window.

I blew out a breath. Was she right? Was I overreacting? I rubbed a hand over my forehead as the creases melted away. "I wouldn't have thrown him into a wall. Not when there was a perfectly good balcony to throw him off."

When I opened my eyes, Ella was looking at me askance. "I guess that was your version of a joke?"

I rested a hand on her leg. "I apologize for overreacting. Tomorrow's meeting has me on edge."

Her fierce expression softened. "You admit you acted nuts?"

Nuts was not the word I would have used, and I still wasn't convinced that any Solano was harmless, but I nodded. "I do, if you admit that he was flirting with you."

She opened her mouth to argue then clamped it shut. "Okay. He might have been flirting with me. I'm never very good at picking up on that type of thing. It's not something I'm used to."

Ella's lack of awareness of her own beauty and charm continued to amaze me. Either she'd been lied to all her life, or her ex-boyfriend had done a thorough job of eroding her confidence. "Trust me on this one. He was definitely flirting with you."

"Then I'm sorry, too." She put her hand over mine. "I never intended to upset you or give you any reason to be jealous. I promise you that I'm not interested in him, even if he has excellent taste in bagels."

I frowned at her, which made her laugh. Then she squeezed my hand. "Do you have to go to the meeting?"

"I do, but as soon as it's over, I won't have to think about work for the rest of the trip."

She gave me a shy smile. "That sounds good. Where else are we going on our trip?"

"I thought we could sail down to Greece. We have an island I'd love to show you."

"An island?" She twisted to look at me head on. "You own a Greek island?"

I chuckled at her shock. "It's not large, but it is secluded." I didn't tell her that the private island was one of our first headquarters, and the ancient fortress on it was still where the Fallen gathered for important occasions or meetings with all two hundred of us. I also didn't tell her that it was where I planned to introduce her to my fellow Fallen.

"Then I can't wait to see your island," she said, facing forward again and resting her head against my arm as the car wound its way back down toward the coast, now glittering with lights from the docked yachts.

My stomach tightened as I thought about the prophecy that had been all but forgotten and might only be a myth. What were the chances that a human with an angelic mark could ever fall in love with a fallen angel? I'd only ever encountered a handful of humans who carried an angelic trace, and none of them had been people with even the remotest chance of falling in love with me.

I still couldn't be sure that Ella falling in love with me would start the Fallen on the path to being restored to our place in heaven, but it was as close as we'd come since our exile. The closest I'd come to redemption or love.

I slipped my hand under the lace of Ella's dress, the warmth of her skin tingling my skin. Even though what I felt for her was real, I couldn't bring myself to tell her about the prophecy and her part in it. As soon as I did, she would doubt my intentions and my feelings. The moment she learned that she could be the key to my personal salvation and the salvation of all the fallen angels, my desire and affection for her would be tarnished as black as my wings.

She would have to know eventually, especially if it was true, but for now I wanted to enjoy my time with her. Once she knew that she was more than the key to my heart, she would never look at me the same way.

You can't tell her until you're sure of her love for you, a dark voice deep in my soul reminded me. I pressed my eyes closed, forcing that voice to go silent. Ella's head resting against me was further rebuke, and another reminder that I was not one of the better angels.

When the car glided up to the dock leading to the ship, I realized that Ella had fallen asleep. Scooping her into my arms, I carried her to the yacht and up the gangway. Rami's car had arrived before mine, so he stood at the top, his dark form silhouetted by the interior lights of the yacht as he waited for me.

I paused before walking inside, speaking in a low tone so as not to wake the woman sleeping in my arms. "I want there to be guards on the ship when we leave for the meeting—Dan and Gad. Tell them not to let Ella out of their sight until I return." I stepped inside, then hesitated. "And find out everything there is to know about that youngest Solano boy."

"Should we remove him from the equation, Dom?" Rami asked, glancing down at Ella.

I thought about the upcoming meeting and what Ella had said, then I thought about the other Solano brother who wasn't so harmless. "Not yet, but I want to know if he's the only brother in town. If Mateo is slinking around somewhere, find him."

40

Ella

The rich aroma of coffee tickled my nose, and I rolled over to see Dominick walking into the master bedroom, holding a steaming mug.

"You're dressed." I pushed myself up in bed, swiping my tousled hair from my face. A quick glance under the sheet told me that *I* most definitely wasn't dressed, then I remembered stepping out of my cocktail dress the night before and slipping naked into bed.

As usual, he looked incredibly put together in his tailored, black suit—and dangerously gorgeous. He pressed a button on the wall and the shades covering the 180 degrees of windows began to lift with a low hum, revealing the bright glint of sunlight off the blue water. "You slept in."

I slapped a hand over my eyes and moaned. "You love to torture me, don't you?"

"You? No." He put the mug in my hand. "I don't mind punishing the truly evil, though."

I groaned again, not sure how much of what he said was in jest and how much was frighteningly true. Dropping the hand shielding my eyes so that it could hold the sheet around my chest, I took a sip of the coffee, letting the warmth and the caffeine give me the jolt I needed to kick off the duvet and swing my legs over the side of the bed. "Do you have to leave so early?"

He laughed, cutting his gaze to the windows. "Early?"

"Fine, it isn't early, but do you have to leave?"

Dominick leaned over, placing his hands on either side of me on the bed. "Trust me. I want this meeting to be over and done with as much as you do." He brushed his lips over first one cheek then the other. "As soon as it's done, we can leave for the island."

Pleasure rippled through me from even his brief touch, and I almost dropped the sheet between us, but I forced myself not to let out the breathy sigh on my lips. Instead, I glanced to one side of the room where I could see the orange roofs dotting the Croatian coastline and the green hills silhouetted behind them. "Not that a private Greek island doesn't sound fabulous, but I'd hoped to see more of Croatia than just the shoreline. The town looks pretty."

He angled his head at me. "You wish to play tourist?"

"I want to play shopper." I took another sip of coffee, peering at him over the rim of the mug. "No way can I jet around Europe and not bring anything back for my best friend. She will officially disown me."

He sighed, rubbing a hand across the dark scruff of his cheeks. "You wish to shop?"

"From the look on your face, I can tell you don't."

Dominick shrugged. "We have whatever we need brought to us. It has been a long time since I felt the need to shop."

I slid off the bed, bringing the sheet with me and depositing the mug on the nightstand. I pressed a hand to his chest. "Shopping isn't something you do because you *need* to, it's something you do because you enjoy it."

"In this one case, our ideas of enjoyment differ."

I drummed my fingers on his chest, inhaling his distinctly intoxicating scent. "Then in this one case, you're like a typical man."

He grimaced and closed a hand over mine, pressing my hand to the heat of his chest as his pupils flared. "I'm going to pretend you didn't say that."

My stomach did a flip from the buzz of his touch and his seductive warmth, and I tugged my hand from his grip and took a step back. "I thought you said you had to go."

"I do." He let out a long, regretful breath. "If you truly wish to shop for your friend, I will leave you some local currency."

"So, I'm not confined to the ship?"

He bit his lower lip for a moment. "I feel relatively confident that the most dangerous people in Croatia will be in a room with me. If you wish to go into the town, Dan and Gad will escort you to keep you safe."

I could agree to that. After all, I'd need someone to tell me where to go so I didn't wander aimlessly or go to the wrong shops. "You've got yourself a deal."

Dominick looked amused. "It was not a negotiation, but I'm glad you agree."

I fought the urge to shoot him a look or snap back with a smart-ass response, reminding myself that there was a demon out there somewhere who held a grudge against me, and Dominick was trying to protect me. Of course, this plan of his could only work for so long. Despite what he thought, he couldn't keep me sequestered forever. I did have a life that I'd have to return to one day, demon or no demon.

Not that I was going to say that to Dominick. Not now, at least. He had bigger things to worry about with his business rival and the demon unrest. Once the summer was over and things had cooled off, I'd remind him that my life was in New York. Besides, once I'd left Dominick, the demon who was obsessed with him wouldn't have any reason to chase me. It was never me she wanted anyway. It had always been about Dominick.

My heart squeezed as I thought about leaving him. It would hurt like hell, but could I really embrace the alternative? A life spent bouncing around the world as the girlfriend of an immortal fallen angel who ran a mafia empire? The whole idea was absurd, aside from the fact that I'd eventually grow old and die, and he never would. No way did I want that. It was already hard enough to accept that someone as gorgeous and perfect as Dominick Vicario desired me. But when I was no longer young and attractive myself? I shuddered. Nope. Better to have fun with it while it lasted, and then go our separate ways.

"Ella?" His voice ripped me from my mental wanderings.

"Sorry." I forced myself to smile at him. "Can I pick up anything for you while I'm shopping? A snow globe, or a shirt that says, 'My girlfriend went to Croatia and all she got me was this lousy T-shirt'?"

He made a face. "Please don't."

Seeing his horrified expression made me laugh. "Now I absolutely have to get you something embarrassing."

Quirking his lips up, he wrapped his arms around my waist and held me flush to his hard body. "It seems you're angling for some punishment, after all."

As one of his hands slid down to dip underneath the sheet and slap my bare ass, my knees wobbled, and desire arrowed through me. Then regret jabbed at me, reminding me that my happiness couldn't last.

Dominick dropped his head to nuzzle my neck and fresh waves of pleasure cascaded down my spine, banishing every rational thought. At least it wasn't ending anytime soon.

41

Dominick

"Everything is ready?" I asked Rami as we walked side by side into The Palace, the wall of black, glass-paned doors sweeping open as if by magic.

It had taken little more than an hour to drive up the coast from the Split harbor, but I was glad to have the distance between the other dons and my yacht. Of course, Ella was being guarded by two of my most trusted Fallen, so my worry wasn't acute.

Doormen in crisp, dark uniforms stood at attention, nodding their heads in deference as we entered. We didn't visit the hotel often, but they recognized us or they'd been properly briefed about our arrival. Or both.

The lobby swept out on both sides; the neutral furnishings punctuated by square, black and white marble columns. Matte gold and crystal chandeliers hung over groupings of upholstered chairs and roll-back settees interspersed with mahogany tables, and arrangements of white lilies spilled from cut-glass bowls, filling the lobby with their heady perfume. It was an eclectic blend of Old-World style and new, and it felt fitting for those who'd lived for millennia. Still, the Roman ruins the hotel was built around were practically modern from our perspective.

"The room on the top floor is prepared," Rami said. "I thought our guests might appreciate the view."

I nodded. "And the guards?"

"At every corner of the room as well as on the roof." His gaze flicked to a pair of Fallen flanking a marble column. "As well as the lobby."

Even though the meeting was the perfect time for an ambush by one of the families, we'd increased the difficulty by holding it in one of our properties. They would expect added security, but they would not know that our security was provided by immortal fallen angels.

"And all the dons and their people arrived yesterday and slept on-site?" I strode to the elevators, not missing a beat, as Rami and I stepped on and the doors glided shut.

My second-in-command gave a sharp nod. "No one has left."

The elevator surged up, giving me a momentary longing for flight. "And the Solano sons? What of them?"

Rami faced the doors as chimes indicated the floors we passed on our ascent. "The Fallen in Venice report that the elder remains there licking his wounds."

I stifled my satisfied grin. "And the other?"

"Gone. Our people tracked him to the airport this morning. He boarded the private plane his father arrived on and left."

A wave of relief coursed through me, although I was aware how foolish it was—and how foolish I'd been to think the boy was any kind of threat. "Good. It's just the don we need to deal with."

The brushed gold doors opened, and Rami stepped out first, sweeping the hallway with his alert gaze. "Well, all the dons."

His reminder was a good one. I'd been so preoccupied with my issues with the Solanos that I'd almost forgotten that there were other families and other dons. I noted two black-suited Fallen at the end of the hallway—one on either side of double doors that stood open. They gave small bows with their heads as we passed.

"Don Vicario!" the thickly accented voice bellowed from across the room as we entered.

It took me only moments to assess the room that featured a wall of glass overlooking the water. Since the hotel was perched on the side of a hill, the view of the harbor was impressive—as was the setup of the room. A single round table was positioned in the middle with a low arrangement of colorful flowers on top of an ivory cloth. Boxes wrapped in brown ribbon sat at each place along with glittering champagne flutes.

I spun toward the booming voice. "Don Raffalo." I walked over to where the stocky, gray-haired man stood with a small cluster of bodyguards and associates. "*Buongiorno*."

He accepted my embrace, rattling off his own greeting and pleasantries as we kissed cheeks. If I did not know that the man controlled most of the drugs and prostitution in the greater Florence area, I might have mistaken him for a kindly grandfather.

"I look forward to Solano telling us why he wanted a meeting." He squeezed me harder, thumping me on the back with his fist before letting go.

"I, as well." I scanned the group that had gathered, making note that the Solano contingent had not yet arrived.

Moving through the room, I greeted each don, paying them the respect they were due and welcoming them to the property. Rami stood off to the side, glancing at the glass walls and then at the doors.

After a few minutes had passed, a murmur of voices drew my gaze to the door as Don Solano swept through it. His bodyguards were beefier and more plentiful than the other dons—a clear show of strength—and he paused at the entrance to allow the others to get a visual of his sizable entourage.

Without waiting for him to step farther into the room, I approached him as the chatter in the room died out. "Don Solano."

He met my eyes with his own beady ones, but he had to look up to do it. Finally, he grunted, and we embraced stiffly. He might hate me for what I'd done to his son, but he wasn't foolish enough to challenge me here, even with all his hired muscle. He also wasn't fool enough to deny that his son had deserved what he'd gotten and had been lucky to survive my wrath.

"Shall we sit?" I swept my arms wide, indicating that the dons should take their seats.

As the men shuffled around the table, distracted by the task of finding where they'd been placed, cries in the hallway made my head snap to the open doors.

Don Solano rose from the chair he'd just taken, pointy a fat finger at me. "Treachery!"

Before I could deny it, a swarm of demons poured through the doors. Moving with unnatural speed, the black leather clad creatures wielded curved blades as they attacked. Outside the room, I heard the Fallen battling more of them, and within seconds, Rami had sprung into action, attacking the demons with his own considerable battle skills.

The bodyguards reached for guns, but they were too sluggish or too caught off guard, the demons disarming them as they slashed their throats. Screams pierced the air, and chairs flew back, crashing to the floor.

I leapt through the air, spinning and tackling a demon as he scampered across the table toward Don Solano. I snapped his neck and threw his limp body to the floor, waving to the don. "Get under the table!"

The glass from one of the floor-to-ceiling panes shattered, as a demon was hurled through it, shrieking as she plummeted to the ground far below. Rami wasn't even breathing heavily from the effort of the throw, pivoting and launching himself at yet another demon.

My mind raced as I fought off the horde. I'd been prepared for a power move by one of the dons, but I had not expected such a coordinated and substantial demon attack. And it was clear from Don Solano's terrified expression and the way he now cowered under the table that he wasn't behind it.

I dodged a swipe of a demonic blade, the steel audibly whistling by my ear. With a speed that even demons couldn't match, I flipped over the creature's head, coming down on the other side of him before he could track me and kicking him hard out the shattered window. It had been a considerable number of years since I'd engaged in a full-on battle, but the moves were ingrained in my muscles. Still, I would have preferred to be outfitted in my angelic armor with my wings unfurled. But with the number of humans still in the room, that wasn't possible.

A flash to my left made me duck and roll across the floor. When I got to my feet again, Jaya stood across from me, her gaze a fathomless inferno of rage.

"I should have killed you long ago," I said through gritted teeth.

"You couldn't." She grinned maniacally as she flipped a pair of arched blades in her hands. "Angels cannot move against us without provocation—even fallen ones."

I growled at her. "Then I thank you for the ample provocation."

Her eyes glinted as they narrowed. "I'm surprised you'd want to waste time killing me, when you should be trying to save *her*."

My rage stalled as her words worked their way into my mind. *Ella*. Had this been a trick to draw me away from her? My first urge was to fly across the room and rip out her throat, but if there was a wisp of truth in what she said, I couldn't waste a moment longer on Jaya.

Terror iced my skin as Jaya gave me a final, cold smile and bolted from the room. I swiveled my gaze to the south. I couldn't see the harbor in Split, but I knew how many winding roads were between me and the yacht. There was no doubt what I had to do. Without another second of deliberation, I leapt from the broken window, falling like a stone toward the rocky ground before unfurling my wings and swooping through the sky. I arched up to fly through the clouds, the cool air rushing over my skin and gliding across the iridescent black of my feathered wings.

Then I heard the pops of gunfire behind me.

42

Ella

"You're sure he wouldn't wear this?" I held up a traditional Croatian cravat, the red fabric silky in my hands.

Gad eyed it and then me. "Positive."

We'd driven from the harbor up into the old town of Split, and I was wandering happily through an outside market in the shade of a stone cathedral, and near the walls of the famous Diocletian's Palace. Long tables were filled with fruits and vegetables and topped with colorful fabric umbrellas, while other stands featured local olive oils or bags of nuts. As tempting as the food was, what I was interested in were the tables of traditional Croatian goods and crafts.

I walked to a display of colorful paintings depicting a Croatian castle overlooking the sea or a whitewashed boat bobbing in the harbor. They weren't great art, but Sara might think it was fun to hang one on her wall. My nose twitched, and I turned to see a narrow shop filled with every type of lavender product known to man—lavender sachets, lavender soap, lavender oil. I liked lavender, but the smell was overwhelming.

Backing up, I bumped into Dan, who stared down at his phone. His jaw was tight, and his hand clenched the device so hard his knuckles went white.

"Is everything okay?"

He didn't answer me, instead glancing up. His gaze locked onto Gad, who was also looking intently at his phone. "Did you get the same message?"

Gad quickly joined us, his head swiveling to take in the people milling about. Then he nodded. "From Rami."

"Go," Dan said, his usual smirk gone from his face. "They'll need reinforcements if it's as bad as it sounds.

Gad hesitated, his gaze darting to me. "Dominick was clear about us guarding her."

"That was before." Dan clutched the other man's arm. "There hasn't been an unprovoked demon attack like this for..."

"A hundred years," Gad finished for him, gritting his teeth in an obvious attempt to quell his anger.

"What's going on?" I looked from one man to the other. "What demon attack?"

Dan shushed me, looking around us furtively and then backing me into the lavender shop. "Not so loud."

I coughed, as I inhaled what felt like an entire field of lavender then glared at both of my guards. "You can't mention demons and tell me to be quiet."

Gad peered back down at his phone and let out a low growl.

"I told you to go." Dan positioned himself in front of me and faced Gad. "I can get her back to the ship on my own."

Without another word, Gad disappeared into the crowd with startling speed.

"So." I folded my arms over my chest. "Are you going to tell me what's going on before I lose my shit?"

He turned and appraised my stance. "First we should get you back to the ship."

I shook my head, my pulse racing. "Not until you tell me what's happening." I lowered my voice. "Was that about Dominick's meeting?"

He scowled at me, which didn't do anything to make him less smoldering. "If you must know, yes. It was attacked by demons."

I gave my head a small shake. "As in actual hellfire demons?"

"Demons do not look like humans imagine them to, at least not the ones who roam the earth. The demons we attempt to control look just like we do." He bobbled his head. "Obviously, not as handsome or alluring."

I ignored his on-brand arrogance. "And demon attacks aren't normal?"

"Not anymore." He frowned and looked over his shoulder. "This one had to be planned."

The thought of Dominick battling demons, even ones that looked human, made my stomach became a hard ball of fear. "Is he okay, though? Is Dominick okay?"

Dan glanced down at his phone and his gaze hardened. He slipped his device in his jacket pocket and raked his fingers through his hair. "No, he's not okay."

"Was he injured?" I gazed out the narrow shop. We hadn't parked the sedan too far away, had we?

"Ella." Dan grabbed me by the arms. "I need you to listen to me very carefully. Dominick is dead. I have to get you out of here and back to the ship so the Fallen can determine what to do next."

Dead? I gaped up at him, then shook my head heard. "That's impossible. He's immortal. He can't be dead."

"Ella." Dan's voice was pleading. "Come with me now."

I jerked my arms from his grasp and backed away, tears burning my eyes and clouding my vision. "I don't believe you. He can't be dead. Angels don't die!" I screamed the last words, but I didn't care. Dominick couldn't be dead. Not after everything. Not like this.

I bent over, my arms wrapped around my middle as I fought off the pain that threatened to bring me to my knees. I might not have known him for long, but it didn't feel that way. As crazy as it sounded, it felt like he was a part of me. Like he was the person I'd always been meant for. The thought of never seeing him again and never feeling the buzz of his touch made bile rise in the back of my throat. The cloying scent of lavender wasn't helping, so I took shallow breaths as I pushed past Dan and stumbled from the narrow shop.

A shout from behind made me jerk upright, but then there was sharp jab in my neck.

"Son of a bitch!" I slapped my hand to the spot, hoping to kill whatever bug had bitten me, but there was nothing to swat. Before I could turn back to find Dan, everything went black.

43

Dominick

Rami skidded to a stop beside me, tucking his wings in as quickly and seamlessly as I had moments before. Luckily, we'd landed behind a small building and out of view of most of the harbor. Not that I much cared.

I'd flown as fast as possible, arrowing through the sky high above the clouds, in order to reach the harbor of Split faster than a car could have driven. Still, it had taken too long and panic filled me as I folded my own wings.

"You shouldn't have followed me," I said as I ran down the dock toward the yacht that towered up above the water. "Especially since they were shooting at me."

"They were shooting at the demons. The shots just went wide. Those bodyguards aren't very good marksmen."

"None of the dons saw me fly away?"

Rami gave a single shake of his head. "They were still under the table. The only humans who saw you are now dead."

I didn't ask him if he'd killed them or if the demons had. It didn't matter to me. The only thing that mattered was making sure Ella was safe. I hadn't even paused to digest the fact that a meeting I'd arranged in a hotel I owned had been violently attacked. None of the family heads knew that it had been the work of demons. They'd only seen black-clad assassins attacking, and they would no doubt level some of the blame at me, even though I'd been fighting off the attackers alongside them. As soon as I located Ella and we'd set sail, I would have a lot of work to do to clean up the mess I'd left behind. Would I even be able to continue as the head of the Vicario family, or was it time to disappear for a while?

I pushed those thoughts away as I ran up the gangway with Rami close at my heels, and we both burst into the main-level salon. It was empty.

I dashed up the spiral stairs, even though no noises came from the master bedroom. Storming through the bedroom and master bath told me that she wasn't there either. The only evidence of Ella was a damp towel hanging on the rack and the faint trace of her scent. As a cool tendril of fear twisted itself around my heart, I pounded back down the stairs.

Rami ran in from the aft deck. "She's not upstairs on the sun deck or in the hot tub."

I glanced at the stairs leading down, but she'd have little reason to go to the crew quarters or spare bedrooms.

"She must have gone shopping early." I pulled out my phone, first dialing Gadriel's number and hearing its muffled ring nearby.

Rami gaped at me as Gad strode into the room, holding out his own phone.

"You're here," I said, disconnecting the call and staring at him. "Where is she?"

Gad shook his head. "I left her with Dan to come help you with the battle against the demons. When I got to The Palace, it was over and you were gone, so I came back here. Dan is probably on his way back with her."

I swallowed my anger as I dialed Dan. "You left her?"

"Dan assured me he would get her back safely," Gadriel said. "From Rami's message, it sounded like you needed all the help you could get."

"I never meant for you to—" Rami started to say.

"It doesn't matter." The call to Dan went directly to voicemail, and my gut tightened. "He's not answering."

"That's impossible." Gadriel punched numbers into his own phone. "I just left him in the market, and he was bringing Ella back to the ship directly. Neither of us saw any evidence of being followed by humans or demons." He frowned as held out his phone, the call also going instantly to voicemail. "Maybe he isn't answering because he's driving. Here, I'll use the phone locator feature." He tapped his screen, his frown deepening. "According to it this, he's still at the market."

I slid my phone in my jacket, tempering my fury. Anger would not make finding her go faster, but if Dan was indeed still shopping with Ella while we frantically searched for them, I would be very displeased. "Show me where you left them."

Instead of going back out to the dock, I led Gadriel and Rami to the top of the yacht and onto the enormous "H" emblazoned on the helicopter pad.

"You're sure?" Rami asked.

It was rare for us to fly so often, and especially in the daytime. I tipped my head up to the white clouds dotting the sky. "I'm sure." Then I cut my eyes to Gad. "Take us."

With a sharp nod, Gadriel's dark wings fanned out behind him —the feathers as ebony as his skin—and he shot up into the sky. Rami and I both followed suit, flying high enough to be masked by the clouds. It was easy to track the inky black of my fellow Fallens' wings as they sliced through the white haze of the clouds. I arrowed across the sky behind him, the deafening wind in my ears louder than the furious rushing of blood.

When Gad begin his descent, I dropped through the clouds and plummeted behind him with Rami a blur next to me. We all landed in a crouch behind a copse of bushes, dirt puffing up around us from the impact as we tucked our wings away. After a moment during which no one screamed, we straightened. Another advantage of being endowed with angelic speed—it was difficult for the human eye to see us when we flew as fast as we were able.

"This way." Gad waved for us to follow him as he weaved through tables with bundles of flowers and displays of berries. The crowd milling about the market parted for us as we strode through the stands and displays, eyes widening at our intensity. Most people were there to mingle and shop at leisure. We were clearly there on a mission.

When we reached a shop that reeked of lavender, Gad spun around. "This is where I left them."

"They're gone now," Rami said, taking long strides first one way and then the other.

Just as I was about to suggest we split up and search the market, my gaze caught on something black and shiny on the floor. I picked it up as Rami and Gadriel both watched me with open mouths.

The screen of Dan's phone was cracked, but the last alerts on it were the missed calls from me and Gadriel. Dread settled over me like a shroud.

"We aren't going to find them." My hand went limp, and the phone clattered back to the ground. "They're gone."

I fought the urge to fall to the ground myself, instead closing my eyes as fury tore through me like a fiery scourge. The sounds of the market faded away, and I could only hear the thundering of my heart. All the desire and tenderness that Ella provoked in me were overcome by my dormant vengeance, wrath waking in me like a slumbering beast.

"You don't think Jaya—" Rami's voice was barely a croak.

I held up a hand so he wouldn't finish his sentence. I couldn't bear to hear it out loud. "The only thing I know is that someone has taken what is mine." I balled my hands into iron fists, darkness stoking the inferno within my soul. "I'm going to find Ella and the person who took her, then I'm going to burn down their world and everything in it."

EPILOGUE

Ella

My head throbbed as I lifted it. What happened? I blinked a few times, letting my hazy vision adjust. I'd been shopping and then Dan had gotten word about an attack at Dominick's meeting. My stomach plummeted.

Dominick.

It all rushed back to me, slamming into me with such force I gasped for breath. Tears stung the backs of my eyelids, and a sharp ache rose in my throat. He was dead. As unbelievable as it seemed, the immortal Dominick Vicario had been killed in the demon attack. That had been the last thing Dan had told me before I'd felt a sharp pain in my neck and then the world had gone sideways.

Despite our brief relationship, the thought of life without the man made a sob escape my lips. How had it taken losing

Dominick for me to realize that I'd fallen in love with him? I'd never felt about anyone the way I'd felt about Dominick—and it had been more than just the burning passion that his touch had provoked. It had been much more, and it had been real.

What couldn't be real was his death, I told myself. He was immortal. But then I remembered him telling me that immortal didn't mean invincible. As powerful as he was, there were ways to kill one of the Fallen, and according to Dan's reports, the demons had done it.

As I blinked away hot tears, I raised one hand to touch my neck where I'd felt the jab after hearing the news, but my arm couldn't lift that far. Glancing down, I saw that my wrist was bound. I tugged my other arm instinctively, and it jerked back. It was also restrained, and a twist of my neck told me that I was tied to the bed.

"What the actual fuck?"

My grief was overtaken by panic. Dominick had never tied me up and I found it hard to believe he would have ordered his people to have me restrained. Unless I'd been a danger to myself, but I had no memories of that. Nope, my last memory had been of getting the news about Dom. Had I passed out?

I shook my head. Even so, I shouldn't have been tied up.

"Hello?" I called out. "Dan? Gad? Can someone untie me?"

There was no response, and it was then that my eyes focused on my surroundings. I wasn't on the yacht. Although the ivory sheets were just as luxurious, this was not Dominick's bed. My heart pounded as I swept my gaze from one side of the room to the other. It wasn't the palazzo in Venice, either.

Even though it was nighttime, moonlight shone through three tall, minaret-shaped windows draped with gauzy fabric. Instead of a headboard for the huge bed I was tied to, there was a recessed, minaret shape carved into the wall behind me with ambient amber light glowing from above. Overhead hung a metallic, Moroccan-style chandelier, and there were matching brass and glass lanterns on either side of the door. Where the hell was I?

When the door finally opened, I breathed out a sigh of relief. Then the breath died on my lips.

"You don't look happy to see me," the demon that Dominick had called Jaya said as she stepped into the room.

My mouth went dry as the dark-haired woman sauntered to the foot of the bed, her glittering eyes feasting on me. She was every bit as terrifying as she was beautiful, her black leather pants and skin-tight vest doing nothing to make me feel better.

One thing I knew for sure. I wasn't with the Fallen anymore.

"Where am I?" I asked once my throat had started working again.

She smiled at me, then twitched one of her shoulders. "Does it really matter? You're somewhere the Fallen can't find you."

"So, you killed Dominick and now you've kidnapped me? Why? Just because I was with Dominick? Well, he's gone now." My voice cracked as I thought about never seeing him again. "You win."

She cocked a severely arched eyebrow. "You're right about one thing." She leaned over and put her hands on either side of my legs that were covered by the sheet. "I always win."

Anger pulsed through me—anger that this crazy, demon bitch had been behind Dominick's murder and that she'd kidnapped me. I flexed my hands, wishing dearly they weren't tied up so I could slap the smirk off the cocky demon's face.

Jaya straightened. "I can see why Dominick was intrigued by you. You've got a spark I wouldn't have expected, especially for one with an angel's mark. Usually, the archangels pick the most boring humans alive, but you're different."

I stared at her. "I have no idea why you've taken me or what you're talking about."

A smile crossed her face, but it only made her look more menacing. "He didn't tell you. Fascinating."

"What the fuck are you talking about?" My voice had become a shriek, and I jerked my restraints, making the bed shake.

She crossed her arms over her chest. "I'll let that be a surprise." Then she spun on one heel and headed for the door, nodding at a man as she walked out, and he walked in.

My mouth fell open as the familiar figure crossed to me, smiling.

"Hi, Ella. I hoped we'd see each other again after we were so rudely interrupted."

"Anthony?" I whispered, confusion muddling my mind and making my head throb again as I stared at the youngest Solano son.

He sat on the edge of the bed and stroked a hand down my cheek. "Now that I've made sure we won't be interrupted, I think we're going to enjoy getting to know each other better, don't you?"

Thank you for reading *Mark of the Fallen*!

Want to read a bonus steamy scene from Rami's point of view (and discover what happened between him and the waitress in Istanbul)? Click below to join my VIP Reader group and get the bonus chapter!

Get My Bonus Scene!

Ready to read what happens after Ella is abducted? One-click Book 2, Curse of the Fallen>

I thought it was the demons I needed to fear. I was wrong.

I'm now a pawn in the deadly game between Dominick and his enemies. But this pawn is done being played. I'm about to show them what I'm made of--and it isn't sugar and spice.

This book has been edited and proofed, but typos are like little demons that like to sneak in when we're not looking. If you spot a typo, please report it to: evearcherauthor@gmail.com

ALSO BY EVE ARCHER

Mark of the Fallen

Curse of the Fallen

Wrath of the Fallen

ABOUT THE AUTHOR

Eve Archer writes sinfully hot paranormal romance with devilishly wicked heroes. Who doesn't love a smoking hot bad boy (or very naughty demon) who meets his match when it comes to true love?

Eve adores traveling and puts as many of the exotic places she's visited into her books as possible (which gives her another excuse to plan more trips)! She's sailed the Adriatic, hunted for secret waterfalls in Bali, and floated in the Dead Sea. When Eve isn't bopping around the world researching books or writing them, she can be found juggling one husband, two teenagers, two moody cats, and one very energetic dog.

Cover Design by Croci Designs

Editing by Tanya Saari

CPSIA information can be obtained
at www.ICGtesting.com
Printed in the USA
LVHW041328030122
707736LV00014BA/54

9 781949 496680